DETECTIVE HELEN GRACE IS

"MESMERIZING!"
—#1 *New York Times*
Bestselling Author Lisa Gardner

"A GENUINELY FRESH HEROINE."
—*Daily Mail* (UK)

"THRILLING AND ENJOYABLE."
—The Crime Scene

3-3-22 ~~4848~~

PRAISE FOR THE NOVELS OF M. J. ARLIDGE

POP GOES THE WEASEL

"Exciting. . . . Readers will root for this admirable if flawed heroine every step of the way."
—*Publishers Weekly*

"Another gripping and action-packed read topped by a final twist."
—*Library Journal*

"Arlidge again leads readers through a twisty, turny mystery. . . . I'd compare [Arlidge] to Elizabeth Haynes in terms of content and tone and Jeffery Deaver in terms of pacing and the can't-put-it-down quality."
—No More Grumpy Bookseller

"Arlidge repeats the successful style of his prior novel . . . a wild ride."
—Curled Up with a Good Book

"A fantastic thriller that will keep you guessing . . . until the very end!"
—Chick Lit+

"Arlidge is my kind of author. Strong characters, a nice story line, just as strong a killer, and a great ending." —Cheryl's Book Nook

"I loved it! . . . I am hooked on this series and am going to anxiously wait for number three to be published." —Kritters Ramblings

"You just get slingshot from one end of the book to another. The story is concise, written in a succinct, efficient manner that digs into the story, fleshes out characters, and doesn't leave room for fat." —Bites

EENY MEENY

"It's almost always cause for skepticism when a book's jacket copy promises an ingenious new variety of serial killer, but amazingly enough it's true of M. J. Arlidge's gripping debut. . . . His story is honest to us and to itself, and boy, do the pages fly by." —*USA Today*

continued . . .

"Dark, twisted, thought-provoking, and I couldn't turn the pages fast enough. Take a ride on this roller coaster from hell—white knuckles guaranteed." —Tami Hoag, #1 *New York Times* bestselling author of *Cold Cold Heart*

"No doubt about it! *Eeny Meeny* debuts one of the best new series detectives, Helen Grace. Determined, tough, and damaged, she must unravel a terrifying riddle of a killer kidnapping victims in pairs to send a particularly personal message. Mesmerizing!"

—Lisa Gardner, #1 *New York Times* bestselling author of *Crash & Burn*

"There are so many things about this novel that are expertly pulled off. It has a devious premise. Helen Grace is fiendishly awesome. It's scary as all hell. It has an ending that's fair and shocking. And it has a full cast of realistically drawn, interesting characters that make the thing read like a bullet. *Eeny Meeny* is a dark, edgy thriller."

—Will Lavender, *New York Times* bestselling author of *Dominance*

"What a great premise! . . . *Eeny Meeny* is a fresh and brilliant departure from the stock serial killer tale. And Helen Grace is one of the greatest heroes to come along in years."

—Jeffery Deaver, *New York Times* bestselling author of *The Skin Collector*

"Engrossing. . . . Readers will look forward to seeing more of this strong, intelligent, and courageous lead." —*Publishers Weekly*

"Fast-paced, terrifying, and impossible to put down, this gripping debut stars a fierce protagonist in Grace. Readers will look forward to the next book in this series!" —*Library Journal* (starred review)

"M. J. Arlidge has created a genuinely fresh heroine in Helen Grace. . . . He spares us none of the dark details, weaving them together into a tapestry that chills to the bone." —*Daily Mail* (UK)

"With an orchestration of tension that is always sharp and cinematic, M. J. Arlidge's debut novel grabs the reader by the throat." —Crime Time

"A fast-paced roller-coaster ride. Every chapter holds new developments, new murders, new clues. . . . I would highly recommend it for any crime fiction fan and I am giving it four stars out of five. A truly wonderful debut novel."

—Life Through Books

"[A] rip-roaring affair . . . pulls no punches with its opening lines and doesn't let go until the very last. . . . This is the first in what may be a long line of Helen Grace books, and I for one am excited about what else she has to come."

—Boy, Let's Talk About Books

"An entertaining read [that introduced] a new star character in the world of thrillers."

—Examiner.com

"This taut, fast-paced debut is truly excellent."

—*The Sun* (UK)

Also by M. J. Arlidge

Detective Helen Grace Thrillers

Eeny Meeny
Pop Goes the Weasel

A DETECTIVE HELEN GRACE THRILLER

M. J. ARLIDGE

NEW AMERICAN LIBRARY

NEW AMERICAN LIBRARY
Published by New American Library,
an imprint of Penguin Random House LLC
375 Hudson Street, New York, New York 10014

This book is a publication of New American Library. Previously published in a Penguin Group (UK) edition.

First New American Library Printing, February 2016

Copyright © M. J. Arlidge, 2015
Penguin Random House supports copyright. Copyright fuels creativity, encourages diverse voices, promotes free speech, and creates a vibrant culture. Thank you for buying an authorized edition of this book and for complying with copyright laws by not reproducing, scanning, or distributing any part of it in any form without permission. You are supporting writers and allowing Penguin Random House to continue to publish books for every reader.

New American Library and the New American Library colophon are registered trademarks of Penguin Random House LLC.

For more information about Penguin Random House, visit penguin.com.

LIBRARY OF CONGRESS CATALOGING-IN-PUBLICATION DATA:

Names: Arlidge, M. J.
Title: The doll's house: a Detective Helen Grace thriller/M. J. Arlidge.
Description: New York: New American Library, 2016. | 2015 | Series: A Helen Grace thriller; 3
Identifiers: LCCN 2015035939 | ISBN 9780451475510 (softcover)
Subjects: LCSH: Policewomen—Fiction. | Women detectives—Fiction. |
Serial murder investigation—Fiction. | BISAC: FICTION / Suspense. |
FICTION / Thrillers. | GSAFD: Mystery fiction. | Suspense fiction.
Classification: LCC PR6051.R55 D65 2016 | DDC 823/.914—dc23
LC record available at https://protect-us.mimecast.com/s/g5ZxBXS1dYqhM

Printed in the United States of America
10 9 8 7 6

PUBLISHER'S NOTE

This is a work of fiction. Names, characters, places, and incidents either are the product of the author's imagination or are used fictitiously, and any resemblance to actual persons, living or dead, business establishments, events, or locales is entirely coincidental.

Penguin
Random
House

THE DOLL'S HOUSE

1

Ruby tossed fitfully in her bed after a disturbed night's sleep. She seemed to have been in and out of consciousness for hours—not fully awake, but not truly asleep either. Wild anxiety dreams collided uneasily with the odd sensation of her mother carrying her to bed. That had felt nice but was impossible, of course. Ruby lived alone and it had been fifteen years or more since her parents had had to do that.

Ruby regretted her session at Revolution last night. Angry with life, she had been in a self-destructive mood, unable or unwilling to turn down the free drinks offered by hopeful lads. There had been pills and cocaine too—the whole thing had been a blur. But had she really drunk so much, taken so much, that she should feel *this* bad?

She turned over again, burying her throbbing head in the sheets. She had important stuff to do today—her mum was coming round soon—but suddenly Ruby couldn't face any of it. She just wanted to hide away from the world, cocooned in her hangover, safe from the intrusion of family, responsibility, betrayal and tears. She wanted her life to go away—for a couple of hours at least.

Putting her head under the pillow, she groaned quietly. It was surprisingly cool underneath—cooler than usual—and for a moment she felt refreshed and soothed. This would be a good hidey-hole for a litt—

Something wasn't right. The smell. What was it about the smell of the sheets? They smelled . . . wrong.

Alarm started to burrow through her hangover. Her sheets always smelled citrusy. She used the same fabric softener her mum did. So why did they now smell of lavender?

Ruby kept her eyes closed, the pillow clamped over her head. Her brain ached fiercely as it spooled back over last night's events. She had snogged a guy, flirted with a few more . . . but she hadn't gone home with anyone, had she? No, she had made it back to her flat alone. She remembered dropping her keys on the table, drinking water straight from the kitchen tap, taking some Nurofen before flopping into bed. That *was* last night, wasn't it?

She could feel her breathing becoming shallow now, her chest tightening. She needed her asthma inhaler. Stretching out her arm, she groped for the bedside table—drunk or not, she always left her inhaler within easy reach. But it wasn't there. She reached out farther. Nothing. The *table* wasn't bloody there. Her hand collided with the wall. Rough brick. Her wall wasn't like th—

Ruby pulled off the pillow and sat up. Her mouth fell open, but only a weak gasp came out—her body frozen in breathless panic. She had gone to sleep in her nice, cozy bed. But had woken up in a cold, dark cellar.

2

The sun was high in the sky and Carsholt Beach looked magnificent, a long swath of golden sand merging effortlessly with the gentle waters of the Solent. Andy Baker patted himself on the back—Carsholt was literally at the end of the road, so even though the beach was beautiful, there was hardly ever anybody down here. Cathy, he and the kids had the place to themselves and were set fair for a perfect Saturday by the sea. Picnic, bit of Frisbee, a few beers—already the stresses of the working week were melting away.

Leaving the boys to dig their trench—a prelude to pitched battles between his boisterous twins—Andy set off by himself toward the water's edge. What was it that was so calming about this place? The isolation? The view? The sound of the sea lapping the shore? Andy let the water run over his toes. He had been coming here since he was a kid. He'd brought his wife—his first wife—and the boys here. That hadn't ended well, of course, but looking over toward Cathy, digging and joking with Tom and Jimbo, Andy now felt blessed.

This place was his sanctuary and he looked forward to it all week. Running a security business sounded good on paper, but it was nonstop aggro. You used to be able to get decent people on your books, but not now. Maybe it was the influx of foreigners or just modern times, but every third employee seemed to have a drug problem or an eye for the girls. Last month, he'd been sued by a nightclub owner who'd caught one of his guys dealing ketamine in the club toilets. He was getting too old for stuff like that—perhaps it was time to think about retiring.

A noise made Andy look up sharply. It came from behind him. From the direction of the boys. They were shouting. No, they were screaming.

Already Andy was sprinting across the sand, his heart beating sixteen to the dozen. Was someone hurting them? He could see Cathy, but where were the boys?

"Cathy?"

She didn't even look at him.

"Cathy?"

Finally she looked up. Her face was ashen. She tried to speak, but before she could say anything the boys crashed into her, holding on to her for dear life.

Andy stared at them, confused and fearful. As Cathy clasped the boys to her chest, her gaze remained resolutely fixed on the trench. Was it something in there that had spooked them? A dead animal or . . .

Andy approached the lip of the trench. He had a sense of what he would find. Could see it in his mind's eye. But even so, his heart skipped a beat when he peered into the hole. The sides were steep, the trench was deep—three feet or so—and there at the bottom, perfectly framed by wet sand, was the pale face of a young woman.

3

Snow blindness studded her vision and her chest tightened still further. Ruby was in the midst of a full-blown asthma attack now, her panic making her breathing short and erratic. She could feel her heart thundering out a remorseless rhythm, as if it were going to explode. What the hell was happening? Was this *real*?

She sank her teeth into her arm. The pain coursed through her fleetingly before she released her grip to try to suck in more air. It *was* real. She should have known by how bloody freezing she was. Shivering, she lay down on the bed and tried to calm herself. The thought of not having her inhaler was freaking her out, but she had to try to control her panic or she would black out. And she couldn't do that. Not here.

Calm. Try to be calm. Think nice thoughts. Think of Mum. And Dad. And Cassie. And Conor. Think of fields. And rivers. And sunlight.

Think of being a kid. And playgrounds. And summers in the garden. Running through the sprinkler. Think happy, happy thoughts.

Ruby's chest was rising and falling less violently now, her breathing a little less desperate. *Keep your cool. It'll be fine. There will be a simple explanation for all this.* Propping herself up on her pillows, she took a deep breath and suddenly called:

"Hello?"

Her voice sounded strange, her words flopping dully off the exposed brick walls. The room was in darkness save for the light that stole under the bottom of the door, providing just enough illumination to reveal her situation. The room measured about fifteen by fifteen and would have looked like any other bedsit—a bed, a table and chairs, an oven and kettle, some bookshelves—except for the fact that there were no windows. The floorboards that formed the low ceiling above were wooden but oddly betrayed no cracks or chinks of light.

"Hello?" Her voice quivered as she fought to suppress the panic that gripped her. Still no answer, no signs of life.

Suddenly she was on her feet—anything not to be sitting there thinking horrible thoughts. She crossed the room, working the handle of the heavy metal door, but it was locked. Frantically she did a circuit of the small room, looking for some means of escape, but found nothing.

She shivered. She was scared half to death and cold to the bone. Her eyes alighted on the cooker. It was an old gas one, with two ovens and four hobs. She was suddenly seized with the thought of turning it on. The four hobs would warm the place up and brighten it a little too. She turned the dial and pressed the ignition. Nothing. Ruby tried the next, then the next. Still nothing.

She walked round the cooker to check out the back. She didn't know the first thing about cookers, but perhaps there was something obvious?

It wasn't connected. There were no pipes at the back connecting it to a gas supply. It was just for show. Ruby slumped to the floor. Tears came fast now as her confusion collided with fear.

What was this place? Why was she here? Questions spun round Ruby's head as she tried to process this strange reality. She was slipping fast into despair, tears rolling off her chin onto the floor.

Then suddenly a noise nearby made her look up.

What was it? Was it upstairs or down here?

There it was again. Footsteps. Definitely footsteps. They were coming closer. Stopping outside the door. Ruby jumped to her feet, alive to the danger.

Silence. Then suddenly a wicket hatch in the door slid open and a pair of eyes filled the slit. Ruby stumbled backward, pressing herself into the corner of the room—she wanted to be as far away from the door as possible.

The sound of bolts being unlocked.

"Help!" Ruby screamed.

But she didn't get any further. The door swung open, flooding the room with light. Ruby clamped her eyes shut, blinded by the sudden burst of illumination. Then slowly, cautiously, she opened them again.

A tall figure stood in the doorway. He was silhouetted by the light behind, so she couldn't make out his features. He was just a shadow—hovering, watching.

Then, as suddenly as it had opened, the heavy door slammed shut again. They were together in darkness now.

Ruby covered her face with her hands and prayed to a God she didn't believe in, pleading with him to have mercy on her. But for all her praying, she couldn't block out the sound of the footsteps approaching her.

4

The wind buffeted DI Helen Grace as she sped along the coastal road. She hadn't been down this isolated spit of land before and she liked what she saw. The wildness, the isolation—it was her kind of place. With the road open before her, she ratcheted up her speed, pushing hard against the strong headwind.

Soon the crime scene came into view and she eased off on the throttle, bringing her Kawasaki's progress down to a respectable thirty miles per hour. DS Lloyd Fortune was waiting for her by the fluttering police tape. Young, smart, the poster boy for ethnic-minority policing in Southampton, Lloyd was destined for great things. Helen had always liked and respected him, yet still it felt odd having him as her number two. Her old friend Charlie Brooks had been temporarily promoted to DS during their pursuit of Ella Matthews, but her elevation had never been made permanent. And as soon as Charlie had announced her pregnancy, it became academic—she would remain at her former rank of DC for the foreseeable future. It wasn't fair, but that was the way it worked, the odds forever stacked against working mums.

The old team was breaking up. Tony Bridges had left the force for good, DC Grounds was due to retire shortly and Charlie was on maternity leave, a few weeks shy of giving birth. Lloyd was the new DS, they had two new DCs—the Major Incident Team had a very different feel now. If she was honest, it made Helen uncomfortable. She hadn't got a handle on the new personalities, was yet to establish an easy rhythm with the freshly assembled team. But the only way to do that was to go through fire together.

"What have you got for me, Lloyd?"

They were already making their way under the police cordon and across the sand toward the trench.

"Young female. Buried about three feet down. Found by a couple of kids an hour or so ago. They're over there with their parents."

Lloyd indicated the family of four, huddled in police blankets, giving their statements to a uniformed officer.

"Any connection to the victim?"

"No, they come here most weekends. Usually have the place to themselves."

"Anybody live near here?"

"No. The nearest houses are three miles away."

"Does it pick up anything from the lighthouse at night?"

"It's too far round."

"Making this a pretty good deposition site."

They walked in silence to the lip of the trench. Meredith Walker, Southampton Central's chief forensics officer, was at the bottom, carefully excavating the body. Helen took in the scene, the white-suited forensics officer crouching sinisterly over a woman who looked completely at peace, despite the wet sand that stuck to her hair, eyes and lips.

The woman's face, shoulders, upper torso and arms had been revealed. Her limbs were painfully thin and the skin very pale, which made her single tattoo stand out even more. Despite the partial decomposition, she was a strangely beautiful sight, her black hair still framing those vivid blue eyes. It reminded Helen of the Grimms' fairy tales, of gothic damsels awaiting true love's kiss.

"How long has she been down there?" Helen asked.

"Hard to say," replied Meredith. "The sand at this depth is cold and wet—ideal conditions to preserve the body. There are no animals or insects to get to her here either. But it's not recent. Given the levels of decomposition, I would say two, three years—Jim Grieves will be able tell you more once he gets her back to the mortuary."

"I'll need the crime scene photos tonight if possible," Helen said.

"Will do. Though I'm not sure how much help they'll be. Whoever did this has been careful. Her earrings and nose studs have been removed. The fingernails have been cut. And you can guess what time and tide have done to any residual forensic evidence."

Helen thanked Meredith and walked down to the water's edge to get a better view of the scene. Already her nerves were jangling. This was a careful, premeditated disposal by someone who knew exactly what they were doing. This wasn't the work of an amateur. Which strongly suggested to Helen that their killer had done this before.

5

"Stay away. Don't come near me."

Ruby was backed into a corner of the room. She held out her arms to ward off attack, but she knew immediately that it was an empty gesture.

Click. A powerful torch beam fired straight at her. Her heart raced as she watched the torch beam run the rule over her, creeping down from her face, over her chest to her thighs and then her feet. Despite her determination to appear strong, she felt her composure abandon her now and she started to sob.

"Don't be frightened."

His voice was measured and steady. She didn't recognize it, though the Southampton accent came through clearly.

"Please let me go," she said through tears. "I won't tell anyone. I—"

"Are you cold?"

"Please. I just want to go home."

"If you're cold, I can get you an extra blanket. I want you to be comfortable."

His calm pragmatism was crushing. He was speaking as if nothing unusual had happened. As if this were *normal.*

"Are you hungry?"

"I want to go home, you motherfucker. Stop . . . stop talking to me. Just . . . take me home. The police will be looking for me—"

"Nobody's looking for you, Ruby."

"My parents are expecting me. My mum's coming round today—"

"Your parents don't love you."

"What?"

"They never have."

"Why are you say—"

"I've seen the way they treat you. What they say about you when you're not around. They want rid of you."

"That's not true."

"Really? You walked out on *them*, remember. So why should they come looking for you?"

The horrible logic of it rendered Ruby speechless. "No . . . no. You're wrong. You're lying. If you want money, they've got—"

"I'm just telling you the truth. They don't want you. But I do."

Ruby sobbed louder. This couldn't be happening.

"I want to go home," she whimpered.

The torch beam moved still closer. He was beside her now. Ruby hung her head, clamping her eyes shut. She could feel his breath on her. She flinched when she felt him stroke her hair.

"That's good to hear, my love."

His voice was a warm whisper.

"Because this is your home now."

6

Alison Sprackling was furious with her daughter. They had made an arrangement to meet at eleven—it was now nearly one p.m. Where the hell was she?

The doorbell had gone unanswered, so Alison had let herself in. Ruby lived alone in a tiny, down-at-heel flat. She was by nature a party girl and often went out drinking on Friday nights, so it was not beyond her to cower under the duvet, nursing a hangover, blocking out the world. There was of course always the chance that she had brought someone home with her—not something Alison liked to dwell on, given her daughter's romantic history—but there was too much riding on this to be bashful.

It had taken so long to get the family back to a point where a reconciliation might be possible—Alison was determined not to blow it now, however unreliable and willful Ruby could be. Months of diplomacy had gone into engineering Ruby's return to the family—today was the day when they were going to contact her landlord, book a removal firm. It was a day of celebration, a day to rubber-stamp a hard-fought victory for common sense over hurt.

It was all Alison craved. A return to normality, a happy united family. So where was she? Where could Ruby be—today of all days? Should she call Jonathan? Get him to come over? No, best not give him any more ammunition when the truce was so fragile.

Ruby's yearlong exile from the family had been awful. Not just the bitter accusations, the tears, the threats, but more the sheer lack of her, their eldest, at family gatherings, holidays, barbecues. It had all just felt *wrong*, as if they—and she—were somehow willfully ignoring a burning building or drowning swimmer.

Alison stalked through the flat again—bedroom to bathroom to living area—but there was no sign of her. What was this? A final act of rebellion? A warning that she could—and would—still be her own woman? Or was this something more serious? Was she reneging on their agreement? The uncertainty made Alison deeply nervous.

Then, suddenly, birdsong—Alison's phone heralding the arrival of a new tweet. Ruby was a regular tweeter—it was largely how Alison kept tabs on her—so Alison rushed over to her bag, pulling out the contents in search of her phone.

It *was* from Ruby. Alison read the tweet. Frowning, she read it again. She couldn't be that selfish, could she?

Need to get away and be by myself. If people had loved me better then I would stay . . . Rx.

She could. Ruby had pulled the roof down on them. And Alison knew immediately there would be no coming back from this.

7

Having finished tweeting, he turned the phone off and stowed it safely in his jacket pocket. He checked again that the coast was clear, but he was being overcautious; no one penetrated this deep into the forest.

Pushing on, he made his way slowly through the undergrowth, careful not to snag his clothes on any of the thorns or brambles. His synthetic clothing was unlikely to leave any fibers behind, but you could never be too careful.

He emerged into a small clearing. The foliage was less thick here, the soil sandy and dry. Perfect for his purpose. Clearing a small patch of vegetation, he retrieved the large bundle of sticks from his rucksack and laid them carefully on the ground. Soon he had a good pile, encircled by the little trench he had dug carefully with his trowel. The trench would catch any stray sparks—a forest fire here would be catastrophic. Safety first, always safety first.

A little crumbling of fire lighter to set it going. This was more dangerous than using newspaper of course, but newspapers could provide useful clues to a half-intelligent police officer, so paraffin it was. It seemed odd to feel the heat of the fire on an already warm Saturday afternoon, but needs must. If anyone did see it, they would think it was holidaymakers having a barbecue—there were loads of them about at this time of year. Anyway, he'd be long gone by the time anyone did find it, so . . .

The thought of discovery, as ridiculous as it was, prompted him to action. He pulled Ruby's pajamas from the bag and laid them on the fire. He watched them burn, riveted by the slow conflagration. They resisted stubbornly at first; then came the first flicker as the fibers began to catch, before eventually they succumbed to the inevitable.

It was stupid to enjoy it as much as he did. But he couldn't help it. It was beautiful—the leaping flames, the glowing embers and finally the gossamer-soft ash. He was moved by what he saw, aware of its wonderful significance. This was the end of Ruby. She was dead and gone now, but from the fire, from the ashes, something new and beautiful would rise.

8

The young woman lay cold and lifeless on the slab. The sand that had encased her for so long had been swept away grain by grain and sent for analysis, leaving the victim looking strangely clean. Now that she was away from the beach, exposed and unadorned in the police mortuary, she was a pitiful sight. She was so thin—skeletal was how Jim Grieves, the pathologist, had put it over the phone. As Helen stared at the corpse, she felt a wave of nausea sweep over her. This had once been a vibrant young woman, but now her skin was gray, her lips cracked and her bones strained everywhere to puncture what remained of her skin. Helen felt profoundly sorry for her.

They had searched the Police National Computer and made the customary missing persons inquiries, but had come up with nothing. So Helen had decided to head straight to the police mortuary to see if Jim could throw any light on who she was and how she had come to this.

"She's been starved," Jim offered as his opening salvo. He was not without compassion, but he was to the point, years of service and hundreds of corpses having eroded his desire to engage in pleasantries. "Her stomach has shrunk to the size of an orange, bone strength has been compromised and I found traces of nonedible objects—wood, cotton, even metal—in her digestive system."

Helen nodded.

"I've more work to do, but so far I can find no obvious cause of death. The neck and vertebrae are intact, there are no bullet or knife wounds, no signs of manual or ligature strangulation either, so for now we'll assume that she starved to death."

"Jesus."

"This would fit with a few other things I've observed. Her skin has a gray, leathery quality—even where it has been well preserved—and her eyes have deteriorated markedly. I would say she was virtually blind by the end. Also, bloods show that she had a total absence of vitamin D in her system."

"Meaning?"

"Taken all together, it suggests that she was kept in total darkness in the final weeks or even months of her life."

Helen couldn't find words to express her horror this time. Had this young woman starved to death in a lightless hell?

"Anything else?" Helen said quickly.

"You'll note the tattoo—a bluebird on the right shoulder—done sometime in the last three to five years. Also, the pitting around the groin area. Looks like historic evidence of an STI—I would hazard molluscum contagiosum, but I'll confirm when I've done more tests."

"How long has she been buried?"

"Hard to say with any real accuracy. As you can see, the body has started to decompose. Skeletalization is about thirty percent complete, but there is still plenty of skin remaining and the hair is largely intact. Heat speeds up decomposition, cold slows it down and it was pretty chilly down there. So I would estimate two to four years."

Helen exhaled—those parameters were too broad for her liking.

"But I do have something else that might help," Jim continued. Turning, he offered Helen a small metal bowl. She peered into it—a small, electronic device lay inside.

"Your victim had a heart condition. This is her pacemaker," Jim explained, wiping rust and dried blood off the unit, "complete with manufacturer's logo and serial number."

Helen mustered a half smile: finally some good news.

"Run that serial number down," Jim continued, "and you've got your girl."

9

DC Sanderson approached the flat in Millbrook with a heavy heart. Increasingly this was her lot in life—sweeping up the cases that no one else in the Major Incident Team wanted. Helen, Lloyd and a number of the others had been out at Carsholt, doing the interesting stuff. What had they left her? A glorified missing persons case. She didn't blame Helen, who had always treated her fairly and encouraged her as a fellow female officer. No, she laid the blame squarely at the door of Lloyd Fortune, whom she felt favored the new DCs over her. It wasn't fair—she was more experienced, knew Southampton better than these blow-ins—but station politics is a fickle business.

The interior of the flat didn't improve her mood. It was amazing what landlords could get away with these days, now that no one could actually afford to buy a property. The one-bed flat was cramped and unprepossessing. Damp hugged the ceiling, the windows were ill-fitting and drafty and she was sure there were things living behind the skirting boards. Or perhaps dying. The whole place smelled of decay.

Still, it was someone's home and the tenant—Ruby Sprackling—was somebody's daughter. Alison, her mother, flanked by her worried husband, Jonathan, paced the floor. Tears were not far off, so Sanderson decided to press on and get as much info as she could.

"There have been a lot of . . . issues over the last couple of years, but she wouldn't take off like this," Alison was saying. "She was due to move back into the family home next week. We'd been talking about it for months. We'd made arrangements . . ."

"Could she have got cold feet?"

"No" was the swift response, although Sanderson detected a hint of doubt. She was also intrigued by the fact that the stony-faced husband had not said a word.

"You said that she had been in contact with her birth mother recently?" Sanderson continued.

"Not recently, but on and off during the last two years." Ruby's father *was* keen to talk about this topic. "She was a terrible influence," he said. "Got her into drugs, skipping school—there was trouble with the police. Ruby completely ballsed up her A-Levels because of that bloody woman."

A sharp look from Alison made him rein in his anger. He ceased his rant but was unrepentant. He knew what he thought of Shanelle Harvey and wasn't minded to change his opinion. His promising daughter had gone completely off the rails in the last year, prompting furious bust-ups and recriminations within the family—all because of an innocent and well-intentioned desire to create a bond with her biological mother.

As he filled her in on the details, Sanderson couldn't help feeling that Ruby would have been better off sticking with what she had. Shanelle Harvey had turned out to be a small-time fence, thief and dealer with questionable hobbies and even more questionable boyfriends. Not the plucky but poor earth mother that Ruby had perhaps been hoping to find.

"You said you weren't too worried at first, but now . . ." Sanderson got the conversation back on track.

"I wasn't," Alison agreed. "Ruby can be unreliable and impulsive—it's not impossible that she would wind herself up and take off for a bit. But she's posted one tweet since last night, and believe me, that is seriously out of character. Her phone's turned off—I've tried her a dozen times . . ."

"What about keys? Purse?"

"It looks like she's got those with her," Alison conceded.

"So she packed a bag . . . ?"

"Her rucksack's not here. And it's true she's taken most of her clothes."

"Was there any sign of forced entry?"

"No, the lock's new and pretty decent and the windows seem okay, but even so . . ."

Sanderson felt herself mentally switching off, dismissing Alison as a mother in denial, then mentally slapped herself back into concentrating. Helen Grace was very hot on missing persons cases—she always said that they were just the stepping-stones to murder cases, rape cases—and Sanderson knew Helen would expect her to leave no stone unturned.

"Her inhaler."

Now Alison had Sanderson's attention.

"She's asthmatic?"

"Since birth. She had several bad attacks when she was a kid.

Ended up in hospital twice. Now she *always* has her inhaler with her. It's her little mantra going out the door: 'Keys, purse, inhaler . . .' She would never take off without it."

"And?"

"And I found it by the side of her bed. It must have fallen off her bedside table onto the floor. Even if she was in a rush, even if she did want to get away, she would be too scared to leave without her inhaler."

"And if she'd forgotten it?"

"Then she'd come back, regardless," Jonathan said firmly, equally concerned, it appeared, despite his checkered history with his step-daughter.

Sanderson asked some more questions, then wrapped things up. This missing persons case had just taken on a more sinister hue. As scrupulous as she was to reassure Alison and Jonathan, the detail of the forgotten inhaler alarmed Sanderson. It was the kind of thing someone else might miss, but not Ruby, who'd been scarred by asthma since birth. Which raised the question: Had Ruby really taken off? Or was a third party involved?

10

Sometimes it was tough being a parent. Scratch that—it was *always* tough being a parent. Detective Superintendent Ceri Harwood mounted the stairs to the third floor of her fashionable town house in a dark mood. She had been nagging her kids to go to bed for nearly an hour now, but still they defied her, finding endless excuses to avoid doing what they were asked. It had been a long day—she didn't need to be marching up and down the stairs all night, when she could be snuggled up on the sofa with a glass of wine.

"If you're not in bed and quiet within two minutes, the PS4 goes into the cupboard for a week."

It felt good to threaten a week—she had never threatened a whole week before. It had the desired effect. The fourth floor suddenly went very quiet as feet scurried, lights were switched off and peace descended. Harwood waited a further few minutes, then crept up to the top floor and poked her head round the door.

Both girls were fast asleep, and despite her irritation and tiredness, this made her smile. They had had busy days with school, swimming, music lessons, but even so Harwood marveled at her kids' ability to drop off to sleep within seconds. It was not a skill she possessed—stress and the fag end of her daily caffeine intake often keeping her awake and restless into the small hours.

It had been a hard year. A year spent swallowing Helen Grace's heroism and popularity day after day. Grace had brought in two serial killers now and had achieved legendary status within the force as a result. Outside, in the real world, it was little better: the subject of Helen Grace often came up at dinner parties Harwood attended, people peppering her with questions about the detective inspector's character and talents. It was all Helen, Helen, Helen.

In the professional sphere, Harwood had behaved impeccably. She had patted Helen on the back, congratulated her on her official commendation and made sure she had all the resources she needed. Her success ultimately reflected well on Harwood—but none of this made her feel any better. She remembered Helen's withering character assassination of her, as they came to blows during the Ella Matthews investigation. Infuriated at what she perceived as Harwood's attempts to run her out of the force, Helen had dismissed her as a glorified politician, unfit to wear the police badge. Helen had not mentioned the row since, but Harwood recalled it word for word.

Still, there *were* some things Ceri had that Helen didn't. The superior rank. A loving husband. Two beautiful daughters. Harwood stared at the sleeping girls now and her despondency ebbed away. She had always been a fighter, and despite having been in Helen Grace's shadow for so long, she felt that where there was life, there was hope.

As she descended the stairs once more, Harwood knew that there would be payback. Someday soon, she would settle the score. She had lost the battle after all. She had not lost the war.

11

The seventh-floor office was quiet as the grave. It was after hours now and the rest of the Major Incident Team had headed home, leaving Helen alone. Which was how she liked it. She didn't need an audience for what she was about to do.

Double-checking that there was no one lurking in the corridors, Helen parked herself in front of a computer terminal and fired it up. Using someone else's machine was a low trick, but a necessary one—it was strictly forbidden to access the PNC for personal use.

Within a minute, she was in the system. She didn't hesitate, typing swiftly "Robert Stonehill." As the system searched for any crimes or incidents linked to that name, Helen tried to ignore the faint fluttering of hope inside her. Her nephew had dropped off the radar nearly twelve months ago now—he had had no contact with his adoptive parents or his friends—and Helen's constant searching for him had yielded nothing. Her feud with Emilia Garanita had prompted the vindictive local journalist to publicly out Robert as the biological son of Helen's sister, Marianne. Learning for the first time that his mother was a serial killer, while the press besieged his poor parents' house, had tipped the young man over the edge. He had fled in order to draw the press pack off. Helen had assumed he would reappear when the furor died down, but he didn't. Robert wanted to stay hidden.

His continued absence was crushing for Helen. He was the only family she had left, and during their brief acquaintance she had made a promise—to herself and to Robert—to be his guardian angel. To protect him from a dark world that had taken his mother's life and blighted hers. But she had failed utterly—and now he was lost to her for good.

The search came up blank. As it always did. Suppressing the deep sadness that rose inside her, Helen turned off the terminal and hurried out.

The short ride to Charlie's house helped restore her spirits. She and Charlie had been through a lot together—good and bad—yet Helen always felt welcome. Steve and Charlie's home wasn't grand, but it was a happy one. Even more so than usual now, with the impending arrival of their baby girl.

"You're looking well," Helen said as they sat in Charlie's living room.

"Is that code for enormous?" Charlie countered.

"No. It suits you."

"Bloated ankles and stretch marks—it's a good look," Charlie replied, casting an envious eye over Helen's trim figure. "Let's hope it catches on."

"How are you and Steve getting on?"

"Outwardly, excited. Inwardly, terrified."

"You'll be fine. You're both naturals."

"Maybe. If Steve and I are still married in twelve months' time, we'll be able to say it's a job well done."

Helen smiled and sipped her tea. Helen never drank, so she was a good companion for a mum-to-be.

"And how are you? McAndrew told me about your beach body," Charlie continued. "Sounds . . . unusual."

Helen could tell by Charlie's tone that she was already missing police work. Steve had been insistent she quit the force after what had happened with Marianne, and Charlie had initially agreed to do so. But the unexpected discovery of her pregnancy had helped Charlie hedge her bets, opting for a backroom role and then a year's maternity leave, taking her out of the firing line. Though she'd never say it aloud, Helen hoped Charlie would come back to Southampton Central when the time was right.

"It is. It was clinically done—and some time ago—which makes me worry . . ."

"What he's been up to since?" said Charlie, completing Helen's sentence.

Helen nodded.

"And how are the team shaping up in my absence?"

"Still finding their feet," replied Helen diplomatically.

"And Lloyd—how's he doing?"

Helen sensed that this was what Charlie really wanted to know. The sudden elevation of this talented but inexperienced officer to the role of DS had stuck in Charlie's craw. She put it as much down to Detective Superintendent Harwood's mistrust of Charlie, as she did to Lloyd's individual merits. There's nothing worse than losing out to politics and, despite Charlie's good heart, Helen knew she was hoping Lloyd wouldn't cover himself in glory.

"Early days," Helen replied, keeping her expression as neutral as possible. Whatever she might feel personally, she could never let on that she was anxious about her current team.

Helen left shortly afterward, wishing Charlie well and promising to return before D-day. She was walking to her bike when her phone rang. It was DC Grounds.

"Sorry to disturb you late, ma'am, but we've had results back on the pacemaker."

Helen stopped walking.

"The dead woman is Pippa Briers. She would be twenty-five now. Next of kin is her father, Daniel Briers. We've got a Reading address and phone number. Do you want me to make the call?"

"No, I'll do it. Text me the details."

Helen rang off. Moments later, Grounds's text came through. Helen steeled herself for what was to come. She couldn't put it off—she owed it to Daniel and Pippa Briers to make the call without delay. Still, she took a second to compose herself. However many times you've done it, it is never easy to tell parents that their beloved daughter is dead.

12

Ruby came to, scared and disoriented. She had been determined not to let her guard down, but had dozed off nevertheless. She scanned the room quickly, alive to the danger despite her continued grogginess and aching head, but there was none. She was still alone.

What time was it? Ruby had no watch and the clock on the wall was frozen at quarter past twelve. She could have slept for five minutes or five hours; she had no way of knowing, which unnerved her deeply. She was like Sleeping Beauty down here, trapped in a living death. Except this lonely girl had no one to rescue her.

Ruby shivered, her body numb with cold. It must be nighttime by now, because the temperature in the room had dropped markedly. It was a horrible damp kind of cold that got into your lungs and head. Ruby knew already that she would become ill here. Or worse. And she'd spent the whole day asking herself why.

She had tried to place her captor—tall, thin, with a curious manner. There was something familiar about him—was it his face, or the smell he gave off?—and she had tortured herself trying to think where she had seen him before. If she could work out who he was, then she could work on him, persuade him to see the harm he was doing. But he eluded her, and her attempts to identify him only served to crush her spirit further.

Why? Why? Why?

Why was she here? What had she done?

At first, she had assumed he was going to kill her. Or worse. But he had made no attempt to harm her. Then she'd assumed he wanted money. But he didn't. He wanted her. This strange room with its pastiche of homeliness—the stopped clock, the empty shelves, the freshly laundered sheets—was designed to be a home, not a prison.

How did he know her so well? Had something she'd done prompted her abduction? Was she in some way *responsible*?

In the shivering darkness, this explanation had made the most sense. She had been a terrible daughter and a bad friend. Since Alison and Jonathan had adopted her, her life had been steady and productive. Unwanted at birth, Ruby could have gone badly wrong, but thanks to the kindness and charity of her adoptive parents she had had a decent start in life. And she had thrown it back in their faces. Her intentions had been good. The knowledge of her abandonment by her birth mother had never left her and she needed to meet her, to see if, years later, she cared for her child at all.

What had she found? A calculating, manipulative criminal, interested only in how her abandoned child could benefit her. Ruby cursed herself for her stupidity in ever having trusted her. Because she swallowed her lies, because she desperately wanted her attention, she had spurned the only people who had ever shown her any real love. And when they reacted badly to her craziness, she had rewarded them with vitriol and abuse. She had called them every name under the sun, spat at them, clawed at them. She was under the influence—in more ways than one—when she committed those crimes against her family, but that didn't excuse her behavior. She had been vile to those who least deserved it.

As Ruby lay on the bed, her surrender complete, she thought she understood. She had done terrible things. She was, and always would be, a terrible human being.

And now she was going to be punished for it.

13

Helen stood stock-still in the shadow of St. Barnabas's Church. How she had got here she couldn't tell. Perhaps she should have gone back to the station to make the call to Daniel Briers, but it was already very late and, besides, she was honor-bound to deliver her terrible news as quickly as possible. So she had made the call there and then. As the conversation progressed, Helen filling the heavy silences with as much detail and reassurance as she could, she had sought out a quiet spot and had ended up here, in a lonely churchyard.

The call had been upsetting, as they always were. Daniel Briers had not reported his daughter missing and had no idea that any harm had come to her. They had fallen out a few years back and though she had moved away, he claimed they had still kept in contact intermittently, through social media if not face-to-face. She had actually sent him a text earlier that day, so to be given news of her "death" was a shock, to say the least. Helen could tell he didn't believe it. Helen had told him as much as she could, then arranged for him to visit Southampton the following day. Perhaps the reality of this tragedy would start to sink in then.

Helen shivered. The silence after the call was disturbing, especially in these surroundings. However you tried you couldn't rid yourself of the image of the person on the other end. What was he doing now? Telling his wife that Pippa was dead? Was he crying? Vomiting? Many did, having been given the news. It was terrible to be the instrument through which such awful pain was delivered.

Half an hour later, Helen was at Jake's door, ringing the bell three times in quick succession—their secret code. The door buzzed and Helen let herself in, hurrying upstairs.

What was it about her conscience? She had done the right thing—the responsible thing—making the call. But now she was plagued by dark thoughts, images of herself as this remorseless engine of misery, tainting everything and everyone she touched.

The first blow landed, jolting Helen from her introspection. Her skin arched deep pink in protest, and as the pain coursed through her, Helen shut her eyes and waited for that familiar feeling of release. Slowly it crept up on her, her demons finally in retreat, beaten away by Jake.

Afterward, he watched her get dressed. Helen had been using Jake's services for a few years now and they were long past the point where he would turn away. They had even spent the night together once and this had briefly promised to lead to greater intimacy, but Helen had run scared. Jake as her dominator was one thing. Jake as her lover was something else altogether. That was more than twelve months ago now and Jake seemed to have swallowed his obvious disappointment and accepted a return to the status quo.

But as Helen pulled the banknotes from her purse, Jake stopped her.

"Don't." It was simply said, but with emotion.

"Come on, Jake, you've earned it."

"This one's on the house," he replied, smiling awkwardly.

Helen looked at him. Was this a genuine one-off—an act of friendship—or was this the first move in something more concerted? Helen didn't know what had prompted this change of tack, but she didn't like it.

"I insist," Helen countered, thrusting the notes into Jake's hand.

"Helen—"

"Please, Jake, it's been a hard day. Take it."

She turned and left—she didn't have the stomach for a fight. The last twenty-four hours had been extremely tough, and though it was still early days in the investigation, Helen sensed that the worst was yet to come. The storm clouds were gathering and she knew from bitter experience that she couldn't fight on too many fronts at the same time. She walked back to her bike, never once looking over her shoulder. Despite this, she knew full well that Jake was watching her from the window, every step of the way.

14

DC Sanderson pressed the doorbell firmly and braced herself for what was to come. She had risen early and been on the M2 by seven a.m., heading east toward Kent. Ruby Sprackling had only been missing for thirty-six hours, but Sanderson was already seriously concerned.

Having arranged to meet her mother to rubber-stamp her long-sought family reconciliation, Ruby had unexpectedly vanished. She had written a brief e-mail to her landlord giving notice, then sent a single tweet to family and friends announcing that she was taking off. This from a young woman who was remorselessly sociable, a girl of the Twitter generation who lived her life in the open, tweeting her every thought, reproach or epiphany. More suspicious still was the fact that her phone had been turned off since she disappeared. For her phone to be out of commission for that long suggested she either didn't want to be found or no longer had the phone in her possession. A nagging fear in Sanderson suggested it was the latter.

Her birth mother, Shanelle Harvey, lived in a run-down block of flats in Maidstone. Sanderson had visited some rough places in her time, but Taplow Towers really was an armpit—bursting with sink estate mums and blokes on day release. Sanderson's mood plummeted as she surveyed the large penis spray-painted on Shanelle Harvey's front door.

Footsteps, then the front door opened a sliver, the chain firmly on.

"DC Sanderson, could I have a word?"

Shanelle Harvey looked at her visitor, cleared her throat unpleasantly (the result landing close to Sanderson's left foot) before reluctantly opening the door.

Inside was worse than out. A sea of cardboard boxes, probably full of knockoff gear, littered the place. There was little room for the usual decoration of a family home. In fact, the only ornaments Sanderson could see were ashtrays, overflowing with the butt ends of hundreds of unbranded cigarettes. The place stank of stale smoke—Sanderson would gladly have opened a window, if she could get to one.

"Nothing to do with me."

Shanelle was quick to deny any involvement in Ruby's disappearance.

"But you don't deny having had contact with her recently?"

"Might have done."

Shanelle had the weary experience of a professional chancer, determined not to admit responsibility for anything.

"We can check your phone records, Shanelle, so let's cut the bullshit, shall we?" Sanderson continued.

"Okay. I seen her on and off for the last two years. She used to like coming here. I'm a bit less stuck-up than the other lot."

"Her parents?"

"If that's what they like to call themselves. Always on at her, they were, telling her what to do, how to be. It's no way to live."

"And this is?" Sanderson responded.

"Yeah, it's easy to look down your nose at me, but at least I let her be," Shanelle spat back. "Instead of coming round here pointing the finger, why don't you ask *him* about it?"

"Who?"

"Her 'dad.'"

"Why would Mr. Sprackling know anything about it?"

"Got a temper on him. Likes to get his own way. Doesn't like naughty little girls. He used to get very . . . cross with Ruby."

Sanderson said nothing.

"He came round here once. Called me all sorts, threatened to take my head off. I stood my ground, but I don't mind telling you I was bricking it. I was alone, I didn't have anything to hand, nothing to stop him . . ."

"So what happened?"

"Neighbor came out. Told us to keep the noise down. He didn't like that. Didn't like being caught somewhere like this. I don't think he'd told his wife he was coming."

This was said gleefully, retrospectively enjoying his discomfort.

"So, why don't you ask *him* about Ruby? Ask him what he wanted to do to the little girl that turned on him?"

Sanderson was irritated by Shanelle, but also disquieted. Most disappearances were the products of domestic disharmony, and Sanderson knew there was no reason why this should be any different. Could

Jonathan Sprackling be involved? Could he be punishing her for disloyalty and disobedience?

"Have you seen Ruby in the last week?"

"No. Last time was about a month ago."

"Did she ever stay here overnight?"

"Yeah, so what?"

"Just the two of you."

For the first time, Shanelle hesitated. Sanderson was quick to press home the advantage.

"Who else was here?"

"Nobody . . ."

"Don't make me arrest you, Shanelle."

"It was just a guy."

"What guy?"

"He came round once in a while. To smoke a bit. I think he was here once when Ruby stayed. He liked the look of her. I told him I'd cut his balls off if he even looked at her."

"Name?"

More hesitation, then:

"Dwayne something. That's all I got," she added in response to Sanderson's evident irritation.

"How often did he come round?"

"Once or twice a month."

"Where can I find him?"

"Like I know or care."

"Had a falling-out, have we?"

"I threw the little shit out."

"Because?"

"Because he stole from me. I knew he was a freeloader. All he did was sit on his arse smoking dope and watching porn, but then he half-inched two hundred notes from me. Said he didn't, but I wasn't born yesterday. So I kicked him out. Told everyone on the estate he was a pedo and I ain't seen him since."

She smiled at her own wit and invention.

"Have you had any contact since?"

"Not face-to-face."

"Meaning?"

"A brick through the window and some dog shit through the door—is that 'contact'? Next time he does it, I'll have him."

It wasn't much to go on, but it was a start. She knew of cases where embittered exes had kidnapped and imprisoned children of former lovers. It seemed unlikely that a low-rent crook could be responsible for something like this—but Sanderson knew she had to pursue it.

The clock was ticking.

15

He didn't like the look of this guy. Not one little bit.

The man had come to the door cursing, reeking displeasure. He was sweating and seemed keen to avoid eye contact, as if visitors were somehow contagious. When he did eventually look up, his expression was full of suspicion, as if the courier were here to rob him, rather than deliver the goods that *he* had ordered.

The courier held out the package and asked the man to sign for it. As he did so, he looked over his shoulder, curious to see what sort of hole this guy inhabited. It was a bomb site. Broken furniture, cardboard boxes, dust sheets, discarded pizza boxes. The tall Victorian property had presumably once been a rich gent's town house; now it was a stinking hovel. The courier jumped at the sight of a rat scurrying out from among the pizza boxes.

He raised his gaze to find the man staring right at him. His piercing aquamarine eyes silently chastized him for his nosiness.

"Good-bye," the man said, offering an abortion of a smile. Always polite, the courier didn't respond for once, simply turning and hurrying away as the front door shut firmly behind him.

Inside the house, the man listened to the van depart, peeking through the dirty curtains to check that he had really gone. Then, sweeping some old newspapers off the sideboard, he set the box down. Ripping off the tape that bound the lid together, he delved inside. He had cursed himself for his stupidity, for his oversight, but the precious contents of this box would rectify matters.

And his new friend would thank him for it.

16

The pain was horrible. It coursed through her eye sockets straight into her brain. Her nerve endings screamed in protest; her head throbbed violently. She buried her face in the bedsheets, praying that it would end.

She had been lying in bed when it happened. The approaching footsteps had not alarmed her, as they had before. She was ravenously hungry and wanted company—even his company—after a long and cold night. The wicket hatch slid open, then shut, and Ruby had expected to hear the key turn in the lock next—already a strange kind of routine was developing.

Instead, she was suddenly and unexpectedly blinded. The main lights in her small cell snapped on without warning. She had clamped her eyelids shut, but the damage had already been done. Her eyes, which had grown used to the darkness, were suddenly assaulted by the three heavy-duty sodium lights that were fixed to the ceiling.

Her eyes crept open, clamped shut again, then very slowly opened once more. Weird shapes and lights danced in front of her as her startled retinas scrabbled for some kind of focus.

He was standing over her.

"Don't touch me."

"Did you sleep well?"

"No. I bloody froze to death, you stupid freak. I'm going to die down here. Is that what you want?"

"I'll get you an extra blanket."

"Please let me go home."

"Get up."

He barked out this order, his tone suddenly impatient and unfriendly. Ruby realized that she knew nothing about this guy or how his mind worked. Could he turn violent? Could he be reasoned with? Was he insane?

"Take off your clothes."

"Please . . ."

"Take off your clothes," he repeated, raising his voice.

He wouldn't look at her. Oddly, his hands were trembling. Ruby tried to speak, but her heart was beating too fast, making her breathless and panicky.

"I don't want to," she managed eventually.

"Do it now or God help me . . ."

As he took a step toward her, Ruby scrambled off the bed.

"I'm doing it. I'm doing it."

Still, he wouldn't look at her. Sobbing quietly, Ruby took off the thin cotton pajama top that he'd given her in place of her own night gear. She hated the feel and the smell of it, but it kept her from freezing to death. Now she shivered, her naked skin exposed to the cold air. Hesitating, another sob escaping her, she removed her pajama bottoms, placing them on the bed next to her.

She felt intensely vulnerable, naked in front of a stranger, her gaunt frame illuminated by the overhead lights. She looked ghostly, her pale skin framed by the darkness of her tresses and pubic hair. She stared at the floor, refusing to meet his gaze.

She could tell he was looking at her now, appraising what he saw. *Go to hell,* she thought, but her empty bravado did little to cheer her. She was exposed and powerless here.

He stepped forward. Still Ruby stared at the floor. Then another step—he was right by her now. His hand reached out, lifting up her chin. She was looking straight at him; they were virtually nose to nose. His peculiar aroma filled her nostrils once more. She refused to blink, or smile.

His hands rose and Ruby flinched. There was something cold pressing against her stomach. She flicked a glance down. It was the end of a tape measure. He was measuring her.

She tried to stay stock-still, but her body was quivering with fear. He measured her hips, her shoulders, her chest. As the cold tape pressed against her nipples, another tear escaped, a sense of rising horror overwhelming her.

He slipped the tape round her neck, pulling it tight.

Then, satisfied, he stepped away. "You can get dressed."

Ruby gathered her pajamas, tugging them on quickly and clumsily.

"I have to go out now, but I won't be long," he said, watching her change. "And because you've been cooperative, I've brought you a present."

He pulled something from his pocket and placed it on the table.

An inhaler.

Ruby took a step forward, then checked herself.

"It's yours now. Don't make me take it away from you."

It was said with a smile but chilled Ruby to the core. It was obvious to her in that moment, as it should have been from the start, that this stranger now wielded the power of life or death over her.

17

He was taller than she had expected. On the phone he had sounded hesitant and lacking in stature. But the reality was very different. Daniel Briers was tall and handsome, with a confident stride and an easy manner. Dark hair, flecked with gray at the temples, framed an open countenance.

"DI Helen Grace. Thanks for coming down so quickly."

"I just want to get this thing sorted. There must have been a mix-up with the serial numbers. Pippa was tweeting again this morning, so it's hardly likely that—"

"May I have a look?"

They were heading out of Southampton train station toward Helen's pool car. Daniel Briers handed her his phone. Helen read the tweet—a brief and anodyne comment about Sunday morning hangovers.

"Have you actually spoken to her in the last two to three years?" Helen asked as she handed back the phone.

Daniel paused, frowned, then said:

"No, I haven't."

He suddenly seemed less assured, the fatigue of a sleepless night catching up with him, eroding his optimism. "I tried many times, left countless messages, but . . . I don't think she was ready to talk, so we had to rely on the occasional tweet and text. She seemed to be doing well in Southampton and . . . I was happy for her."

As they drove to the mortuary, Daniel filled her in on the cause of their estrangement. Helen could have guessed before he said anything: a new wife.

Pippa's mother had died of breast cancer when Pippa was six, sending the family into a spin for several years. But when Daniel had married again, all seemed set fair. However, Pippa and his second wife did not get on. Kristy brought two children to the party from a previous marriage, and to her mind, where they were constructive and polite, Pippa was hostile and unhelpful, unwilling to accept Kristy as her new mother. The situation had only worsened during Pippa's teenage years, and as soon as she was old enough to leave school *and* home, she did.

"I tried to reason with her," Daniel explained, "but she just wanted away. So she dossed down with an old school friend who was at college in Portsmouth and eventually she moved to Southampton. Got a job, a flat. She was making a go of things. It broke my heart when she left. I missed her every day, but I hoped over time we could repair the damage. That I could encourage her to come home."

They parked in the mortuary car park and headed inside to see Jim Grieves. As soon as they stepped into the building, Daniel's manner changed. He had been chatting sixteen to the dozen previously, but now he seemed affected by the cold sterility of the place. He was silent, focused, his body rigid. Helen had seen this many times before—the anxiety that affects all civilians when they are about to come face-to-face with a dead body for the first time.

The pleasantries were kept to a minimum—there was no point delaying the inevitable. Jim Grieves lowered the sheet slowly, revealing the young woman's face.

The effect on Daniel Briers was terrible and instant. A horrid, pained intake of breath. He looked like he had momentarily stopped breathing and Helen put her arm on his to check that he was okay. He turned to her, his face now drained of color, a man visibly aging in front of her.

When he did finally speak it was in a whisper and through tears: "That's Pips."

18

Andrew Simpson ran his finger down his tie and regarded the young lady sitting opposite him. It was unusual for him to have such pleasant company during the working day.

"So Ruby e-mailed you two days ago, giving notice?" Sanderson asked. Simpson Rentals had a broad portfolio of properties for rent in Southampton, most of them one- and two-bed flats in shoddily converted houses. They were cheap, but like Andrew Simpson's office, they were also unloved.

"That's correct. It was brief to say the least." Andrew Simpson turned his laptop round for Sanderson to see. As he did so, a strong odor of stale sweat drifted toward her. He was a thin man, with precise features and a very meticulous manner, but there was something about him that felt oddly washed out.

"I hereby give notice. Ruby Sprackling." Sanderson read the e-mail aloud.

"It's supposed to be in writing obviously, but nobody bothers with that anymore," Simpson said.

"Did you have any warning? Any sense of why she was leaving?"

"No, it was completely out of the blue. But then, she was a scatty girl. Always losing things, forgetting to pay her rent on time—"

"And do you have any idea where she might have gone?"

"No. I don't see my tenants very much."

Sanderson could well believe it. Out of sight, out of mind. "Do you have a set of keys to her flat?"

This was what Sanderson had been building up to. It seemed logical that if a third party was involved in her disappearance, then he or she must have had access to Ruby's flat. There had been no sign of forced entry, detritus from her night out had been found in the bin, the door had been double-locked on the way out—everything was in order, apart from the forgotten inhaler. If she had been taken, it was more of a . . . removal than an abduction or struggle.

"Yes, I do, but they are not in my possession at the moment."

Sanderson knew of four sets of keys in existence—Ruby had a set, as did Shanelle Harvey and Alison Sprackling. The latter two sets had been accounted for. Ruby presumably still had hers, so that left one set out there. "Where are they?"

"I gave them to my builder on Thursday. We've had a few problems with leaking pipes in that property. I'd asked him to go in over the weekend and paint over the damage."

Two days ago. Time enough to plan and execute an abduction. "And what's his name?"

Andrew Simpson looked uncertain, hesitating for the first time in their conversation, as if scared of the consequences, before finally replying:

"His name is Nathan Price."

19

He was a strange sight in the tattoo parlor. Clutching his New Look and M&S bags, he looked like any number of beleaguered dads on a Saturday afternoon shopping trip. Except it wasn't Saturday and he wasn't in a shopping center. He was in Angie's tattoo parlor—a forgotten dive in the shadow of the Western Docks that specializes in cheap body art and drug dealing.

The place had only been open five minutes when he entered. It was still a mess from last night's trade—sailors, hookers, stag parties—and the grumbling owner seemed irritated to have business so soon. She was still half-asleep and more than half-intoxicated. She offered him her body art menu with a shaking hand:

"Choose your poison," she said without smiling.

He looked her up and down before replying, "Actually I'd like to buy some needles."

She paused with her tidying and turned to face him. "You want kit?"

"I need round liner needles, flat shader needles, some curved stacks and inks too, of course."

"Any particular colors?"

"The full palette, please."

Angie looked him up and down—he hadn't a tattoo anywhere and didn't look the type—then rooted around for the items. He watched her intently, alive for any signs of curiosity or suspicion on her part.

But he had chosen his quarry well. Money was all that mattered to Angie.

She placed the items on the counter, but as he reached out to take them, she slammed her hand down to stop him. "Money first. No cards, no checks."

He handed over the cash and departed with his purchases. As he walked through the back streets of this forgotten part of town, he afforded himself a small smile. He now had everything he needed and though he didn't normally go in for such cheap amusement, he had to admit to a small thrill at having paid for it with Ruby's own money. She wouldn't thank him for it—who would, given the pain that lay ahead?—but he was prepared to face down any protest or defiance. After all, she had been put on this earth to make him happy. And the best way to do that was to learn how to submit.

20

They were caught in a strange kind of hell. This one came complete with plastic flowers, a statuette of Jesus and tired sofas. Many people, having discovered the worst, fled the mortuary, wanting to get as far away from the reality of their tragedy as possible. Others, like Daniel Briers, simply didn't have the strength in their legs. Which was why Helen now found herself sitting by his side in the mortuary relatives' room.

"It doesn't make any sense." Daniel Briers hadn't said a word since he identified his daughter. Now, a full thirty minutes later, he was trying to process the awful news, cradling a full cup of cold tea.

"She texted me, wrote tweets," he continued. "I replied to her texts, for God's sake."

"Did she ever reply directly to your texts? Within the following day or so, say?"

Daniel looked at her but didn't speak. It was as if he didn't understand the question.

"Daniel, I know that none of this seems real, that you're in shock, but it's really important that you answer my questions, if you can."

He looked at her for a moment, his mind scrolling back, trying to connect to his past with his daughter. "No. It's true, there were always large gaps between the texts. And the tweets."

His mind was whirring with the awful possibilities this presented.

"It did seem odd," he continued. "But she'd left under such a cloud that I thought this was her way of keeping control of the situation, of letting us know that she was in charge."

At this point, he finally broke. The last words cascaded from him and were then swallowed up by huge, racking sobs. His misery was primal, elemental—a towering, imposing man howling in grief for his lost daughter. Helen had witnessed this scene many times before and always felt deeply for those left behind. She knew what it was like to lose a loved one and feel responsible. But this time her sympathy was particularly acute.

Not only was Daniel Briers grappling with the fact that his daughter had died before they could be reconciled—he was also beginning to realize that all recent communication between them had been fake, fabricated by a devious killer. Someone had been keeping his little girl alive from beyond the grave.

21

"Put them on."

Ruby stood by the bed, under the glare of the sodium lights that had suddenly snapped on. It seemed part of her captor's technique now to half blind her before opening the door.

She turned her gaze to the bed, where he had laid out a complete outfit for her. Knickers, tights, a short denim skirt, low-cut top, hoop earrings. A funky Saturday night outfit or a hooker's uniform, depending on how you wore it.

"Now."

His raised voice made her jump. This time she kept her nerve—though her bottom lip quivered as she picked up the skimpy black thong—she was not going to give him the satisfaction of crying again. She undressed and dressed quickly, not wanting to be naked for long. Even so she faltered as she put the earrings in. Unlike the clothes, these were not new—they looked tarnished and old. Somehow they felt like death to Ruby.

"Let me look at you."

She turned to face him. At first he didn't react, but then a smile crept over his unshaven features.

"Good."

He stared at her, enjoying the moment. All the while Ruby tried to swallow down the bile that crept up her throat.

"As it's Sunday," he continued cheerily, "I thought we'd eat together. I know how you like a roast."

Ruby now spotted the tray on the table. It had drinks on it and two plates covered with plastic food warmers. Ruby didn't want to play ball, but she was so, so hungry. He removed the covers to reveal a ready-meal Sunday lunch. It was a travesty of the real thing . . . but the gravy smelled good. Ruby sat down and fell on the meal, cramming great forkfuls into her mouth.

"Don't give yourself indigestion."

He seemed amused by her hunger. She slowed her intake slightly but was not about to let a feast like this go begging.

"It's good you've got your appetite back, Summer. You always were a good eater."

Ruby paused momentarily, then carried on eating, trying to quell the fear rising inside her. "Don't call me that."

"Why not? It's your name."

"It's not my n—"

"What else would I call you?"

Ruby's fork clattered down onto the table, gravy splashing messily around. Tears were already streaming down her face, her strength suddenly evaporating. "Please don't do this. I want to go home. I want to be with my family—"

"You are home, Summer."

"I want to see my mum and dad. And Cassie and Cono—"

"Will you fucking shut up!"

As he bellowed this, he struck her hard across the cheek, the rings on his fingers connecting sharply with her cheekbone. She stumbled a little, falling back off her chair, but before she could hit the floor, he had hauled her back up, dumping her unceremoniously back on the chair.

"Just shut the fuck up and eat—your—lunch."

His eyes were blazing as he screamed at her. Ruby froze, the thought that she might be only moments from a brutal death paralyzing her completely.

"Eat," he said more quietly, fighting to contain his rage.

Slowly Ruby lifted the fork to her lips. But the cold meat now felt alien and unwelcome in her mouth. She held it there but didn't chew it, powerless to do as she was told.

"That's better," he continued, placing a small grayish potato in his mouth. "Now, let's *try* to enjoy the rest of our lunch."

22

They ate in silence, pushing the food around their plates. The leg of lamb, Maris Piper potatoes and posh broccoli had been bought with a celebration in mind—Ruby's return home. But in her absence, the family Sunday lunch felt more like a wake. Jonathan had wanted to throw the food in the bin and forget the whole thing, but Alison had refused. It wasn't in her nature to bin expensive food and, besides, she couldn't give up on Ruby yet.

Did she really think that by cooking the meal she could make Ruby somehow appear? She couldn't answer that question, couldn't really explain what she was doing, but she felt compelled to keep the home fires burning nevertheless. As she basted the meat, as she trimmed the broccoli, she kept one eye on the front door, hoping against hope that the key would turn in the lock and Ruby would enter, full of excuses and half-baked apologies.

It's funny how these things turn out. She had waxed and waned in her attitude to Ruby, one minute castigating her for her unpleasant behavior, the next trying to understand what she was going through. Now Alison knew she would forgive her anything—never say a word in reproach ever again—if she just walked through the door. Would Jonathan do the same? Alison found it hard to tell. Usually such a ball of energy, he had been oddly quiet since her disappearance.

Was it possible that Ruby had run off? Changed her mind about coming home? Surely it was, as there had been so much fuss and upset recently. Alison cursed herself for ever having supported Ruby in her quest to find her birth mother. It had seemed the right thing to do at the time—it's what liberal parents should do, isn't it?—but look where it had got them.

She and Jonathan had fought so hard for their family. They'd always wanted three kids, but Alison couldn't conceive. When they first found out, Alison feared Jonathan might leave her, in search of a more fertile mate. But oddly it had drawn them closer together. Terrible though the adoption process was, she and Jonathan had been determined not to be beaten by it and over the years they had managed to create a loving, stable home for Ruby, Cassie and Conor. Until Alison—or, more truthfully, Shanelle—had torn it apart.

Conor and Cassie were scared—that much was obvious. They read the news, watched TV—they knew how stories of missing girls sometimes ended up. Alison had worked overtime to convince them that this wasn't the case here, that things would be okay. Sometimes she even believed it herself. In the absence of fact, of certainty, all that was left was hope—and the stupid superstitions of a heartbroken mum.

Which was why the four of them now sat in silence in the dining room, eating food nobody wanted and thinking about the girl that everybody missed.

23

Nathan Price was not at home. His wife had been very certain on *that* point. On everything else, she was frustratingly vague. Sanderson had pushed Angela Price as hard as she could, but had learned only that Nathan worked away a lot and was currently on a job—though she didn't know where he was or when he'd be back.

Price was a freelance painter and decorator who went where the work took him. He had a few regular maintenance contracts with local landlords—Sanderson had checked these out, but they too had yielded little. So she was left with Angela as her "best" hope of a lead.

Scanning the small flat, Sanderson felt curiously depressed. The place reeked of defeat and despair. Angela and Nathan didn't have kids and, as far as Sanderson could tell, didn't have much of a relationship either. They had been together several years and yet there were no photos of them anywhere, no signs that they were a happy, committed couple. Angela didn't work and was reliant on Nathan for cash to top up her benefits. She was overweight and lacking in confidence, spending her time waiting to see if her errant husband would return. Sanderson sensed a sadness in her, as though she knew she was second best. For once in her life, Sanderson was glad to be single. Better to be alone than somebody's doormat.

Sanderson left empty-handed, her frustration simmering. Who was this guy that he left such a small footprint on the world? Was it deliberate? If it was, it would make him hard to find. Which was bad news for Sanderson.

And even worse news for Ruby.

24

The Great Southern Hotel was not the plushest hotel in town, but it was central—just off Brunswick Place—and, more important, quiet. The Saturday night revelers had checked out by now and the whole place had a peaceful Sunday feel. It had been Helen's first thought when Daniel Briers insisted on staying in Southampton, rather than returning home.

Daniel was still in shock, so Helen did the formalities for him, checking him in with the minimum of fuss. Moments later, they exited the lift on the fourteenth floor and entered Daniel's well-appointed room. Helen knew she should really have asked a Family Liaison officer to do this bread-and-butter stuff, but something told her not to abandon Daniel today. This strong, optimistic man suddenly looked very fragile. Having wrecked his world, Helen felt responsible for his safety and well-being. She couldn't leave him until she was sure he was okay.

Sitting on the bed, his raincoat still on, he stared into space, seemingly oblivious to Helen's attention.

"I'm going to stay," he said suddenly, interrupting her. "For the duration."

"Of course. You must do what feels right," Helen replied. "But you should be aware that our investigations take weeks, sometimes months—"

"I abandoned Pips once. I'm not going to do it again."

It was said without self-pity. His tone was one of quiet determination.

"I need to understand what happened to her," he continued. "Where I . . . went wrong."

His voice quivered a little now, before he went on:

"She was my little girl, Helen. I want to stay here until you catch . . ."

He petered out, grief robbing him of the breath to finish his sentence.

"And we will," Helen responded quickly. "We'll catch whoever did this to Pippa. You have my word on that."

It was a stupid thing to promise and Helen knew she would regret it, but it was what Daniel needed to hear now. The only thing he could hear that would give him the strength to keep going. He looked up at Helen, his eyes full of gratitude, the color suddenly returning to his cheeks. It was as if her words had briefly brought him back to life.

He reached out a hand and took hers. "Thank you, Helen."

The pair sat in silence for a moment. Then, having checked once more that Daniel had everything he needed, Helen left. Daniel had phone calls to make—the worst phone calls he'd ever have to make—and Helen had work to do.

Walking away from the hotel, Helen was suddenly fired with determination to get justice not only for Pippa, but for Daniel too.

25

"So, what do we know about Pippa Briers?"

Helen was addressing the team who had now assembled in the incident room at Southampton Central.

"Born in Reading in 1990 to Daniel and Samantha Briers," Helen continued. "Her mum died when she was six. Shortly afterward Pippa was diagnosed as suffering from brachycardia—her heart beat too slowly—so she had a pacemaker fitted when she was ten. Her dad remarried shortly afterward. It didn't go down well and Pippa moved south following a bust-up with her stepmum, staying first with her friend Caroline Furnace in Portsmouth—have we tracked her down yet?"

"Spoke to her on the phone this morning," DC Grounds replied. "Caroline's had the occasional text, read the occasional tweet, but hasn't seen Pippa for over three years now."

Helen let this thought settle before continuing:

"So she ends up in Southampton, having got a job at the Sun First Travel Agency in WestQuay shopping center. What are they saying?"

"She worked there as a travel agent for nearly six years," DC McAndrew replied. "Quiet girl, good worker, well liked. Great appraisals and attendance records. Then one day she just didn't turn up. Sent them a brief e-mail from her BlackBerry saying she'd had enough of organizing other people's holidays and wanted to travel herself. And they never heard from her again. They were irritated because she was supposed to work a month's notice, but . . ."

"When was this?"

"Three years ago."

"Which is within the time frame of her abduction. Where did she live?"

"She moved around a lot," piped up DC Stevens, one of the new officers on the team. "Bitterne Park, Portswood, St. Denys. Mostly studio flats or bedsits, nothing very high end. Last known address was in Merry Oak. We're checking it out."

"Quick as you can, please," Helen said with just the right mixture of admonishment and encouragement. They needed facts, not possibilities.

"Friends? Boyfriends?"

"We've taken a look at her phone records, her e-mail accounts," DC Lucas, the new female DC, offered. "Plenty of socializing and lots of Internet dating. Nearly all short-lived apart from one—an on/off boyfriend whom she dated for a year, then dumped when he turned out to be married."

"Name?"

"Nathan Price."

26

His eyes remained glued to her as she crouched over the bucket. She hated being watched while she urinated and consequently she had held off as long as she could. But her bladder was in agony and he had made no move to leave, so in the end, she had relented, tugging down her knickers and emptying her bladder into the old builder's bucket as quickly as she could. The sound of her urine hitting the plastic echoed round her brick prison.

Finishing, she tugged up her knickers and headed swiftly back toward the bed.

"Come here."

He had been watching her silently for a long time, as if plucking up the courage to say something, so she was startled by this sudden instruction. She paused, flicking a glance up at him, afraid of what he might want.

"Come," he repeated.

She walked slowly over to him.

"Sit."

She did as she was told, sitting next to him by the battered dining table.

"Roll up your right sleeve. Higher. I want to see your shoulder. Good, now put your elbow on the table. Like that. Grip the top of my chair with your right hand and keep your arm steady."

"Please . . ."

"It may sting a bit at first, but it won't do you any permanent damage."

He reached down now and brought out a leather case, which he opened and unfolded on the table. Needles, inks, designs—a tattoo artist's instruments.

"Please don't do this. I don't want you to do this."

Ruby was begging now. She had always had a massive thing about needles—she had fainted several times when faced with injections—and she was sickened by the thought of him taking a needle to her bare flesh. In response, he gripped the underside of her arm, pinching and turning her skin so fiercely that it brought tears to Ruby's eyes.

"Don't fight me, Summer," he said calmly, twisting the skin round still farther.

Ruby screamed and cried, but it made no difference. He refused to release his grip. Through tears, she saw the fierce intent in his eyes and the long needles that lay on the table before her. Though the thought of what was about to happen horrified her, she knew that there was no point resisting. She hung her head, whimpering quietly.

"That's better."

Releasing his grip, he set about his work. Carefully, he opened the jar of black dye. Slipping the steel tip and barrel onto the body of the tattoo gun, he chose a needle, dipped it in the dark ink and readied himself to begin.

Ruby shut her eyes, tensing herself against the inevitable pain. As the needle punctured her skin, she swallowed down a yelp. He moved it over the surface of her skin and the pain immediately increased—it felt like a cat's claw dragging across her flesh. Despite her obvious discomfort, he didn't hesitate, his concentration never wavering, as he meticulously carved out the outline of his design. After ten minutes' patient work he paused, smiling briefly at Ruby, before moving on to the blue ink. Ruby's respite was brief and he applied himself again, the same sharp pain jagging through her as he worked.

Ruby closed her eyes, hoping that it would be over quicker if she didn't focus on it. The worst was over—she had consented to be decorated—now there was nothing to be done but see it through.

"You can look now."

When she opened her eyes, she found he was holding up a small mirror for her to admire his handiwork. For a brief second, she stared straight into his eyes, defiant, refusing to look in the mirror. But his intense gaze was too strong and, defeated, she dropped her eyes to the mirror. She didn't know what she had been expecting, but the result still surprised her.

Her pale skin looked sore, a wide red circle of irritation adorned her shoulder. And in the center of the circle, innocent and strangely at odds with its unhappy surroundings, was a small bluebird.

27

DC Sanderson sat across the desk in Helen's office, files spread out in front of her. The door was firmly shut, the blinds down—this was not a conversation for public consumption. In some ways Helen's desire for privacy was pointless—several officers in the team knew that Nathan Price was a person of interest in the Ruby Sprackling case and had no doubt made the connection themselves, but Helen didn't want anyone speculating about a possible link between the two investigations until they were sure there *was* a connection. The lowered blinds and closed door made this point eloquently.

"I need exact times," Helen said as Sanderson skimmed Ruby Sprackling's phone records.

"Ruby sent her first good-bye tweet yesterday at around one p.m.," Sanderson replied.

"Where was it sent from?"

"Still trying to pin the exact location down, but it's somewhere on the eastern fringes of the New Forest."

Helen kept her expression neutral, despite the fear rising inside her. "And the second?"

"Sent this morning at around ten, Southampton city center."

There it was. An exact match to the times and locations when Pippa Briers had texted and tweeted *her* latest offerings. The relative briefness of the messages and the generalized, anodyne contact were concerning, as was the fact that both phone signals were on only briefly before vanishing again, presumably having been switched off. It looked very much like a third party was keeping the girls' digital presence alive. The killer obviously didn't know that Pippa's body had been found and identified. Helen was glad that this discovery had been kept away from the press, as it now gave the lie to these fake tweets and texts.

"I want this link kept quiet for now," Helen continued, after she'd filled Sanderson in on her thinking. "But Nathan Price is now our number-one suspect in both cases and I want him found. Give his photo to uniform, get people back to his house, circulate his van registration details to traffic—and get Stevens down to Pippa Briers's flat in Merry Oak. There may still be tenants in the building who remember Pippa and Nathan. We need as much info as we can, as fast as we can."

Sanderson nodded and hurried off to do Helen's bidding. Helen watched her go, her emotions churning. They were making progress and Helen could already see Sanderson's orders energizing the team—the latest developments *could* herald the safe return of Ruby Sprackling if they moved with speed and purpose. On the other hand, their latest breakthrough had confirmed Helen's very worst fears. They were dealing with a serial offender. A skilled and experienced predator. Helen had caught two serial killers already in her short career. But would her luck hold a third time?

28

"The body was found on Saturday morning and has since been identified as being that of Pippa Briers from Reading, a woman in her mid-twenties. The family have been informed."

Detective Superintendent Ceri Harwood's delivery was crisp and authoritative. Sitting next to her, Helen privately conceded that Harwood was made for this sort of thing—the massed ranks of the press spread out in front of her like an adoring audience—and she always came across as calm and in control. Helen by contrast often found it hard to suppress her impatience in these situations. She knew the press was a valuable tool for an investigation, but she hated the inactivity of sitting here answering questions, when she could be out chasing leads.

"How did she die?" Emilia Garanita asked.

As ever, the crime correspondent of the *Southampton Evening*

News got the first question in. She had an uncanny ability to talk over her colleagues in the press. Her question was aimed directly at Helen, but before she could answer, Harwood jumped in.

"The postmortem examination is ongoing. We will release more information as and when we have it."

"Is the beach safe? Should the public be worried?" Emilia asked with hesitation. Helen could see her searching for the story, the sensation. But once again Harwood played a straight bat.

"The beach is *perfectly* safe. I must stress that the body appears to have been buried several years ago—this is not a recent incident. The beach has been reopened and the public should feel free to use it as usual."

"Any leads, Inspector?" asked Tony Purvis from the *Portsmouth Herald*, nipping in just ahead of Emilia.

"We're pursuing several lines of inquiry," Helen replied, "and we would ask anyone who knew Pippa Briers socially, or who worked with her at the Sun First Travel Agency, to contact the incident room. Any details—no matter how small—about her life in Southampton could be extremely helpful. She had several piercings and a tattoo, an image of which is in your briefing notes, which we believe was done during her time in Southampton. If anyone recognizes it or knows where it was done, we would ask them to get in touch."

"Any suspects? Anyone you'd like to talk to?" Tony continued.

"Not at this time," Helen said firmly. "But obviously we'll let you know if that changes."

Helen had debated long and hard about whether to release Nathan Price's name to the press. But Harwood had urged caution and for once Helen had agreed with her. Naming him might drive him further underground, which was the last thing they wanted.

The briefing wound up shortly afterward. As Helen was leaving, she felt a familiar tap on the shoulder. She turned to find Emilia Garanita facing her. They were old foes, but Emilia had nevertheless gone out of her way to be publicly supportive of Helen recently. During the investigation into the Ella Matthews murders, Emilia had seriously overstepped the mark, illegally tracking Helen's movements during the hunt for the killer—and she was still eating humble pie because of it.

"Any further tidbits for the *News*? We'd love to help in any way we can."

Helen smiled inside. Emilia clearly found it quite a struggle to be friendly—full-frontal assault was her default setting.

"Nothing yet, Emilia. But I've got your number."

Emilia watched her go. She had had precious little from Helen since they called a truce a year ago, and the pain of being nice was beginning to tell on her. She was working her ass off to get some new purchase on Helen, but it was abundantly clear that she was still frozen out. Irritated, she gathered up her things and followed the rest of the assembled journalists toward the exit. She'd hoped this case might be a way back in—a chance to get her career back on track—but already it was looking like another horrible dead end.

29

She was going to break his neck this time. She was going to march right in there and break his stupid neck. What a mug she'd been. Sticking up for him, lying for him, when all the time he'd been lying to *her*. About where he was, what he was doing, who he was with . . .

Angela Price's fury was at fever pitch, yet still she hesitated. A girlfriend had tipped her off that she'd seen Nathan in Southampton city center, when he'd specifically told Angela he would be working the week in Bournemouth. He'd probably been up to no good—boozing, chasing girls, being the faithless little shit he always was. Why did she put up with it?

She'd been round his usual haunts—the builders' cafés, pool halls, drinking dens—and eventually found him in the Diamond Sports Bar. There he was—not thirty feet away—watching the rolling TV news intently, totally oblivious to her presence. Her hand was on the bar door; she could walk in there right now and call him out. Embarrass him in front of his mates, call him every name under the sun, let the world know what he was really like . . .

"Out of the way, love."

A thirsty punter barged past her, irritated by her hovering presence at the doorway. Who was she kidding? She wasn't going in there. She looked like death—lank hair, no makeup, bags under her eyes—and would only embarrass herself. It was all blokes in there and they'd only laugh at her pathetic display. She would be the one who'd end up looking ridiculous, not him.

Tears pricked her eyes as she walked away. Why was she such a massive waste of space? She would never be anything but a doormat, something for Nathan to pick up and toss aside whenever he wanted . . .

She slowed as a thought occurred to her. There was one way she could get her own back on the faithless bastard, one thing she could do to scupper him once and for all.

Summoning her courage, she pulled out her battered Nokia and after a moment's hesitation dialed 999.

30

"Get your hands off me, girl." It was said with a smile, but the aggression beneath was clear. "I know you want to get in my trousers, but I'm a married man, so get your fucking mitts off me."

Sanderson didn't dignify Nathan Price's outburst with a reply. He'd been effing and blinding since she picked him up, and besides, she wouldn't put it past him to do a runner. One hand on his cuffs, one hand on his collar—that was the best way to keep hold of him. If she was honest, this was one of the small perks of the job, cutting violent, unpleasant men down to size. She bustled him roughly through the doors, only releasing him when they reached the custody sergeant.

"Got a nice one for you, Harry," Sanderson said, depositing Price at the front desk. The formalities were soon done and they were buzzed through to the custody area. As they neared the interrogation suite, DS Lloyd Fortune approached.

"All right, fella, what did they get you for?" Nathan asked with mock sympathy.

Ignoring Price's racist gibe, Lloyd turned to Sanderson. "I'll take this charmer off your hands."

For a moment, Sanderson said nothing. Price was her suspect and, more important, her collar.

"It's all right—I've got it."

Sanderson should have backed down immediately, of course, but something—pride? anger?—stopped her.

"DI Grace suggested that she and I lead on this one."

Was this true? Was she being elbowed aside? Whatever the truth of the matter, she couldn't argue the point with Nathan Price hanging on their every word, visibly enjoying the tension between the two officers.

"Lovers' tiff?" he offered helpfully. "Like a bit of black, do you?"

"Watch your mouth," Lloyd barked back, hauling the grinning suspect away toward the custody suite.

Sanderson watched them go. There was prejudice here all right, but it wasn't just coming from Price. Sanderson was the more experienced, better-qualified officer, with far more investigation hours and convictions under her belt, yet Lloyd Fortune had still been promoted over and above her. He'd only been at Southampton a little over a year—to her four—and already he'd shot past her. She knew the reason why—though of course she could never say it in public. It was political correctness pure and simple and it made her blood boil. Lloyd was keen to justify his promotion, to get a high-profile conviction under his belt, and Sanderson would suffer as a result. She understood this; she might even have done the same if she were in his shoes. But was Helen complicit too? She didn't go in for that kind of thing normally, but had the landscape changed?

Walking back to her desk, Sanderson felt the ground subtly shifting under her feet and she didn't like it one little bit.

31

"Tell me about your relationship with Pippa Briers."

Helen sat opposite Nathan Price, flanked by Lloyd Fortune. Now facing a detective inspector, Price had lost a little of his cockiness, the seriousness of the situation finally impressing itself upon him. Helen was keen to press home the advantage.

"What do you want to know?"

Answering a question with a question. Price had never been charged with anything, but Helen didn't doubt he'd been in a custody suite before.

"How long were you seeing her for?"

"Nine, ten months."

"Did you live together?"

"On and off. I had a wife at home, so you know . . ."

He was unrepentant, enjoying his status as a low-rent seducer.

"And how did you get on?"

"Good. She liked a drink, a dance. She was all right."

"Did you argue?"

"Sometimes. When she went on about things."

"Like the fact that you had a wife and hadn't told her about it."

Nathan shrugged—he wasn't going to deny it.

"Am I right in thinking Pippa ended the relationship, when she found out you were two-timing her."

"Three-timing her, actually. I don't know what it is about the girls round here."

"And how did you react when she dumped you?"

Helen clocked the tiny reaction from Price, a little spike of anger at the word "dumped," which he quickly suppressed.

"What are you going to do?" he replied casually, but Helen wasn't buying it.

"You went nuts, didn't you?"

"No. I di—"

"You didn't like being dumped and you blew your stack. I have a witness statement here from one of Pippa's colleagues at Sun First. Says you barged in there, caused a massive scene."

"Bullshit."

"Apparently you had to be hauled out by security. We also have a statement from a long-term tenant at Bedford Heights in Merry Oak who confirms that you turned up drunk several times, banging on Pippa's door, demanding to be let in."

"She'd changed the lock and I didn't have a key. It was no big deal."

"Why had she changed the lock, Nathan?"

For once, Nathan didn't have a ready reply.

"Because she was scared of you? She told colleagues she was scared of you. Said you were stalking her."

"No way."

"You didn't want to let her go, did you, Nathan? I think you *liked* her. Where did you take her?"

A long silence, as Nathan stared back at Helen. Then he dropped his gaze. "I want a lawyer."

"A duty brief is on the way. She should be here in a few minutes. But I'd like to keep going with these general questions, unless you'd specifically like me to stop for some reason."

Another long pause, then a dismissive shrug.

"Tell us about Ruby Sprackling," Lloyd said, taking up the baton.

"Don't know her."

"Pretty girl. Similar look to Pippa. You're fixing a leak in her flat."

"Oh yeah, I got you."

"Still got keys to her flat, have you?"

"I did until you took them off me."

"And where is Ruby now, Nathan?"

Another long beat, then:

"No idea."

"When did you last see her?" Helen countered quickly.

"A couple of days ago. She was heading out to the shops or something—"

"She disappeared on Friday night, hasn't been seen since. Did you see her Friday night, Nathan?"

"No, I was off to a job in Bournemouth."

"So you weren't at Revolution, then? On Friday night?" Helen fired back.

Finally a flicker of fear in Nathan's expression. Helen slid a photo across the table toward him.

"This is a CCTV still of you queuing up to enter Revolution, a club off Bedford Square. Look at the date and time code. Friday night. Ruby was there that night."

"Piss off."

"We see you going in, but we don't see you coming out. A place like that must have emergency exits, somewhere you can slip out. Is that what you did? Before you followed Ruby home."

"I never saw her."

"Your van was parked in Ruby's road. Traffic cameras pick you up entering the road just after six p.m. Same camera sees your van driving away at four a.m. But the club shut at two a.m. What were you doing in the intervening two hours, Nathan?"

"I want a lawyer." His tone was angry now.

"Why won't you talk to me, Nathan? What have you done?"

Nathan stared at the floor, saying nothing.

"This is your one chance to come clean. Any denials or lies will play very badly in court," Helen continued. "We can't do anything for Pippa now, but if you give up Ruby, then maybe I can help you. So please, Nathan, tell me where she is."

A long pause. Helen shot a look at Lloyd, then back at Nathan. Slowly the suspect raised his head. All the attitude was gone now; he looked like a cornered animal.

But when he spoke, he simply said:

"No comment."

32

The sharp pain had subsided, to be replaced by a dull ache. Ruby lay on the bed, cradling her defiled shoulder, wishing the whole thing would just go away. After he had finished tattooing her, he had seemed quite emotional. Tears hugged the corners of his eyes as he leaned forward and kissed her gently on the head. He left soon after, as if not trusting his composure to hold.

Ruby's despair was total, her mood black—those early hopes that she might bargain with him, bribe him, were now in tatters. She had cried and cried, the pain of her recent tattoo amplified by her feelings of hopelessness. She realized now that she was his toy. She was his plaything in this doll's house where everything that looked real was fake.

She had examined every inch of her surroundings now. There was little else to do in the long hours alone and she had spent the time hunting for anything that could be used as a weapon, should the need arise. Though she tried to deny it, she had seen the intense emotion that gripped him when he looked at her, had felt his eyes crawl over her body. If he did force himself on her, how would she fight him off?

There was a kettle on the rickety sideboard, but that was made of plastic and would be cumbersome to wield. There were other strange additions to the room—framed pictures on the walls, a calendar from 2013 and hooks on the walls on which to hang a hat or coat—but nothing of any use. She had tried to rip the hooks off the wall, but they were sealed in concrete and impossible to budge. Why were they there in the first place? It wasn't as if anyone was going to visit. So why? Why go to such trouble to create a picture-perfect room that was just for show? Ruby buried her face in the sheets, trying to stem a rising wave of nausea.

Try to stay calm. Don't give in. Ruby forced herself to think of happier things once more. She had only been here a couple of days, but already her anxiety about going mad in this hole was real. Total despair would lead to insanity, Ruby felt sure of that, so she once more turned her thoughts to her family. It was Sunday—what would they be doing? The washing-up from Sunday lunch would have eventually been done by Conor and Cassie—begrudgingly, as always—and Mum and Dad would have taken Max out for a walk—

It hit Ruby like a train, suddenly and without mercy. Her mum. It was her mum's birthday in two days. She would miss her mum's birthday . . .

What would she go through this year? Ruby could picture the stifling mood of anxiety and distress, the total absence of presents or cards, the paralyzing awfulness of a birthday spent missing a daughter who wasn't there to give her a birthday hug. The horror of it took

Ruby's breath away. This was *real.* This was happening. She had been ripped from the heart of a family who loved her far more than she deserved and would probably never see them again.

Swallowing down her tears, Ruby tried to conjure up their familiar faces again. To relive those moments of family happiness that already seemed a lifetime ago. It was desperate stuff—her family existing only in these pointless imaginings—but this was her lot now. Retreating inside her memory, Ruby felt empty but oddly comforted. This would be her cocoon now.

33

"My client has told you as much as he knows—"

"Your client hasn't told us a single thing," Helen barked back, already irritated by the by-the-book primness of Price's duty brief. "And let me give you both a piece of advice. 'No comment' is not a good defense. It makes you look guilty."

Helen stressed the last word.

"Do you know what you get for abduction and murder, Nathan?" she continued, determined to keep the pressure up. "Fifteen to twenty minimum. How does that sound?"

"I think we should take a break now," the brief resumed predictably.

"We still have time," interjected Lloyd dismissively. "More important, we still have questions. The *same* questions. What happened in those two hours, Nathan? Did you let yourself into Ruby's flat? Overpower her? Or had you already slipped something into her drink at the club?"

Still nothing in response.

"Your client should know," Lloyd carried on, "that we have impounded his van. We found some interesting things in the back. The usual pots, tools, building stuff, of course, but also a bedroll and several blankets. What are the blankets for?"

"I sleep in there sometimes when I work. I need blankets," Nathan replied.

"Four of them? In the height of summer? There were hairs on the bedroll, black hairs. You look to me like you're a natural blond, Nathan, so why are there black hairs there?"

A long pause. Nathan's brief shot a look at him, clearly waiting for his next move.

"I've nothing to say," he eventually replied.

"So I suggest you charge or release my client," his brief followed up quickly.

"We're just getting started," Lloyd said, his professional politeness falling away now.

"You've got nothing. You know that, we know that—"

"Let's see what the forensics team turn up in the van, shall we?" Helen replied abruptly. "Silly to count our chickens before then. I make it we still have . . . almost forty hours left to hold your client. Which I'd say is more than enough time for a night in the cells, wouldn't you, Nathan?"

Not for the first time that day, Helen enjoyed wiping the smile off Nathan Price's face.

34

Night was slowly stealing over Southampton. The landmarks that had looked unfamiliar and workaday in the daylight now took on a more sinister appearance. From his viewpoint on the fourteenth flour, Daniel Briers looked out over the city. To some, the twinkling lights against the night sky would have looked exciting, full of promise. To him, it was just a world of shadows. He imagined all sorts of depraved characters out there—murderers, rapists, thieves—exploiting the darkness, using the cover of night to commit numerous unspeakable crimes.

Pippa had come here and been swallowed by this place. Though he was compelled to stay here now, to see justice done, he already hated Southampton with a passion.

Since Helen had left him, the day had seemed to drag on and on. He had made the necessary phone calls immediately, but they had been brief. He couldn't trust himself to hold it together during a long conversation. There was no question of him trying to analyze events with others yet. He just imparted the dreadful news and made his excuses. As soon as he had finished the calls, he turned his mobile off, had a whiskey and tried to get some rest.

He was exhausted from a sleepless night and the awful events of the day, but he couldn't switch off. A kaleidoscope of images and memories swirled round his mind—Pippa's birth, her bitter grief at her mother's passing, the way she used to make him "Dad of the Year" cards when she was small, her pride in her school prizes, the later arguments and recriminations—most of which had been his fault, he now realized. An endless carousel of thoughts and feelings, some bad, but mostly very, very good. *His* Pippa living on, as she would have to now, in his memory.

Was it a wise move to stay here? Kristy, his wife, clearly wasn't sure—"Wouldn't you be better off here with me and the boys?"—though she left the final decision up to him. It was hard for her, Daniel now thought to himself. Kristy was deeply shocked by Pippa's death, as they all were, but she didn't really *like* Pippa—Kristy felt she was self-oriented and needy—and her grief was necessarily compromised by her feelings, whatever she might say to the contrary.

Even now Pippa was a source of tension between them—someone Kristy didn't much care for but whom Daniel couldn't give up on. The ties that bind a parent to a child can never be broken; however awful their relationship might be, those ties just *are*. Even in death, that doesn't change, which was why Daniel had to stay. There would be many awful things he'd have to face here—he hadn't yet been to the beach where they found her—and he hoped he would have the strength to see it through, for Pippa's sake if not his own.

But looking out over the bleak vista of Southampton, he felt his courage wavering. This place was so alien to him, so threatening. And hanging over everything was the terrible knowledge that out there somewhere, shrouded in darkness, was the person who stole, killed and buried his only child.

35

It was chaos. As she had expected it would be. A wall of noise assaulted Emilia Garanita as soon as she entered the hall—a cacophony of shouts, recriminations, laughter and more. Knackered, she plonked her keys down on the hall table and made her way toward the source of the anarchy.

Her father was serving out the remainder of a lengthy prison sentence and her mother had done a runner nearly a decade ago, meaning that Emilia—the eldest of six children—had been in loco parentis now for more years than she cared to count. She was still young herself, shy of thirty, but she felt much older, particularly today. The briefing at Southampton Central had yielded nothing concrete, and the rebuff from Helen Grace had rankled, setting her on edge for the rest of the day. Some days were like that—fruitless, irritating and depressing.

She entered the kitchen to a litany of accusations and counterclaims. The youngest of her five siblings was only twelve, the closest in age to her not twenty-five, so there were lots of fragile, oversize egos to create conflict and consternation. As ever, Emilia's presence calmed things and slowly the grievances of the day were put to bed. As the family sat down to eat together—pork and chorizo stew, a legacy of their Portuguese heritage—Emilia's mood slowly began to improve. As exasperating as her siblings were, they nevertheless loved and accepted Emilia for what she was, warts and all. Some people didn't like her character, other people despised her because of her job and everyone reacted to her face, half of which was badly scarred following an acid attack by her father's drug-dealing employers. She had learned to ignore it, then later taken advantage of it, deliberately testing people with her disfigurement to see if they'd react. But as bullish as she was, the frowns her face provoked still hit home. Not here, though—not at home—where she was abused, teased and cherished just the same as everyone else.

Slowly the younger children sloped off to bed. Her closest sister, Luciana, kept her company through *Game of Thrones*, and then she too called it a day. Leaving Emilia alone with her thoughts.

Her career—her life—had stalled. Her disloyalty in selling the sensational Ella Matthews story to the *Mail*, rather than to her employers, had not gone down well and she had very nearly lost her job at the *Southampton Evening News*. The job that had been promised at the *Mail* never materialized, leaving Emilia in the undignified position of having to beg to keep her old job—a job that she still thought was beneath her. She had always hoped regional crime reporting would be a stepping-stone to greater things, and even her worst enemies couldn't deny that she was good at her job. But here she was, still stuck in Southampton, with much less chance of getting a promotion than she had had before.

She needed a scoop. Something big that could put her front and center again. The body on the beach had sounded exciting at first but would probably end up being some depressing drug murder or the like. And Helen Grace—the one police officer round here guaranteed to create news—was determined to give her nothing. As she drained the last of her wine, Emilia felt sure that the answer to her present conundrum lay with Helen Grace.

She had to get her back onside—by means fair or foul.

36

Charlie took a deep breath and stepped inside the pub. She had been inside the Crown and Two Chairmen so many times—this drinking hole was a second home to most Southampton Central coppers—but tonight she felt nervous. As she made her way through the crowds toward the knot of familiar faces in the corner, she felt the color rising in her face, the heat of the pub mingling with her anxiety to give her a distinctly pink hue.

Charlie was greeted with warmth and affection, every man and woman there trumpeting, patting and generally drawing attention to her enormous bump. Charlie smiled and received their inquiries in good humor, but in truth she felt uncomfortable and ridiculous. The baby was particularly active tonight, pummeled her from the inside, pressing down hard on her pubic bone in agonizing fashion. Charlie felt uncomfortable, unattractive and dispirited. She had hoped a night out would raise her spirits, but just getting to the pub had exhausted her and now she found herself chatting to people she barely knew. Helen smiled over at her but was kept at a distance by the persistent attention of Detective Superintendent Harwood, who was clearly grilling her about operational matters.

The cause of all the merriment was DC Grounds, a career copper soon to retire from the force. He was a solid, old-fashioned kind of policeman whom you couldn't help liking—a sort of dad to the team, persistently uncool but well-intentioned. It was being spun that they were rewarding him with retirement after twenty-five good years of service, but Charlie saw it differently. Grounds was being elbowed out to make room for fresh blood.

Charlie knew that this was at Harwood's instigation. Over the last two years, most of Helen's allies had gone or been sidelined. Mark, of course—Charlie pushed that thought away quickly—Tony Bridges, Charlie herself and now Bob Grounds too. They had been replaced by shiny, fast-track coppers of the type beloved by Harwood—Lloyd Fortune, DC "Call me Ed" Stevens and the person Charlie now found herself talking to—DC Sarah Lucas.

The ambitious, shiny Lucas only increased Charlie's discomfort. She was young, slender, university-educated and going places. She had joined the police late, having completed a degree in criminal psychology at Durham, one of the new breed of fast-track CID officers. Harwood had come across Lucas at her previous station and had fought hard to get her transferred to Southampton Central. The rumor was that she was Harwood's heir apparent. Charlie could well believe it—like her superior, she had no discernible sense of humor and little more sincerity.

"You look amazing, Charlie." It was Lucas's third lie in as many minutes.

"I feel horrible," Charlie countered, smiling bravely.

"How long is it till . . . ?"

"Any day now."

"I'm not surprised" was the neutral reply, as Lucas eyed Charlie's bump.

The conversation carried on in this fashion until Charlie feigned a weak bladder to make her escape. To her consternation, on returning from the loo she was cornered by Harwood, who felt duty-bound to engage her in some small talk. They talked about birth, babies and child-rearing, Harwood full of helpful tips that she had no doubt picked up from her nanny. The conversation continued pleasantly enough but was an exercise in window dressing. Charlie had crossed swords with Harwood a year ago and hadn't been forgiven. Would she ever make it back into the golden circle? Tonight Charlie seriously doubted it.

DC Sanderson was making her excuses, and as Charlie glanced over Harwood's shoulder at the thinning crowd of revelers, she noted few friendly faces. Helen was of course the notable exception, but Charlie now realized that her former boss was no longer present. As Harwood bore on, Charlie suppressed a smile—Helen hated these things even more than she did and if someone was to escape the forced bonhomie and excessive drinking, Charlie was glad it had been Helen. Typical of her to slip away unseen, though, Charlie thought to herself.

Forever the enigma.

37

Hurrying through the night air, Helen felt herself relaxing once more. Harwood had been particularly persistent tonight, interrogating her about the Pippa Briers case. Harwood had heard rumors of a connection to the Ruby Sprackling investigation and clearly suspected Helen of withholding information from her. Harwood was right, she *was*, but Helen had worked hard to convince her superior that there was no established connection yet and no cause for alarm. Since they first started working together, Harwood had been convinced that Helen *looked* for these connections, as if obsessed with serial offenders and somehow willing to manufacture them if they didn't actually exist. It said something about Harwood's insecurity that she believed Helen would "create" serial killers just to burnish her already impressive reputation.

"You had a lucky escape, Harry," Helen offered breezily as she buzzed herself back into Southampton Central. "If you see any of my team propping up the lampposts tonight, do me a favor and sling them in the cells, will you?"

"It will be my very great pleasure," Harry replied, grinning.

Helen was soon on the seventh floor and back in the incident room. For a moment she paused to look at the board. Pippa's young face stared back at her, full of promise, but now snuffed out. Helen couldn't help wondering what Daniel was up to right now. He was in a hell of grief and bitter self-recrimination and it would be incredibly hard for him to find some kind of normality again. Dark thoughts would eat him up for months and years to come, torturing him with what-ifs. It was the mystery of Pippa's last few months that was torturing her father now—as she stared at the board, Helen vowed privately to uncover the truth of this poor woman's final days and see that justice was done.

She grabbed her bag from her office and was about to leave the empty incident room when she paused. It was stupid really—worse than that, it was pointless—but still something compelled her to sit down at the vacated computer terminal and log in to the system. She used DC Lucas's personal codes this time, which wasn't on, but needs must. She typed Robert Stonehill's name into the PNC and hit Search. Why did she do this to herself? She blamed herself entirely for ruining this innocent young man's life, but even so, what was achieved by this endless trawling? It was a fruitless search, which always ended in bitter disappointment.

Except tonight it didn't. The computer suddenly came alive with times, dates and, more important, a case number.

There was a match. Robert Stonehill. The nephew whom she had loved and lost was back from the dead.

38

He slipped the key into the lock and turned it silently. He had stayed out late—and drunk too much—and he didn't want to wake his father by crashing around. Stepping inside the door, Lloyd Fortune listened. He had expected, and hoped for, silence, but the TV in the living room was still on, despite the late hour.

"Evening, Dad. What's on?" Lloyd said brightly, perching on the vacant end of the sofa.

"The usual fools," his dad replied, gesturing at the talking heads on a late-night politics show.

"Tea?" Lloyd continued.

"Yes, I will. I expect you could do with one too," his father replied evenly.

Lloyd headed to the kitchen, the earlier fun of the evening already starting to recede. Lloyd loved his father as much as any son could or should, but his father was a hard taskmaster and Lloyd often bridled at his implied criticism. And *he* was the success story of the family, for God's sake. His brother and sister were work-shy, living off benefits, unwilling to work as hard or as diligently as their father had done when they were growing up. Lloyd knew they resented the fact that their father had seldom been present when they were small, often leveling this at him during furious family rows. Lloyd understood their grievance, but he never backed them up. His father had brought the family over from Jamaica with nothing—he'd *had* to work all the hours God sent just to keep the family in food and clothing.

It had been backbreaking work too—twelve-hour shifts down at the Western Docks as a stevedore—the legacy of which still made itself felt now. At one time or another Lloyd's father had strained, fractured or broken most parts of his body—Lloyd particularly remembered one nasty fall that had resulted in a broken back that had laid his father out for weeks. His mother had cried pretty much nonstop during that time, as the family stared destitution in the face. But his father had eventually risen from his sickbed and returned to work. He carried on doing just that until they handed him his cards some time later.

So even though he was a hard man to live with, especially now that their mother had passed away, Lloyd refused to criticize him. His brother and sister he was less equivocal about, especially as their failure to live up to the hardworking strictures laid down by the previous generation meant that Lloyd was now the sole repository of his father's dying hopes and ambitions. His father, Caleb, was extremely tough on Lloyd, pushing him to get the best examination results, to pass out of Hendon top of his class, to climb the ranks from PC to DC to DS, faster, faster, faster. Nothing ever seemed to satisfy him. Lloyd kept on achieving, only to find he had still not earned his father's approbation. He had already gone further and faster than most of his peers, but still he fell short.

Lloyd handed his father a full cup of tea and settled down to watch the politicians insinuate and evade.

"Look at this one. Lying through his teeth and he doesn't even bother to hide it."

His father had no time for politicians, but he still watched these shows. Caleb was a man who took life seriously, who set the highest standards and always seemed to be on the lookout in case someone fell short. Especially his own son, Lloyd thought to himself, as he drank his tea. Especially his firstborn son.

39

Helen stared down at the file, her heart breaking. She hadn't slept a wink and had been on edge all morning, waiting for the file she'd requested on Robert to be faxed through. But now that she had it in her hand, she was no further on and her fragile hopes lay in tatters.

There had been some kind of assault in Northampton city center, which had resulted in Robert's arrest and detention. A fight outside a pub between Robert and another individual over a trivial matter. The injuries were relatively minor—thank goodness—but that was about as much as Helen could make out. The rest of the two-page report had been heavily redacted, great swaths of it blacked out, so that only scant details of the incident remained. There was no clue as to whether charges had been brought, where Robert was living or what had happened to him. It promised so much but, obscuring its precious content from view, delivered only bitter frustration.

"I know it's an unusual request, but in the circumstances a justified one." Helen's tone was even and controlled, as she addressed Ceri Harwood.

"But why, Helen? To what end?"

Helen wanted to say, "I would have thought that was bloody obvious," but swallowed her derision.

"He's been off the radar for nearly a year now. No contact with his parents, no benefits collected, no e-mails, nothing. I'd like to find out if he's okay, where he's living—for their sakes, as much as my own."

"I understand, Helen, of course I do. But you know the rules. The unredacted file is classified."

"Why?"

"I don't know why—that's Northamptonshire Police's business, not ours—but even if I did, I couldn't tell you. I don't need to remind you of this, surely."

"I know the protocols for undercover work," Helen said, just about keeping her voice steady. "But I would argue that this is a special case. He's a young man with no support network—"

"You don't know that."

"He doesn't have any contacts in Northamptonshire, any relatives to turn to—"

"It sounds like he's been there for nearly a year. Time enough to make friends, put down roots—"

"Oh, come off it," Helen spat back, finally losing her temper. "When he left here he was in pieces. He'd just found out his mother was a serial murderer. His adoptive parents' lives had been turned upside down; he was full of anger, grief, resentment . . . He wasn't in a frame of mind to 'make friends.'"

The last phrase dripped with sarcasm, which Helen instantly regretted, as she saw Harwood's expression harden. Harwood was her only hope here—she had to keep her onside.

"I don't wish to appear aggressive or disrespectful, but you must understand that I have to find him. It was my fault he left—" Helen continued quickly.

"You didn't out him. Emilia Garanita did," Harwood said coolly.

"To get at me. I feel responsible, which is why I'm asking for your help here. Every day since he disappeared, I've been expecting the worst. He has nothing to live for, no one to care for him, no reason to go on. I know it'll cause a fuss, that it goes against well-established protocols, but you can make this happen. So help me. Please."

Helen had never been so open or vulnerable in front of her superior before. Harwood looked at Helen, then rose and walked round her desk. She put a comforting arm around her and instantly Helen knew she had lost.

"I hear your pain and I sympathize. But I cannot compromise ongoing operations out of sentiment. I'm sorry, Helen; my answer has to be no."

Helen stalked away from Harwood's office. She had the distinct impression that Harwood had enjoyed slamming the door in her face, despite the mock sympathy she ladled on as a sop to Helen's feelings. It left Helen with so many unanswered questions. What had Robert got himself mixed up in? Was he assisting the police? They had taken the trouble to redact any details of his place of residence, job, acquaintances, which strongly suggested that they wanted to protect him. But why? Was he an asset? If so, how had he come to their attention—as a witness or an informant? Helen's mind was running riot with a dozen competing scenarios, each as disquieting as the last.

Marching into the incident room, Helen ran straight into DC Sanderson—the latter had clearly been waiting for her boss to arrive. Her news sent Helen's mood plummeting yet further.

"The DNA from Nathan Price's van isn't Ruby Sprackling's. And SOC can't find any traces of *his* DNA in Ruby's flat, so . . ."

In her characteristically gentle way, Sanderson was telling Helen that they had nothing. Was Price innocent or just a very canny operator? It made no difference now—they would have to let him walk.

40

He drove steadily, but one eye remained fixed on the rearview mirror. He hadn't believed it when they told him he was free to go and he had been right to be wary. He wasn't off the hook yet.

Nathan Price noticed he was being tailed as he drove up Shirley High Road—a dark Vauxhall saloon following at a discreet distance. Unsure at first whether he was being paranoid, he diverted up Winchester Road. It was out of his way but would serve his purpose. The road opened up in front of him and he stabbed the accelerator sharply. His speed leaped to fifty miles per hour. He was comfortably breaking the speed limit now and was amused to see the Vauxhall increase its speed to keep pace.

Instinct now took over and he turned sharply into Dale Road, heading in the direction of the hospital. The road was full of parked cars as always, but Nathan spotted a single space ahead and maneuvered the van deftly into it. With no other spaces nearby, the Vauxhall glided past, eventually stopping at the top of the street. Their view of Nathan's vehicle was now blocked by the van in front. Nathan had no doubt that they would be out of the car in a flash and heading back down the street. But he had time enough, if he was quick.

Killing the engine, he leaped into the back of the van, taking care not to trip over the building detritus that littered the van floor. Easing the back door partially open, he slipped out and, crouching down behind the sides of the parked cars, scurried along the street.

Reaching the end of the street, he took cover behind a green Fiat and paused. This last bit was the most important—he could blow it now if he was rash. Counting to ten, he chanced a look round the back of the Fiat toward his van. Sure enough, a plainclothes copper was peering through the van windshield, searching for his mark.

"Imbecile," Nathan muttered to himself, as the police officer ran back up the street toward his colleague.

Seeing him turn his back, Nathan took his chance, darting out of his hiding place and around the corner. Now he picked up his pace, sprinting down Winchester Road again, before cutting sharply left into St. James's Park. Pulling his hood up over his face, he slowed to a quick walk now, moving steadily but with purpose. Soon he was on Church Street and finally safe from pursuit.

As he walked home, Nathan felt no temptation to congratulate himself. He had had a lucky escape and from now on he would have to be very, very careful. One slip, one small mistake and the whole house would come crashing down.

41

The sun shone down on the water so brightly that Ruby had to raise her hands to shield her eyes from the glare. It was punishing, but it was a ravishingly beautiful sight nevertheless.

Steephill Cove was a perfect horseshoe bay and it looked resplendent today in the fierce spring sunshine. Ruby and her family had been coming to the Isle of Wight since she was small, and this was their favorite place on the island. Ruby knew every detail of it, right down to her favorite rock pools and climbing crags.

Mum, Dad, Cassie, Conor and their border collie, Max, were haring about on the beach, playing Frisbee and splashing in the surf as a prelude to their picnic. They never did these by halves and though it was a pain to lug the hampers down the steep steps to the beach, it was always worth it. The kids would be allowed a swig of the sparkling wine—Dad always fired the cork up into the sea, much to Mum's consternation—to wash down the pies, crisps, sandwiches, homemade cakes and biscuits that Mum had assembled the night before. They always felt sick afterward, of course—but in a good way.

Stripping off to her bikini, Ruby ran into the surf, the foaming water jumping up at her as she hurdled the waves. Diving in, she swam hard—her arms cutting gracefully through the water—and before long she was far out to sea, her family now distant figures on the beach.

Holding her breath, Ruby plunged under the water. Down, down, down she went, kicking hard away from the churning surface and into the depths below. It was part of a game she'd invented to wind up her mother. She would swim out a long way, then disappear under the waves for as long as she could. Her mother, who wasn't a confident swimmer and hated the sea, never failed to react, pacing the shoreline, calling to her. Her father, who was used to her tricks, never reacted, which irritated Ruby a touch, but at least she could always rely on Mum.

When she did finally surface, she would wave cheerfully to her as if she couldn't hear her mother's cries, before plunging under again. She would keep this up until she eventually took pity on her. Swimming back to shore, she could always be sure of a cuddle and an affectionate reprimand.

Her breath was running out now, her lungs bursting for fresh air, so she turned and kicked hard for the surface. She hadn't achieved much in life, but she had always been a strong swimmer and Ruby felt elated now as she arrowed upward, her sleek form cutting through the water.

Bursting through the surface, she took off her goggles and trod water, while drinking in great gulpfuls of air. Sure enough, she heard her mother's plaintive cries. Smiling to herself, she prepared to dive again. Her mother's cries were louder now and she resolved to ignore them, but suddenly she felt her mother's arm on her shoulder, pulling her to shore. How had she got out here? It was miles from—

"Summer."

Already her dream was starting to fragment.

"Summer."

It wasn't her mother pulling her to shore; it was him shaking her awake from her reverie.

Her jailer had returned.

42

"So, what do we do now?"

Harwood was to the point as usual. Helen had informed her that Nathan had escaped his surveillance team, with predictable results.

"Watch and wait," Helen replied evenly. "We've tagged the van, so if he comes back we'll know and I've sent teams to his home, the job he's currently on—"

"And are we sure he's worth all these resources? I've no doubt he's a nasty piece of work, but he has no record to speak of—"

"He's the only face in the frame. He has a history of violence and an unhealthy interest in young women, and had access to both women's flats. If we watch him, I think we'll get results."

Helen had soft-pedaled the possible connection between Ruby Sprackling and Pippa Briers until now, but with Nathan Price slipping off the radar, the need for extra resources had forced her to come clean with Harwood.

"Possibly," Harwood said without enthusiasm. "Two days max and I want to be kept up to speed, right?"

"Of course," Helen countered, refusing to react to the implied criticism.

"Was there something else?"

Harwood was clearly keen to get back to her paperwork and was both confused and mildly irritated that Helen showed no signs of leaving. Helen sized up the situation—it was far from ideal—then plowed on nevertheless.

"I'd like to take a POLSA team back to Carsholt Beach."

"What on earth for? The beach has just been reopened to the public. We've got school holidays coming up. What could we possibly gain from sending a full search team down there?"

"I'm worried about the interval between Ruby's disappearance and Pippa's," Helen continued quickly. "There could be a gap of four years or more between them and, well, that just doesn't feel right."

"What doesn't *feel* right?" Harwood countered.

"Both these girls share a look; they are vulnerable and lonely; both have vanished without a trace. Furthermore, they have both been kept 'alive' through the use of texts, Twitter and the like. It looks like it's the same perpetrator, and if it is, then we can say that this guy is organized, determined and, most of all, driven. He's looking for a certain kind of gratification that only these girls can provide and is clearly willing to go to great lengths and take great risks in order to get it. Stranger abduction of grown adults from the home is incredibly rare."

"So?"

"So, do we believe he would abduct and murder Pippa, then wait another three to four years before trying again? The level of organization that goes into these abductions suggests to me a degree of compulsion that is unlikely to come and go. All the studies show that these sorts of predator—"

"Please don't quote your courses at me. I know how well qualified you are in this territory," Harwood said coolly.

"I'm worried he may have targeted other girls—"

"And do you have any proof of this?"

"Not yet. But—"

"Then we'll leave things as they are. I don't want to alarm the public, and until we know more about what we're dealing with, we sit tight."

Helen said nothing.

"It does seem to be my day for saying no, doesn't it?" Harwood added breezily. "But you know what our budgets are like."

Helen left shortly afterward, with as much grace as she could muster. Was she being punished for her earlier outburst? For past crimes? Either way, Helen had the nasty feeling that they had just made a very bad decision and that their failure to act would cost more lives.

43

They stared at each other, neither saying a word. Ruby was still furious at being dragged from the warm cocoon of her dream and enraged by her captor's patronizing kindness.

"I'm sorry to have left you alone for such a long time."

He clearly wanted a response, but she wasn't going to give him one. What right did he have to wake her up? To keep her here? He was a sick fuck, who deserved nothing but her scorn.

"Summer?"

Still she stared at him.

"Are you feeling okay? You look pale."

"I'm *fine.* How are you?" Her tone was withering and she was amused to see that she had hurt him.

"I'm trying to be nice, Summer."

"Go to hell."

She had wanted to sound angry, but her voice wobbled slightly. She cursed herself for her weakness.

"Well, aren't you going to say something?" she continued, eyeballing him.

He looked at her for a long time, saying nothing in response. Then with a small shake of the head, he rose and walked back to the door.

"Don't go."

Ruby found herself rising, the thought of being alone suddenly too much for her to bear.

He paused at the door to look over his shoulder. "You brought this on yourself, Summer."

Then without another word he left, slamming the door behind him. The first bolt was pushed firmly into place. Then the next. Each one seemed to go right through Ruby.

"Please. I didn't mean it. Please stay."

Ruby could hear him walk away. Then the dull sound of another door closing in the near distance.

"Please," she moaned.

But there was no one to hear her now. And Ruby knew as she lay there that it was *she* who was in hell, not he. With him, she was scared and uncertain; without him she was desolate. Like it or loathe it, there was no escaping the fact that he was her world now.

44

Charlie drummed her fingers on the table, shooting nervous looks at the entrance. Steven often passed by this way on his way to work. If he happened to spot her holed up in a coffee shop with Helen, when she'd explicitly told him she was meeting her mum, she would have some explaining to do.

According to Steve, their life was now back on track following past traumas. The right decisions had been made, with the right results, and now a long and happy life lay ahead of them. Was it just fear—of the birth, of what followed after—that made Charlie uncertain? Or was it that she was a worker at heart, someone with a vocation that could not easily be discarded?

She had been surprised—and excited—by Helen's text. It read simply:

Can you meet this morning? Urgent and discreet if you can.

With surprising ease, she found herself lying to Steve, slipping on her coat and heading out the door. Did she really miss police work so much that she would drop everything and deceive her husband because of a brief text? Suddenly Charlie felt a pang of guilt, but before her misgivings could take hold, she saw Helen hurrying toward her.

"I'm sorry I'm late. Blame Harwood."

"I usually do," Charlie said, their shared antipathy for their station chief drawing a smile from her boss.

"And I'm sorry to be so secretive, but what I'm about to ask you to do breaks all the rules and could land you and me in a serious amount of trouble."

"Sounds fun," Charlie said gamely, but was already a little unnerved by Helen's manner.

"If you want to say no—and you probably should—then that's totally fine. But there's no one else I can confide in."

It had been a long time since Charlie saw Helen like this. There was clearly a lot resting on this meeting. Helen didn't keep her guessing, filling her in on her recent "discovery" of her missing nephew and her subsequent clash with Harwood about her refusal to formally request the unredacted file. Charlie could already see where this was going.

"I know it's a lot to ask, but I don't have any meaningful contacts in the Northamptonshire force, no one I can trust at least. I know this is completely irregular, but—"

Helen's voice wavered slightly as she spoke, so Charlie put her out of her misery:

"It's okay, Helen. I know what you're asking."

Charlie's oldest friend from police college had just taken a high-profile desk job with Northamptonshire Police. DS Sally Mason was the keeper of the administrative gates up there—if anyone could lay their hands on the unredacted material, she could. But Charlie had no idea how she would react to such an outrageous request.

"Let me mull it over," Charlie said.

"That's all I ask. If I could think of another way, I would. But . . . I need to know if he's okay, Charlie."

Helen left soon after, Charlie promising to be in touch. Truth be told, she already knew that she would do what Helen asked. Because she felt for her. Because it was the right thing to do in the circumstances. And perhaps—just a little bit—because it would be fun.

45

An hour later, Helen strode into the incident room. She was pleased to see that everyone was busy, the team finally finding its rhythm in the heat of battle. A major investigation had a way of forcing everyone to up their game, make connections and forge new ground together. It always gave Helen a quiet sense of satisfaction to observe it taking place.

Seeing that everyone was fully occupied, Helen seized the moment, pulling Sanderson aside. Marching her into the office would have excited people's attention, so Helen guided her subtly to the watercooler and, lowering her voice, outlined her plans. For the second time that day she was committing an act of gross insubordination.

"I need you to do a bit of digging—for my eyes only, right?"

"Of course, boss, whatever you say."

Helen had grown to trust Sanderson over the last couple of

years. She wasn't Charlie, but she was the closest thing to her at present.

"I think our perpetrator will have abducted—or attempted to abduct—other girls during the last five years or so. Someone who's this committed, this driven, isn't going to fall in and out of obsession. He'll be compelled to stalk, abduct or kill."

Sanderson nodded, so Helen continued.

"Detective Superintendent Harwood isn't minded to agree, hence the need for discretion. Choose your moments, but I want you to go through the crime reports on the PNC, as well as trawling the missing persons lists for Southampton, Portsmouth, Bournemouth looking for young women who might fit our profile. Limit yourself to single girls who are isolated and vulnerable, perhaps just out of a relationship. They probably live alone, are not massively well-off and for now let's assume they have the same look—black hair, blue eyes. Do it discreetly, but do it quickly. I hope I'm wrong, but if this guy is a serial predator, I want to know. Any crime—or attempted crime—might help us find him. Okay?"

Sanderson nodded and hurried off to begin her task. Helen watched her go. She hoped she was doing the right thing trusting her; she was skating on very thin ice with Harwood already.

Helen was so engrossed in her thoughts that she didn't notice DC Lucas approach.

"Good news, ma'am."

Helen turned, surprised by her sudden appearance.

"Nathan Price is on the move."

46

The van sped along the road, its tires spitting rainwater up off the slick surface. It had been raining solidly for an hour now and the storm showed no sign of relenting. Normally Helen would have cursed such weather, but not today. It reduced driver visibility, making it easier to tail the van unnoticed.

The windshield wipers swept back and forth, beating out the rhythm of Helen's anxiety. Nathan Price had been driving for forty minutes with no sign of stopping. Where was he heading? He had done a couple of laps of the ring road, presumably to throw off anyone following him. If that was the purpose, he had signally failed. The three unmarked police cars were still on his tail, changing positions at intervals to avoid detection.

The van headed south now through Northam and Itchen, leaving behind prosperity and aspiration. The van was crawling along and Helen had to drop her speed to avoid giving herself away. They were in Woolston now. What had once been an affluent prewar suburb was now a forgotten wasteland—never having recovered from the brutal bombing it sustained during the Second World War. The rickety houses round here had been left to molder and were inhabited now by squatters, illegal immigrants and petty criminals. It was a nasty, forgotten place.

Finally the van slowed to a stop. Helen glided past and parked up out of sight round the street corner. She was out of the car in seconds and rounded the top of the street just in time to see Price step inside a house not fifty yards away.

Helen, flanked now by DC McAndrew, hurried toward it. She could see DC Lucas and Lloyd Fortune approaching from the other direction and signaled them to hold back. She would take the lead on this one.

Gesturing to McAndrew to follow, she slipped round the side of the house, keeping below the line of the windows. The back door banged quietly in the wind. Helen hesitated, listening. Voices. She could definitely hear voices. Price's was raised in anger, but who was the other person? Who was he talking to?

Teasing the door open, Helen slipped inside. Edging across the room to the open doorway, she could hear the voices more clearly now. Price and a young girl, who was crying and remonstrating. She seemed to have done something wrong, though Helen couldn't tell what, as the voices had now gone quiet.

A nasty bang made Helen jump—the crying that followed making it clear that Price had struck the girl. Helen didn't hesitate. Pushing the door open and raising her baton, she stepped inside.

It was time to bring this game of hide-and-seek to an end.

47

Ruby screamed for all she was worth. She shrieked, whooped, ranted and raved—anything to break the awful silence that filled the small room. Her captor had only been gone a few hours, but it felt like an eternity. What was he doing? How long would he punish her for? How long would she be left alone down here?

She bitterly regretted her outburst now. She had no power here, no bargaining chip, so why had she pushed him away? As she'd lain alone in the half darkness after his departure, the minutes crawling by, the worst kinds of thoughts had seized her. Thoughts of herself slowly withering to dust in this dreadful place. So she screamed to distract herself, to keep herself company in her lonely cell.

Tiring of this, she now found herself stalking the room again. It was more in hope than expectation—she had already explored her confines several times—but she had to do *something*. Passive resignation would only lead to madness or worse. She had to think. To act. To find a way out.

Clambering onto the table, she ran her fingers over the ceiling. The floorboards were wooden and could perhaps be prised apart . . . But, for all her probing, they refused to budge. They had been sealed with solid silicone mastic that stubbornly resisted her attempts to remove it. It was presumably some kind of DIY soundproofing. Ruby shivered at the thought. Why did he need soundproofing down here?

Jumping down, she completed another circuit of the walls, but giving up quickly, she turned her attention instead to the other items in the room. She pulled the pictures off the wall and yanked fruitlessly at the metal coat hooks. She pulled the pointless cooker and fake basin away from the wall, then, in a final fit of pique, grabbed the clock that hung above the bed and tossed it across the room. It was a flimsy children's clock, designed to help kids learn to tell the time, and it stared down at her day after day, mocking her with its idle hands, which remained resolutely locked at a quarter past twelve. It landed with a clatter on the far side of the room.

Ruby breathed out heavily. All that was left now was another assault on the door. It was solidly built with a heavy lock. There was no way she could pull it off its hinges or ram it with her shoulder. The only way to open it was to force the lock with some kind of implement. But what could she use? She would need something heavy and solid, which she could smash down on it . . .

Bricks. She was surrounded by bricks. The mortar had been touched up in places, but the brickwork was probably a hundred years old or more, so . . . Ruby ran her hands over the cold surface of the walls, forensically searching for signs of weakness in the mortar. Round and round she went, her nails scraping at the mortar, but every brick held firm. Had her captor thought of everything? Had he left nothing to chance?

Ruby was tired now and about to give up when she spotted one place she hadn't tried. Pulling the bed away from the wall, she dropped to her knees to examine the brickwork that lay behind.

As she leaned down to take a closer look at the mortar, she felt a trickle of cool air brush over her face. She kept her eyes closed, reveling in it for a moment. It felt as if someone were stroking her face, like an act of kindness. It felt like a lifetime since she'd received one of those.

The air was coming through the brickwork. She dropped down onto her front and crawled closer to the wall. Sure enough, the brick was loose. Her damaged fingers protested, but she jammed them into the crumbling mortar round the edges and tugged for all she was worth. To her surprise the brick came out easily.

The cavity behind it was stuffed full of paper. Confused, Ruby pulled the papers out but was disappointed to find the cavity was shallow, hardly more than the depth of the brick itself. She pulled at the bricks next to the opening, but they refused to respond, and three broken nails later, she gave up.

She was about to pick up the brick to begin her assault on the door when her eyes alighted on one of the many pieces of paper that now littered the floor around her. On it was a drawing—crudely done in felt-tip pen—of a green tree decorated with baubles.

Curiosity now got the better of her and Ruby read the contents of the homemade card. It was a Christmas card to her mother from a girl called Roisin. In it, she wrote about how much she missed her family, how they were not to worry about her sudden disappearance and how much she was looking forward to the day when she could put this card in their hands herself. The latter section of the text was stained with tears and the card was dated a little over two and a half years ago.

Ruby dropped it like a stone and sank to the floor. In an instant, the full desperation of her situation became clear. She was not the first girl to have been abducted and held down here.

Which raised the question: What had happened to them? And where was this "Roisin" now?

48

"You're not in trouble, Lianne. But you will be if you don't start talking."

Helen was already in a dark mood, and the teenage girl's refusal to talk was only exacerbating her bad humor. When she had burst into the room to confront Nathan Price, she found him manhandling a teenage girl. A teenage girl who was definitely *not* Ruby Sprackling.

"You're telling us that Nathan Price is a friend of the family."

"That's right."

"And do friends of the family usually pop round when you're home alone?"

Nothing in response.

"We'll find out either way. Your parents are coming in—if they can confirm that Nathan Price is a friend of the family—"

"You haven't told them, have you? About him?" Lianne interrupted.

There was real alarm in her face now. Helen felt bad about lying, but needs must. "I didn't have much choice, did I, Lianne? If you won't talk to me . . ."

"I haven't done anything wrong."

"So talk to me. I know you're scared. I know that he hurt you."

A livid bruise covered the girl's right cheek.

"But he can't touch you here. Tell me what's been going on and I swear he won't come near you ever again."

Helen held her hand out to the young girl. Lianne looked at it; then, dropping her gaze to her lap, she muttered, "I met him on Friday night."

"Where?"

"Revolution."

Sanderson shot a look at Helen but was ignored.

"And?"

"He bought me drinks, you know. Asked me stuff."

"He took an interest in you."

"He was nice. He had money too. So we chatted until midnight, then went off."

"Where, Lianne? It's really important you tell me—"

"We went to his van, okay?"

"You slept with him?"

"What do you think?"

"How old are you, Lianne?"

"Sixteen."

"How old are you?" Helen repeated more forcefully.

"Sixteen."

"Lianne . . ."

"Fourteen, okay, I'm fourteen."

The girl started to cry. Helen reached out to take her hand and this time the girl didn't resist. "How long did you stay with him?"

"A few hours."

"He was with you the whole time?"

"Yeah."

"Then what?"

"He dropped me home."

"What time was that?"

"Just after four o'clock."

"Just after four a.m. Are you absolutely sure?"

"I saw the clock as I came in. I was pleased—my folks are dead to the world at that time."

Helen concluded the interview shortly afterward, the young girl having agreed to make a formal statement about the events of Friday night. There was some comfort in the fact that Nathan Price would face criminal proceedings—sex with a minor was a serious offense that would land him on the Sex Offenders Register—but it was of little solace to Helen. Lianne Sumner had just cleared Nathan Price of any involvement in Ruby Sprackling's disappearance.

Like it or not, they were back to square one.

49

He tried to focus, wrenching his mind back to the tasks in hand, but still he couldn't settle. His unpleasant exchange with Summer had left him unsettled and disturbed—it was hard to concentrate on work today. Clients came and went as usual and he dealt with them in his usual professional manner, but he was on autopilot, getting the job done with the minimum of effort and interaction. He just couldn't stop thinking about her. Why was she hostile to him? It didn't make any sense. Why was she so . . . ungrateful? Didn't she understand what he'd had to go through? The risks he'd taken?

News of the discovery of a body at Carsholt Beach had knocked him for six. He'd watched the local news repeatedly since, bought every edition of the local paper, scouring the reports for details. Images of a large police forensics team on-site had unnerved him, as had the confirmation that local hero DI Grace would be leading the investigation. Ever since he saw the news, he'd been on edge, half expecting a knock on the door. He knew that this was unlikely—he'd been so careful, so meticulous in his work—but it just served to underline the lengths he'd gone to, the sacrifices he'd made, to do right by her.

Why wouldn't she give him the love he craved? The love he was *owed*? For the first time, anger flared in him. It could all be so perfect. It was so perfect. So why did she insist on denying him? She was an ungrateful little b—

As fast as his fury rose, he forced it back down again, striving to gain control of his raging emotions. She had behaved badly—very badly—but now was not a time to lose faith. He must be patient—there was no rush. She would come round. After all, time was on his side, not hers. One way or another, she would learn to love him again.

50

Ruby's hands shook as she rummaged through the pile of papers, digesting every horrifying word. She had read cards, letters, confessions from three women now—Roisin, a Pippa somebody and another girl who simply signed herself "I." Three women who had been torn from their loved ones and dragged away to this strange hell.

Roisin's birthday card to her four-year-old son had made Ruby cry. She didn't know this woman—had never met her—and yet even in spite of her own suffocating sense of terror, she had been moved by Roisin's plight. It must have been horrific for her, lying down here alone, imagining her little boy calling for a mother who didn't come. Did the boy think that his mother didn't love him anymore? That she had abandoned him? It was clear that Roisin had begged to be given a pen and paper so she could write to her young son and explain her continued absence. But the cards and letters that she'd written had never reached the intended recipient. The cruelty of her captor's actions in keeping Roisin here took Ruby's breath away.

Pippa's testimony was in diary form. She had less to say; she was just marking the passage of time, trying to keep herself sane by detailing the different phases of her life down here with her captor. There had been arguments, abuse and, worse still, rapprochements. Pippa had clearly hated herself for what she had to do down here, what she had become, and Ruby could see why. In the end, she had had to put Pippa's diary down—it presented a vision of *her* future that she wasn't strong enough to contemplate.

Grim curiosity drove her on to "I"'s writings, but they turned out to be the worst of the lot. They were dated a little over a year ago and were obviously written after she had discovered Roisin's and Pippa's hidden letters and cards. This discovery had been a sledgehammer blow for "I"'s morale, robbing her of any resistance or hope. Her letters thereafter were a mixture of apologies to people she'd loved and wronged in her old life and long, rambling descriptions of her suffering and incarceration—records that she hoped would be found one day.

"I"'s deepest fear was that her fate would never be known. That her parents would remain forever in the dark about what had happened to their little girl. The last letter, dated from May, began in a bleak mood, "I" declaring her avowed belief that she would die in this cellar, before going on to offer her final thoughts, her final expressions of love, as she faced the end of her short life. Horrifically she never managed to complete her good-byes to her family—the green felt-tip pen that all the girls had been using finally running out before she could write her last words.

Each letter was like a physical wound to Ruby. Each word a death knell. Ever since her abduction, she had feared she was going to be her captor's slave. Now she knew she was going to be his next victim.

51

Hidden in a remote interrogation suite, DC Sanderson set about her work in earnest. Helen had tasked her with absolute secrecy, so she'd lied to the rest of the team, telling them she was heading home with a headache. In fact, she had scooped up the impressive number of missing persons files she'd amassed during the day and spirited them away to a forgotten part of the station that was awaiting refurbishment.

It was an odd, lonely space to be and Sanderson's mood of disquiet was deepened by the numerous sad stories she encountered as she pored over the files. Family breakups, child abuse, domestic violence—the various scenarios that had prompted these young people to go missing were uniformly depressing and yet the faces that stared up at her from the files were all smiling. Anxious relatives always gave their "best" photos of their missing loved ones, photos that suggested happiness and hope. Sanderson suspected these moments were fleeting at best and probably wholly unrepresentative of the subject, who had in all likelihood fled, committed suicide or been murdered. And yet for all that, and in spite of Sanderson's battle-hardened cynicism, the photos were still affecting. The beaming, optimistic faces proved that the subjects *had* been happy once, that at some point they had occupied a space that was joyful and forward-looking, before their lives caved in on them.

With each file, Sanderson's spirits sank a notch lower. It wasn't just the unpleasant details of these young women's lives—though those certainly were upsetting—it was also the sheer volume of cases. Sanderson wasn't naive. She knew the statistics on teenage runaways; she knew how many young women ended up walking the streets or worse to escape a difficult home life. But statistics are just numbers—they don't mean very much until you add up the individual cases one by one, until you are confronted with tiny details of scores of young lives gone awry. She had only trawled Southampton's, Portsmouth's and Bournemouth's missing persons lists, as Helen had instructed, but that had proved enough—more than enough—to keep her busy for the day.

She was now down to the last few files and there were currently six individuals who gave Sanderson cause for concern. Cheryl Heath and Teri Cafolla had the look but were frequent runaways who usually resurfaced when the money ran out. So despite some residual concerns, Sanderson had made the decision to put them on the back burner for now. Which left Anna Styles, Roisin Murphy, Debby Meeks and Isobel Lansley.

There was no question that these girls bore a strong resemblance to Pippa Briers. Long, straight raven black hair, piercing blue eyes and something enigmatic in their expression. They were all somehow beguiling, hinting at deeper layers if you could only get to know them better. Their appearances were different for sure—some were punkish and low-rent, some straitlaced and professional—but they all inhabited their look with the same spirit. If Helen was right—if Pippa's abductor was a serial offender following a pattern—then Sanderson was in no doubt he would be drawn to these vulnerable women, most of whom came from difficult backgrounds.

Even as Sanderson thought this, she found herself self-editing, bridling at her own euphemisms. "Serial offender" was a loose term that covered a multitude of sins and was generally used to reduce alarm by softening the reality of the situation. But there was no point dressing things up. If Helen's hunch was right—and increasingly Sanderson felt that it was—then they weren't pursuing a serial offender. They were hunting a serial killer.

52

Ruby smashed the brick down with all her force. Then she lifted it and brought it down again. She was in a frenzy, beating out the rhythm of her terror on the door that kept her locked inside.

The letters lay scattered where she'd dropped them. She had been unable to move for the best part of an hour after reading them—her head spinning with the darkest thoughts. The earrings that her captor had made her wear—they weren't new. They were tarnished and damaged in places. What was so special about them? Had they . . . had they belonged to one of the other girls? Or to this Summer?

With each passing minute, Ruby's anxiety had spiked still higher. She'd pulled hard on her inhaler, but it had little effect, so abandoning caution, she'd thrown herself into a full-on assault on the steel door.

Her blows rained down on the lock, producing small dents but failing to make any significant impression. Ruby wound her arm back and redoubled her efforts, bringing her weapon down with sudden, savage force. She heard a crack and for a brief, thrilling moment thought she'd been successful—until she looked down and saw the half brick in her hand. The other half lay broken and useless on the floor nearby.

Dropping the remnants, Ruby slid down the cold door to the floor, resting her head against the metal. There was no way out. She was beaten, locked for good or ill into this absurd pantomime with a man who abducted women, imprisoned them and then what? What had he done to those girls? If he'd let them go, surely she would have heard about it on the news or whatever, so what . . . ?

Should she ask him? Ask him what happened? Would she gain anything by confronting him? Probably not, but even as Ruby dismissed this thought, another idea rose in its place. She pushed it away immediately, too scared to test it, lest it proved fruitless, but it forced its way back into her mind again, demanding to be heard. It made her feel sick to even contemplate it, but what choice did she have? She *had* to find a way of getting her captor onside, if she was to have any chance of escaping certain death.

Climbing to her feet, she gathered up the letters and stuffed them back into their secret cavity. Ramming both halves of the brick into the hole to conceal them again, Ruby pushed the bed up against the wall, returning the room to its normal state.

Sweeping the brick dust from the floor, she spat on the dented lock and rubbed it with her sleeve. It was only slightly dented and if she could remove the bright redbrick dust, perhaps he wouldn't notice on his return.

Soon the room was back in some kind of order—even the clock was back in pride of place above the bed. There was only one thing left to do now and Ruby hurried over to the chair where her clothes lay. She changed quickly, pausing only at the end when she picked up the battered earrings. She hated these things more than life itself now, but there was no room for weakness, so swallowing her repugnance, Ruby closed her eyes and slipped the dirty hoops through her ears. Sitting down heavily on the bed, she exhaled long and hard. The worst was done.

Now all she had to do was wait.

53

"Are you completely insane?"

It was a valid question and one Charlie had been expecting. It had taken her two hours of chitchat and reminiscing to build up the courage to ask her old friend to do something that would cost her her job if it came to light. Predictably DS Sally Mason's response was one of shock and anger.

"I've only been here six months and it's a bloody good job. I can't believe you would even ask me that."

Charlie was momentarily lost for words. She knew Sally loved her job, but still the strength of her reaction surprised her. They had gone through police training together, surviving the experience largely thanks to their shared sense of humor and plenty of corner-cutting. They were coppers, not form-fillers, happy to break the rules when necessary. But sometime in the interim, Sally had become a responsible grown-up, a career copper with a decent rank, position and pension. Sally was right—she would be a fool to risk all that.

"I know and I feel awful suggesting it, but there's no other way—"

"Do you really want to skewer both our careers in one go? What have you done, Charlie, that would make you risk that?"

"It's not me . . . ," Charlie continued, then hesitated to go further.

Sally regarded her. Now she looked intrigued, rather than angry. "Then who?"

"Helen Grace."

"*The* Helen Grace?"

"Yes."

"But you're off work. And she can go through the normal channels, right?"

"She's being blocked. It's . . . it's about her nephew, Robert Stonchill."

Now Sally was silent. The name was familiar to most coppers, if only through newspaper reports and anecdotes.

"His name was mentioned in a crime report—a fight in Northampton city center—but the original's heavily redacted. No one's helping her, everyone wants her to just forget him, but he's her flesh and blood, the only family she has. So I know it's a lot to ask—too much—but I hope you can see I had no choice. Despite everything, she's . . . she's the best copper I've worked for and one of the best people I know."

Sally looked at Charlie for a long time. Then finally she said:

"*If* I do this for you, it'll be on one condition. You never got it from me—on pain of death, you never got it from me."

"Of course. I'd rather quit the force than get you into trouble because of me."

"And if it does lead somewhere," Sally continued, "you make *sure* Helen Grace does right by me."

So that was it. The power of Helen's reputation had people queuing up to join Hampshire CID—far more than could ever be accommodated. First-rate support officers, however, were at a premium and if Sally fancied the reflected glory of working alongside Helen, then Charlie was sure it could be arranged.

The pair separated shortly afterward, agreeing to meet an hour later in the McDonald's opposite the station to make the exchange. As Charlie watched Sally go, she was suddenly full of nervous excitement. Against the odds, she had pulled it off. She had done it. But what would it mean for her and Sally?

More important, what would it mean for Helen?

54

"So tell me all about her. I'm dying to know the details."

Not for the first time, Ceri Harwood's heart sank. Stuck in another interminable dinner party, she had tried her best to entertain—regaling her guests with stories of the colorful villains she'd nicked, the surprising scrapes she'd survived, while provoking peals of laughter by threatening to frisk them all for banned substances. It was an act—she was dog-tired and couldn't be bothered—but she performed it well. It was important for her husband's firm that the local councilors and business leaders look kindly on him, and she was happy to do her bit, but it always ended the same way. People seemed to look past her for something more interesting—and that something was always Helen Grace.

The woman quizzing her was blond, attractive and good company. Divorced, she ran a local advertising agency and made a lot of money out of it. One in the eye for her unfaithful ex-husband. Ceri had been enjoying their chat together, but as they discussed her police work, Ceri could feel the conversation being steered toward her bête noire.

"She's a good copper," Ceri replied graciously, "if a little unorthodox and prone to hug the limelight. When you've achieved a level of noteworthiness, I'm afraid there is always a part of you that craves adulation and attention. She's highly effective—don't get me wrong—but she occasionally forgets that police work is teamwork."

Her guest—Lucy—seemed little interested in Helen's ego or procedural misdemeanors. What she wanted was a blow-by-blow account of what had happened during the fatal shoot-out when Marianne Baines died. Did she really pull the trigger on her own sister? And what about Ella Matthews? Did she die at Helen's hand? And what was it about this DI that meant she had such a nose for these cases?

The questions rushed out in a torrent. It was as if her guest were a little in love with Helen, Ceri thought uncharitably. And she was about to say something deeply disappointing—she liked to pretend these details were classified despite the fact that they'd been all over the newspapers—when she caught Tim's eye. He was studying her closely. Did he know the subject of the conversation? Either way, he was giving Ceri the eye, tacitly encouraging her to give Lucy what she was asking for.

So, taking another large gulp of Cabernet Franc, Ceri dutifully trotted out the details of Helen's heroism. It stuck in her craw, but there was nothing for it but to play ball. Another evening ruined, Ceri thought to herself.

One more night languishing in the shadow of Helen Grace.

55

Helen slammed the front door shut behind her and hurried into the living room. She didn't even bother to turn the light on—she simply opened up the file Charlie had given her and began to devour it.

The unredacted file was still frustratingly short on detail. It described an altercation outside the Filcher and Firkin pub in Northampton city center between Robert and a local thug named Jason Reeves. Drink had been taken and an argument over a girl spilled into violence. A broken bottle was used—making it a serious offense—but the injuries were minor.

The arresting PC had scented a good collar—assault with a deadly weapon. However, twenty-four hours after Jason Reeves had made his statement—in colorful language—he suddenly withdrew the charges. There was no statement retracting his earlier one—just a brief coda written at the end of the report. Charges withdrawn because of mistaken identity.

Helen read the file from top to bottom again. It was obvious that someone had got to Reeves, as he'd been clear about Robert's involvement in his initial statement. And as Robert didn't really have any friends in Northampton and wouldn't have had time to build up the necessary flying hours with the local criminal fraternities, Helen could only conclude that the police had leaned on Reeves.

What had Robert become involved in that he would have that kind of backing? Helen could only infer that he was an informant and the thought made her shiver—things seldom ended well for informants, however careful they might be.

Amid so much mystery and uncertainty, there was one small clue, however—the name of the officer who had signed off the charge sheet, effectively exonerating Robert. His rank was intriguing—too senior to be a desk sergeant or beat copper—as was his name: DI Tom Marsh. Did that name ring a bell? Should Helen approach him directly or employ subterfuge? Not knowing the character of DI Marsh, she found it hard to know which way to jump.

Helen was still considering her next move when her phone rang. This day that was full of surprises had one more left in store. The caller was Daniel Briers.

56

He'd taken the number 76 bus out to Otterbourne, waiting almost until the end of the line before turning on Ruby's phone and sending the customary tweets and texts. Normally this little charade amused him, but today it made him anxious. Had he tweeted from Pippa's phone *after* the police discovered her body? If so, had they made this connection?

So many questions he couldn't possibly answer, and the not knowing was torturing him. Exhausted by the day's events, he found no satisfaction in the dance of death today—he just wanted to be home. One stop before the terminus, he got off and crossed the road to take the number 38 back into town.

Stepping inside the old house, he collapsed onto the sofa, sending a cloud of dust into the air. The whole place was in a state of chaos—half-finished bits of DIY, creeping patches of damp and empty pizza boxes everywhere, which the rats visited nightly. Coming home had failed to raise his spirits in the way he'd hoped, and he felt curiously despondent. What if Summer was as recalcitrant and hostile as she'd been earlier? He wasn't sure he could face another round of that. Putting off the moment of their reunion, he grabbed a bin bag from the kitchen and started shoveling rubbish into it, determined to get a grip on a house that was falling down around his ears.

Soon he was dusty, thirsty and even more exhausted than before. His body and his mind were urging him to go to bed, to get some rest. But still he resisted. She was down there, underneath these floorboards, waiting for him. Try as he might he couldn't resist her pull. She was his drug. The one thing he couldn't do without.

He paused and looked at himself in the mirror. Where once he had been young and handsome, now he appeared careworn and tired. No wonder she struggled to accept him. But still, was there any need to be so cruel? If she carried on like this, he would have to impose sanctions. He would take away her inhaler. If she needed to be broken, then so be it . . .

He found he was already halfway to her cell, his feet guiding him there on autopilot. It was as if he were in a dream—unable to control his actions or events. Pulling himself back to reality, he slipped the wicket hatch open. For once, she wasn't lying on the bed, despondent. It was hard to make out details in the gloom, but she seemed to be sitting up, waiting for something.

Sliding the wicket hatch shut, he switched on the main lights and slipped inside. To his surprise, there was Summer, just like he always pictured her, sitting on the bed in her skirt, earrings and top, a pretty smile spread across her face.

This is *a dream,* he thought to himself. *But finally it's a good one.*

57

She hated lying, but sometimes you had no choice. At least that was what DC Sanderson told herself as she dialed Sinead Murphy's number. Having already lied to her team about what she was up to, she was now about to lie to an unsuspecting member of the public.

"It's about your daughter, Roisin."

The voice on the other end of the line—which moments earlier had been warm and welcoming—suddenly went quiet.

"There's no need to be alarmed. This is just a routine follow up call," Sanderson continued, keen to put Roisin's mother at ease. "Our records show you reported your daughter missing nearly three years ago. Is that correct?"

"Yes, for all the good it did me."

"I take it you've not seen her since you made the report?"

"No" was the brief and sober response.

Sanderson ran through the particulars on the forms—occupation, family, physical descriptions, past behavior—before asking the only question that mattered. "Has there been *any* contact between you and Roisin since she went missing? Anything at all?"

There was a long pause, then:

"I suppose you could call it contact."

"Meaning?"

"She sends the odd text or tweet. But she never replies when I text back."

"Have you tried calling her on that number?"

"What do you think?" was the withering response.

"And?"

"Always straight to voice mail."

"Can you remember the last time she tweeted?"

"Why do you want to know? Why are you asking me all these questions?"

Sanderson paused—how to respond? "We're just trying to make some progress on Roisin's case. Frankly too little has been done so far and her communications are the best hope we have of finding out where she is."

Another long silence, then:

"She tweeted earlier today actually."

"Saying?"

"Nothing of interest. Just a gripe about having a bad day."

"Can you remember the exact time?"

"Hold on," Sinead replied. Sanderson could hear her rummaging through her bag for her phone. *Come on, come on,* Sanderson thought to herself, casting a nervous eye over the sheet of timings that lay on the table in front of her.

"Here we are," Sinead responded. "She tweeted at . . . six fourteen p.m. today."

"And the one before that?"

"Yesterday. Just after ten a.m."

Sanderson took Sinead back through a few more of Roisin's tweets, then ended the call, promising that she would be back in touch shortly. Sanderson had a nasty feeling that she would honor that promise and when she did, it would be with the bleakest of news. The timings of Roisin's last five tweets matched exactly with the timing of Ruby Sprackling's latest communications.

Helen had been right all along.

58

"So, how was your day?"

The words sounded so alien, but she forced them out, all the while maintaining her broad smile.

"It was fine, thanks."

"Were you working? Do you work?"

"You know I work, Summer."

His knowing reply rattled her, but she was not going to be weak. Not today. "What do you do?"

He looked at her and smiled.

"You look pretty tonight," he eventually said.

"Thank you. I . . . I wanted to make an effort."

"It shows."

Ruby hesitated, looked at her lap, then, lifting her gaze to his, carried on:

"I also wanted to say sorry. For being unkind. I didn't mean it."

He was watching her, as if unsure whether to believe her or not.

"I want us to be friends."

He looked at her but still said nothing. Not a smile, not a rebuke, nothing.

"I get lonely down here, so if we could spend more time together, then . . ."

"That's all I want, Summer. That's all I've ever wanted."

The fervency in his voice took her by surprise. She tried to speak, but fear was creeping up on her again now, robbing her of the power of speech.

"It's a clean slate for both of us, then," he went on. "So why don't we spend the evening together? I'll cook for us."

He looked straight at her. He had a fire in his eyes that she hadn't seen before. "It'll be just like old times."

59

Helen had no idea what she was doing here. But here she was—sitting in the Great Southern's rooftop restaurant, opposite Daniel Briers.

"I feel a bit of a fraud," Daniel Briers was saying as he topped up her coffee. "I don't have anything new to tell you and I'm sure you'd have been in touch if there'd been any developments. I guess I just wanted the company of someone who knew what I was going through."

"It's fine. I wasn't doing anything important," she lied.

"Have I dragged you away from your family?"

"No, nothing like that," Helen replied, artfully avoiding the question.

"You get a bit stir-crazy sitting in this room all day. I've tried to get out, but I don't know my way around and . . . and truth be told, I don't really want to get to know this place. I feel happier here."

"I understand. It's hard. And if you ever feel you'd rather go home, then I won't think any the less of you. There are many different ways to show your love and commitment to Pippa."

He looked at her for a second. "I'd rather stay."

Helen nodded and for a moment neither of them spoke. Daniel looked out over Southampton while Helen surveyed the other guests in the restaurant. Immediately she caught the eye of a middle-aged woman who was staring at her. The woman was obviously intrigued by them—was she trying to work out if they were on a date? Married? Friends? The realization made Helen feel foolish.

When she turned back, she was surprised to find Daniel smiling at her.

"If it's awkward for you to be here, then just say so. I don't want to make your life difficult, Helen."

"I want to help," Helen said. And it was true. Daniel had given her her cue to leave, but she didn't *want* to abandon him here, a grieving man in a lonely city.

"I know what you're going through," she continued. "When you've lost someone close . . . it kind of surrounds you, doesn't it? It's hard to see a way through it."

Daniel nodded. "She's all I think about. She's as alive to me now as she ever was."

Helen smiled. Reaching out, she took his hand. "And that's fine. It's not weird or morbid. It's natural. You loved her. You *love* her. Nothing that's happened can change that."

"Thank you, Helen. I thought I was going a bit crazy, but—"

"It's not crazy and you must think of her. You must always think of her."

Daniel nodded his thanks, just about keeping his emotion in check. "Pippa was always so boisterous when she was little. They say boys are the troublesome ones, but that wasn't true in our case. She had this great mate—Edith—and together they would create havoc. They would dress up as pirates, soldiers, whatever, and create elaborate games in the living room. The sofas would be turned into hideouts, skipping ropes would become lassos, cardboard tubes would become rocket launchers—they could play like that for hours."

As Daniel lost himself in tales of Pippa's childish exploits, Helen thought back to her own childhood. Among all the horror, abuse and degradation, there had been odd moments of contentment. Holidays on the Isle of Sheppey, shoplifting trips with her mum and sister, cider-fueled hysterics with Marianne and their mate Sam. Brief slivers of happiness.

The one character who was always absent from these memories was her father. She tried to think if he'd ever done anything loving or kind, but nothing came to mind. The only thing he had ever given his children was bruises and broken bones. To him, children were first an irritant and expense and later a commodity to be passed around fellow pedophiles. Perhaps he had suffered when he was young, perhaps there were experiences and demons that had driven him to behave the way he did, but Helen had never wanted to go there. She refused to entertain the idea that his brutality could ever be excused or justified.

He was a far cry from the decent, wounded man sitting opposite her now. Helen knew that was why she was still here, drinking coffee late into the night with a man she barely knew. The fact that he did care—that he *loved* his daughter—really hit home with her. And though she chided herself for not passing Daniel on to a trained

Family Liaison officer, she didn't blame herself for it. She was enjoying the rush of his memories—there was an innocence and warmth to them that Helen found irresistible. Neither seemed keen to break up the evening or to acknowledge that—minutes later—they were still holding hands.

60

He reached out and took her hand, running his finger over her knuckles. "Isn't this nice?"

Ruby smiled in response, forking another mouthful of pasta in her mouth. She didn't know what she had been expecting, but the food was good—pasta carbonara, rich, creamy and comforting. She cleared her plate, then picked up her wine, draining the plastic beaker it had been served in. Despite the absurdity of the situation, the wine felt good—a brief spike of exhilaration surging through her before drifting away again.

"Pudding?"

Ruby nodded and within a minute had wolfed down a bowl of trifle. Stuck down here as she was, all she could think of was how hungry she was.

"I wanted to ask you something," she said suddenly. "I . . . I get bored down here waiting for you, so I was wondering if I could have some books."

He regarded her for a second, then said:

"What sort of books?"

"Anything."

"You're not fussy."

"I just want to read."

Another pause.

"Tell me some titles and I'll see if I can get them for you."

Ruby racked her brain, reeling off a list of favorites that would make her feel a little less alone. Books her dad loved, that Cassie was obsessed with. They would be her family down here. Finally she ran out of ideas. Her captor swallowed a yawn, fatigue finally overcoming him.

"Thank you, Summer. I enjoyed myself tonight."

"Me too," Ruby said. There was a small part of that which was true at least.

"And if you're good to me, we'll see about those books."

He took a step forward. Ruby's natural instinct was to step back, but she forced herself to stand her ground. He took another step toward her, wrapping his arms round her and pulling her into a hug. She allowed it, though she was screaming inside. She felt his lips find their way to her ear.

"All good things come to those who wait," he whispered.

Suddenly Ruby had tears in her eyes. She could feel his erection pressing against her. She just wanted to be away, away, away from him. As he disengaged, she wiped her eyes quickly—refusing to throw it all away by losing her cool.

"Good night," he said as he headed toward the door. "And thank you."

Ruby stood stock-still as he departed. She remained there for a full five minutes until she could be sure he was gone—smiling her rictus grin, wanting to be a good girl for him, despite the fact that she was shaking like a leaf.

61

Hurrying straight into his bedroom, he locked the door and lay down on the bed. Unzipping his fly, he slipped his hand inside his trousers. The feeling of flesh on flesh made him shiver.

He knew he should resist, but there was no fighting it tonight. He had returned home in such a low mood, riven with doubts and fears, so this evening had totally ambushed him. Where he had been expecting defiance, hurt and acrimony, he had in fact found compliance and kindness.

Was he foolish to think that Summer was starting to love him again? Things had been so difficult and distressing, but suddenly she seemed to have turned a corner. She *wanted* to be with him and took pleasure in his company. And tonight he had responded, in a manner that surprised and energized him. He had felt so aroused in her company that the greater part of him had wanted to take her to bed there and then.

Normally he managed to contain his urges. But not tonight. He climaxed quickly and fiercely. Lying on the bed later, he felt happy but oddly dissatisfied. It had been so long since he allowed himself even the release of fantasy—so fearful was he of ultimate disappointment—but even that failed to satisfy his needs now. With the realization that Summer might finally be coming home to him, his desire to be with her was growing stronger. He would not rush her—he had made that mistake before—but his feelings spurred him on. The dark days were coming to an end, his salvation was at hand and everything was prompting him to act.

Soon the waiting would be over. Soon their love would be real.

62

Alison Sprackling stood in her daughter's bedroom and stared out the window. She often came here once everyone else in the house was asleep. Had *she* slept at all since Ruby had gone missing? She supposed she must have, otherwise she wouldn't still be able to function, but it certainly didn't feel like it. Jonathan was no different, tossing and turning from dusk till dawn, but this was little comfort. They seemed to be talking to each other less and less.

Alison sat down on Ruby's bed and opened her bedside drawers. She knew she cut a sorry figure sitting on the old John Lewis duvet, rooting through drawers she had once been banned from opening, but what else could she do? She had been through Ruby's stuff three or four times now, searching for some small clue as to her whereabouts—leafing through shoe boxes of old letters, discarded shopping receipts, old school reports—but to no avail. Ruby continued to elude her.

She knew the police no longer had a suspect in custody. There had been a brief surge in optimism when they were questioning that builder, but that had turned out to be a dead end. How she'd cursed them when she found out. Jonathan had counseled her against false hope, but Alison had already played out the narrative in her head. A speedy investigation, a swift arrest and Ruby returned to them safe and well.

The truth was that there weren't many obvious culprits, and that was what unnerved her. Shanelle had been exonerated, as had this other guy, and, despite all of Alison's desperate searching, no one else had come out of the woodwork. They said it was often family members who were responsible for these things, but that was impossible, surely? She had contacted Ruby's boyfriends and schoolmates, but they were all awkward, surprised and innocent of any wrongdoing as far as she could tell.

So who? Who would do such a thing? Alison sensed the answer must be obvious and simple: she didn't believe in bogeymen or stranger danger, but this was baffling and dispiriting. Ceasing her searching, Alison curled up on Ruby's bed. Just the smell of the pillow made her cry. It smelled of Ruby's perfume. Alison had always privately disliked Ruby's choice of scent—it was one of those celebrity-endorsed products that cost nothing to make and everything to buy—but it smelled sweet to her now. It smelled of *her* Ruby. Burying her face in the pillow, Alison sobbed quietly. Another sleepless night beckoned, but tonight for once she wouldn't feel so desperately alone.

63

Dawn was yet to break and the streets were dark and deserted. Recession cutbacks meant the city's lampposts were switched off after midnight, with the result that Southampton felt a lonely and threatening place in the small hours. Oddly Helen liked it that way, enjoying the cloak of anonymity that it gave her. Cutting through the streets on her bike now, she felt relaxed and at ease—despite the early hour. And despite what lay ahead of her.

She was soon on the ring road, then on the motorway, heading north. Pushing past London, she skirted Northampton, before heading toward a village just to the west of the city. Bugbrooke was an old Norman village, populated by young families and retired workers—it was a pleasant, relaxed village with a friendly vibe.

Georges Avenue was just waking up as Helen parked her bike across the road from number 82. The curtains of the house remained closed, but all around the early birds were heading out to work—firing up the vans and swigging coffee from thermoses in expectation of a long day ahead. Helen watched them go, taking in their curious looks, well aware that she stood out like a sore thumb, leaning against her Kawasaki in her biking leathers.

She didn't have long to wait. She suspected DI Marsh would be working the early shift and at seven a.m. on the nose, he left the house, kissing his wife good-bye as he went. Helen watched, waiting until he'd actually opened the car door before marching over.

"DI Marsh?" Helen asked, flashing her warrant card at him as he looked up. "DI Grace, Hampshire Police. Could I have a quick word?"

"How do you know where I live?"

"Detective work, Tom. Can I call you Tom?"

They were sitting together now in the car. Marsh didn't answer either way, so Helen pressed on.

"Your Facebook site is a bit more informative than it should be."

Marsh said nothing, conceding the point with a grunt.

"I'm sorry for the cloak-and-dagger," Helen continued, "but I wanted to have a chat with you and it couldn't be done officially, given the nature of the inquiry."

Tom Marsh looked at her, intrigued.

"I know you're involved in undercover work and I'm not looking for you to betray any promises you've made or risk compromising your operations, but there's an informant of yours I'd like more information on."

"Robert Stonehill," Marsh said evenly.

"You obviously know who I am and who he is too. And I'd like to know if he's been working with you."

Marsh reached into his jacket pocket, pulling out a packet of fags and lighting up. He was clearly contemplating whether to tell his interrogator to sling her hook. Then again, Helen thought as she studied his face, he was also a family man and perhaps not unsympathetic to her plight.

"I can't give you any names or specific details, as the operation is still ongoing. But it's about drugs, okay? Far as I can work out, Stonehill rocked up here without much of a plan. He fell into company with some folk from the wrong side of the tracks and before long was running their errands. Doing a bit of dealing and the like—the crews around here are always looking for new runners, fresh meat to take the risks for them. Turned out he was good at it—kind of used to keeping his head down by now. And he gained the trust of a few middlemen, even met a few of the big suppliers."

"Who are the ones you're really interested in."

"Exactly."

"How did they pay Robert? Cash? Drugs?"

"Mostly cash. He dabbles in drugs but isn't that interested."

"And you pay him too?"

Marsh smiled and looked out of the window. He wasn't going there.

"Is he still on your books?" Helen asked.

"I'm sorry. I'm not at liberty to say—"

"Okay, but is he still in Northampton?"

A long pause as Marsh debated whether to say anything. Then:

"You didn't hear it from me and we never met, but . . . yes, he's still here. He uses the alias Mark Dolman."

"Any idea where he lives?"

"Somewhere in Thorplands. I couldn't say for sure. Thorplands is—"

"I know where it is," Helen said quickly, pleased for once to be ahead of Marsh.

It was tantalizing. To know he was in Northampton, but not exactly where.

"And where do you two meet?"

"No" was Marsh's blunt response.

"I'm sorry?"

"I know what you're going to ask and I'm afraid the answer's no."

"Come on, Tom. Think about it from my point of view—"

"I'm sympathetic to your plight—I really am. But I'm not risking compromising a yearlong investigation for you. I've already told you enough—more than I should have—so if it's all right with you, I'd like to be on my way, okay?"

His tone was firm and final, so, thanking him, Helen took her leave, watching his Ford C-Max burn away from her into the distance. He had gone as far as Helen could reasonably expect, but still she felt frustrated. She had no idea when he had last seen Robert, or what state her nephew was in. Nor did she have an address. That said, she did finally have some pieces of the jigsaw. It wasn't enough—but it would have to do for now.

As she was biking back to Southampton, Helen's head was full of thoughts of what she might do next. As ever her life was a precarious balancing act. Her number-one priority had to be Ruby Sprackling—somehow, somewhere, they had to find a break that would bring them closer to her—but the pull of Robert was strong also. Even if she had to work round the clock, she would have to find a way to achieve both. For her own sanity if nothing else.

These thoughts were still spinning round when Helen noticed the small dark car in the side mirror. She had just reached the outskirts of Southampton and was arrowing toward the hospital when she spotted it a few cars back. There was something about the number plate—its distinctive EKO ending—that she recognized. Was she imagining it or had she spotted the same car following her down the M1 from Northampton? Upping her speed, she took a sharp left, then left again, ripping the throttle back to enable her to spin round the block in quick order and rejoin the main road a good hundred yards from where she had been.

The car was gone. No sign of it on the main drag or any of the side roads. Had Helen imagined it all? Or was someone interested in her movements today? Suppressing her anxiety, Helen hit the indicator and dived off the main road toward Southampton Central.

64

Sanderson was onto her the minute Helen entered the incident room. Moments later, they were camped in Helen's office with the blinds down and the door firmly shut.

"Sorry for the amateur dramatics," Sanderson said in reference to the closed blinds. "But I thought you ought to see this."

She passed a file across the table, which contained four sheets of paper—all of them with a woman's photo attached to the top right-hand corner.

"I've spent the last twenty-four hours going over the local missing persons registers and liaising with the relevant agencies. And it's thrown up four possibles."

Helen kept her expression neutral, but she didn't like the sound of that number.

"They all have the right look—dark hair, blue eyes—all live alone, are low-income and have been missing for some time. Two of them—Anna Styles and Debby Meeks—seem to have vanished completely, no communication of any kind. The other two—Roisin Murphy and Isobel Lansley—send the occasional text or tweet."

"How occasional?"

"Not very often, but always at virtually identical times."

"Before their mobile signal goes off again?"

"Exactly," Sanderson replied, nodding, her expression somber now.

"Do the timings of the communications tally with those 'sent' by Ruby and Pippa?"

"Yes. They're a perfect match."

Helen looked at their pictures—Roisin was a single mum, studded with piercings, rough around the edges, but with stunning aquamarine eyes, while Isobel was a very different kettle of fish. Her eyes were equally striking, but they were hidden behind a long black fringe. Isobel's gaze was sidelong, as if she was unkeen to be photographed at all. Helen exhaled long and hard, suddenly struck by the fact that she might already be looking at the faces of two corpses.

She was on her feet now and marching to the door.

"I'll take full responsibility for pursuing this line of investigation," she said over her shoulder. There was no time to wait, no time for indecision, and Helen knew exactly what had to be done.

65

He was already sitting on the bed when she awoke. Ruby sat upright with a start, freaked-out to find him staring at her.

"You've had a rough night," he said sympathetically.

He was right. Ruby had spent a sleepless night, kept awake by hope, but also by fear. Her captor's obvious desire for her still haunted her waking thoughts.

"I was cold," she lied, pulling the sheets up around her.

"I'll get you some extra blankets," he continued, "and I will try to pick up those books for you today."

"Thank you," she said, earning a smile in response. "If you were feeling kind, there are a couple of other things you could get for me too," Ruby went on, as casually as she could.

Immediately a frown passed across his face. Was he suspicious? Did he sniff trouble? Keeping her expression as meek as possible, Ruby continued. "I would really like some makeup. I would love a hair-brush, some lipstick, some eyelash curlers and, if you don't mind buying it, some nail polish."

He looked at her, saying nothing.

"I just want to look nice for you. And I think I deserve it, don't you?"

Another long, painful pause; then he finally broke into a broad smile. "Were you nervous about asking for these things?"

Ruby looked at her shoes, fearful her expression would betray her.

"There's no need to be. I don't mind it when you're assertive. It's more like the old you."

He rose at this point. "I'll get those things for you. You'll . . . you'll look pretty as a picture."

With that, he departed. As soon as he'd gone, Ruby sank back down on the bed. It had cost her her last remaining ounce of composure to play her part, but it had succeeded beyond her wildest dreams. She had expected more suspicion, more resistance, but actually he had played right into her hands.

The first phase of her plan was complete.

66

"This is fucking out of order and I will not stand for it."

Ceri Harwood seldom swore. It was strangely enjoyable, watching her superior lose her cool, and Helen privately resolved to provoke her more often.

"DI Grace knows the chain of command," the incandescent Harwood continued. "She knows she should have come to me first."

Chief Constable Stephen Fisher nodded, before turning his attention to Helen. "Would you care to explain to me why you didn't, DI Grace?"

Because Harwood would have told me to go jump in a lake, Helen thought, but swallowed that down. Her decision to go direct to Harwood's superior was deliberate—a calculated gamble.

"Detective Superintendent Harwood and I have already had this discussion and she's made her feelings clear—"

"So why are we having it again?" Fisher interrupted.

"Because the situation has changed," Helen replied. "Further investigation—"

"Investigation that was not authorized," Harwood interrupted.

"Further investigation has revealed a number of potential victims," Helen continued. "I have always believed that Pippa's killer had the potential to be a serial offender, and the evidence now points that way."

"Evidence?" Harwood queried witheringly.

"Roisin Murphy and Isobel Lansley. Two young women with the same look, the same profile, who've been missing for over a year and who text and tweet *at the same times of day and the same locations* as Ruby and formerly Pippa. The geography doesn't make sense—the New Forest, then Southampton city center, then Brighton, then Hastings—their movements are so random and unlikely that the only explanation is that someone is deliberately trying to throw the young women's families off the scent. Furthermore, what are the odds that four unconnected girls would be traveling around in the same seemingly random pattern?"

"So you want to go back to the beach?" Fisher interrupted decisively.

"Yes. That's the only deposition site we know of, and serial murderers are creatures of habit. It's a discreet, out-of-the-way location, which regularly washes away surface evidence, footprints and so on. It's perfect for his purposes and he'd be a fool not to use it again."

"He? You keep referring to 'he.' Who is he? You sound like you know him."

"We don't have anything concrete so far—"

"But still you want us to close a public beach, exhaust our

resources digging up great swaths of it and create an unholy storm of public concern and negative publicity in the process. All because of your gut instinct."

"Because of the pattern of his offending. There is almost zero chance he won't have attempted to abduct more victims in between Pippa and Ruby—and Roisin and Isobel fit the bill perfectly."

"We need more time, Stephen," Harwood countered, now turning to her superior. "Let's investigate the circumstances of the girls' disappearance and then see—"

"It's already been done," Helen returned aggressively. "Roisin had a one-year-old baby when she went missing. She tweeted saying she couldn't handle being a mum anymore and it's true she *had* struggled at times, but her family is totally convinced that she would never have willingly abandoned her baby boy. They've spent the last two years searching for her. They've used the police, missing persons, local charities. They even hired a private detective—none of the 'leads' provided by her tweeting check out. She simply hasn't been seen anywhere since she went missing *over two years ago*."

"Even so, the investigations of a local family are no substitute for proper police work," Harwood fired back. "Let us pursue this line of investigation in a measured, methodical way and see if any of these 'hunches' bear fruit. Rushing headlong into a major search operation only risks making us look very foolish indeed."

Both women had finished now. Fisher regarded them, weighing up his options. Harwood had been his appointment and it had worked out well for him. Which was why Helen was surprised when he said:

"You've got one day on the beach, Helen. Make the most of it."

67

The girl in Boots shoved his purchases into a plastic bag and took his cash without once looking up. While he'd been walking round the shop, he felt a sudden pulse of fear—would people look askance at a guy with a basket full of makeup? The local paper was still going to town on the Pippa Briers story, urging its readers to keep their eyes peeled for any suspicious activity that might lead them to her killer. They'd even gone as far as publishing a detailed offender "profile," describing his likely race, background, body language and psychology. It was all rubbish, of course, but some of their lucky guesses had made him uneasy. So he'd prepared a detailed cover story—even slipping a scratched old ring onto his fourth finger to make him look like a solid husband and father—but in the event these precautions had proved utterly unnecessary. Like most young people, the shop girl was only interested in herself—lazily picking up her smartphone the minute she had finished serving him.

The sight of the girl checking her messages reminded him of an important task he had overlooked. Usually he would have caught a train or bus somewhere before work—he'd had Bournemouth in mind this time—to carry out a swift round of texting and tweeting before returning to Southampton on the same train. It was a good way to throw people off the scent, without taking too much time out of his working day.

But having made a detour to Boots on an extended lunch break, he wouldn't have time for that today. So seeking out a quiet spot on the Common, he began to send the customary messages. In days gone by he'd enjoyed this guilty pleasure—climbing inside these girls' identities and speaking for them—but yet again he felt tense doing it. He was taking a risk tweeting so near his place of work, no question about it, and it robbed the little routine of its pleasure.

Funny how life keeps kicking you when yr already on the floor. Gettin used to it, he tweeted from Roisin's phone. He was always careful to factor in the misspellings and abbreviations that these girls were so fond of. Roisin had always been a bit of a Jeremiah, would think herself into dark holes, so it was definitely in character for her to be bleating about life's unfairness. He added a few more cynical thoughts, sent a couple of texts, then turned her phone off and slipped it back in his bag.

The sound of conversation made him look up. Two mums were jabbering loudly as they pushed their strollers along. Startled, he slunk back deeper into the undergrowth. He waited until they were long gone before pulling Ruby's phone from his bag. He did the necessaries, but his mood failed to lift. He couldn't escape the feeling that significant things were happening—things over which he had no control. Previously he had kept these girls alive safe in the knowledge that no one was even aware they were dead. He had reveled in this freedom and total lack of suspicion. But the discovery of Pippa Briers's body had changed everything. Now a major murder investigation was under way, led by DI Helen Grace. For the first time in his short life, he now understood what it felt like to be hunted.

68

The two women were virtually eyeball to eyeball, neither backing down. Sanderson didn't normally do all-out assault, but she was too enraged to back down. DC Lucas clearly felt the same, snarling at Sanderson to "get back in her box."

Sanderson could happily have swung for her colleague. It had been *her* idea to put the mobile phone companies on alert for any sign of the missing girls' phone signals, and now that this plan had paid off, she was buggered if she was going to stand aside and let DC Lucas run with it. The mobile signals had briefly sprung into life, somewhere on or near Southampton Common, and the smart thing to do was to get down there as fast as possible, to canvass witnesses, source CCTV footage, search for any signs of their killer.

"DS Fortune specifically left me in charge," Lucas was saying.

"If anything significant came up while he was at the beach, I was to handle it."

Sanderson was about to come back at her, but DC Lucas was not finished yet.

"And every minute you spend arguing with me reduces the chances of us bagging this guy and bringing Ruby home safe and well. Do you understand, DC Sanderson?"

Lucas had enunciated the syllables of Sanderson's name deliberately slowly—to underline her point. The eyes of the rest of the team were on her now and there was no way she could continue the fight, without looking irresponsible. With bad grace, she backed down and returned to her desk.

Ever since the investigation had widened to include Roisin Murphy and Isobel Lansley, Sanderson had been busy compiling dossiers on both women, climbing inside their lives to test Helen's theory about their abduction. She had made good progress, but she flicked through the pages listlessly now, still fizzing with anger over her confrontation with Lucas. She had never liked the humorless fast-tracker whose ambition was so ill-concealed, but now she was growing to loathe her. This sort of conflict was unnecessary and counterproductive. It risked turning the team against one another, which could only hamper the investigation. It was outrageous of Lucas to accuse her of risking lives, when *she* was the one whose ego could prove costly.

Sanderson returned to the task in hand, wrenching her mind away from crucifying Lucas to the important police work in front of her. She mustn't compromise her own work through anger or bitterness—that wouldn't be fair to Ruby or Pippa. So she continued to leaf through the files, diligently comparing the life of Roisin—a single mother of Anglo-Irish extraction who lived off benefits in a small flat in Brokenford—with that of Isobel Lansley, a student at Southampton University about whom they knew almost nothing. She had few friends, little money, no jobs or hobbies. All they did know about her was that she lived in a one-bed flat in—

Sanderson stopped in her tracks, her heart suddenly racing. Checking the details again, she skimmed back fast through Roisin's growing file, searching for the relevant entry. And there it was. The discovery took Sanderson's breath away.

Finally they had the break they needed.

69

The three figures stood alone, whipped by the wind that roared in off the Solent. Helen was on one side of the trio, Harwood on the other, with an uncomfortable DS Fortune in between. The two women had hardly spoken to each other since arriving, and the atmosphere was tense. Helen got the feeling that Lloyd would rather be anywhere else but here, but that was too bad. This was too important not to have her right-hand man by her side.

The beach had been deserted when they arrived, so securing it wasn't hard. Given the brief window she'd been allowed, Helen had pulled out all the stops, dragging a dozen uniformed coppers off the beat, so that the beach could be taped off swiftly and the necessary public notices erected. Nobody was swimming off this beach today.

A POLSA team had been scrambled from Kent Police, making it

to Carsholt in under two hours—Helen had impressed upon them the urgency of the situation. They were now at work, the metal detectors, cadaver dogs and ground-penetrating radar scouring the broad expanse of sand for any signs of burial, deposition or human remains. The occasional bleep from the metal detectors was all Helen could hear above the wind.

The beach presented in a very different light from the last time Helen had been here. When they had found Pippa, the weather had been incongruously glorious, the sun beating down on the SOC officers as they'd completed their painstaking forensics work. Today the sun had disappeared behind looming gray clouds, hiding its warmth and cheer from the scene. Even the sea seemed to be getting in on the act, raging and crashing on the surf nearby.

DS Fortune snuck a look at his watch.

"How many hours of daylight do we have left?" Helen asked him.

"About seven," he replied quickly. His voice was clipped, infused with the anxiety of a man serving two masters.

"Seven hours before we can bring this charade to an end," Harwood added. "Are you planning on staying down here all day, DI Grace? Or do you have some police work to do?"

"I'll stay as long as is necessary," Helen replied evenly. She wasn't going to embarrass herself by squabbling with Harwood in front of a junior officer. "After all, we only have limited time."

Harwood didn't respond, so Helen took this as her cue, heading down to the water's edge. Once there she turned, taking in the full panorama of Carsholt Beach. Harwood and Fortune were chatting easily—more relaxed now Helen had left them—in sharp contrast to the men and women from Kent, who had worked out a grid and were now combing every inch of it.

Helen felt the tension within her rise as she watched their patient, diligent work.

Had she been too hasty in ordering the search? She had little credit with Chief Constable Fisher and even less with Harwood, so it would be hard now to ask for extra resources later in the investigation, if today's search proved fruitless. For a moment, Helen berated herself for her characteristic impatience. It was like an obsession for her, the desire to chase down leads, to complete the story, to find out what had happened. Once you climbed inside an investigation of this magnitude and urgency, it was hard to wrench your mind from it, as you constantly checked and double-checked your assumptions to see if there was something you could be doing better or faster. Sleep was hard to come by and it was almost impossible to relax, but that was as it should be. You didn't come into this line of work for an easy life—you did it because you wanted to make a difference.

Helen snapped out of her daydreaming, because one unit of the POLSA team had suddenly stopped. They weren't combing anymore; they were digging. Helen raced across the sand, making it to the quartet of officers, just before DS Fortune. The looks on their faces said it all.

"We've found something."

70

Southampton Common looked bleak and sinister under the gray clouds. A suitable place for a killer to roam, DC Lucas thought to herself. She was new to Southampton and still didn't know it well, so she'd brought as many uniformed officers as she could muster. Good, honest guys who knew every inch of this terrain and could be her guides.

Fanning out, they set about their task, stopping joggers, mums, businessmen, even council workers cutting the grass, asking them what they were up to and who they'd seen on the Common that morning. A vast majority were baffled by the questions; others were taciturn and suspicious, afraid of getting dragged into something that was nothing to do with them. It was an exhausting and potentially fruitless endeavor—so many people used the Common during the course of the working day. But he was here somewhere.

The mobile signals had sprung to life just under forty-five minutes ago. If Lucas hadn't had to face down DC Sanderson, she would have been here even sooner, but she was still pleased by the speed of their response. She now had six CID officers in addition to herself and fifteen uniformed officers combing every inch of the Common. They might get lucky; they might not. But something in her waters told Lucas that they would be lucky today.

She had ventured off the beaten track now, walking away from the body of the search party into the denser undergrowth near the Wildlife Center. It was oddly beautiful here, despite the gray sky that framed the woods. The trees were old with characterful hanging branches and thick foliage. And they were full of birds, who called to one another as Lucas picked a careful path deeper into the woods.

Crunch.

Lucas froze, her senses suddenly alert. She cast around her, but couldn't see anything. "Police. Who's there?"

Still nothing. A silence that seemed to go on for ever, then:

Crunch. Crunch. Crunch. Where was the sound coming from? She strained hard to hear but, finding it impossible to locate the cause, made a snap decision and plunged through the foliage to her right.

Suddenly it happened. A figure bolted. The *crunch, crunch* had obviously been him creeping away, but now he was in full flight. Lucas was after him in a flash, sprinting over the forest floor and hurdling fallen logs in pursuit. Lucas had always been a good sprinter and she needed every ounce of her ability now, as the fugitive darted gracefully under branches and round bushes, intent on escape. He knew the forest far better than she, so while he seemed to glide unimpeded through the woods, Lucas was whipped by thorns and branches, scratching the skin from her face and arms. The trees were thinning now, however, and Lucas spotted her chance.

Cutting off the corner of the wood, she raised her speed a notch further. She was taking a calculated gamble that the man she was chasing would bear left on leaving the sanctuary of the wood, heading for the busy city center rather than exposing himself to capture on the open ground of the Common.

Sprinting free of the woods, the man turned sharply left and sprinted for the park exit. Wham! Lucas took him down, wrapping her arms round his legs, bringing him down hard on the concrete pathway. She was swiftly up on her feet and pressing him hard up against the park notice board. He was already cuffed and compliant by the time the other officers arrived to assist.

Lucas's pulse was racing, but her triumph was short-lived. The "man" she was chasing turned out to be sixteen years old. A teenager with a taste for soft drugs and two decent-sized baggies of cannabis in his pocket. What he didn't have, it soon became clear, was any mobile phones.

Cursing, Lucas turned him over to uniform and returned to the hunt. Another twenty minutes had passed and it was clear to her now that unless their killer had a pathological desire to be caught, he would be long gone.

71

Helen stood on the lip of the trench as the team continued their excavations. Their ground-penetrating radar had picked up two bulky forms buried deep below the beach at locations that were only a stone's throw from each other. Helen's whole body was rigid—she hoped she was wrong, but she feared that they'd found what they'd come for.

"It's a young female."

The words were simply said but affected everyone who heard them. Some things you never got used to, and the loss of young life was always particularly upsetting. Helen lowered herself into the trench, taking care not to impede the team's efforts or trample on potential evidence. As with Pippa, the cold sand had done a good job of preserving its charge. There was only slight decomposition and the young woman looked as if she had simply gone to sleep four feet below the beach. Strange that people who have met their ends in such awful circumstances could look so peaceful.

Using fine tools and brushes, the team had now revealed the woman's face and the damp black hair that framed it. Helen examined it closely. There were two small holes in her right nostril, but, as with Pippa, the jewelry had been removed. Any makeup there might have been had also vanished, the moisture and movement of the sand effectively scrubbing the young girl clean. There was a stark simplicity to her face, the features proud and undisguised. It was beautiful, but also crushing. Helen had seen the photos, read the files, and looking down at the face below, she had no doubt in her mind that she was now looking at the remains of Roisin Murphy.

Helen was tempted to leave Roisin now. The rest of the team was at the other dig site, twenty-odd yards away, disinterring another form, and it was important to establish as swiftly as possible whether she was their other missing girl—Isobel Lansley. Yet something made Helen pause. It's strange the connection you can make with someone you've never met before, someone whose life has been snuffed out months, possibly years, ago. But Helen wasn't alone in wanting to cleave close to the poor girl, now that she had been discovered. Her family had been searching for so long, hoping against hope that she was okay, wondering if Roisin would ever return to her baby boy. The uncertainty was over now—they would never see their bubbly, troublesome daughter, mum and friend again. She had been let down by those around her and cruelly let down by life and—though there was nothing that could be done for her—it seemed wrong to abandon her now.

It didn't make much sense, but no one would leave the trench until they had delivered the young woman from her tomb. There was something tender about the way the team eased her shoulders and arms from the sand. It was obviously done to preserve both the evidence and the scene, but it was oddly moving, a final act of kindness in a brief, brutalized life. Helen made a mental note to thank the team later for their professionalism and care.

Already Helen's mind was scrolling forward, drafting the words she would use to tell Roisin's family the terrible news, but what she saw suddenly banished all such thoughts. Roisin's left shoulder and arm had now been fully exposed, and the sight of it made Helen's blood run cold.

There, standing proud on her bare, pale shoulder, was a small bluebird tattoo.

72

Ruby looked at her reflection but saw a stranger staring back. On the back of the improvement in their relationship, Ruby had persuaded her captor to leave the main lights on during the day and had pushed her luck still further by asking for a mirror. He had refused, of course—there was no way he was going to give her glass, or anything else that might be fashioned into a weapon.

But, in deference to her wishes, he had found a couple of sheets of Mylar and made a mirror of sorts. It had only taken him a few minutes to find the reflective sheets upstairs, and it set Ruby wondering what kind of job he did. Mylar was used to make those shiny silver helium balloons—was he some kind of children's entertainer? Did he work in a gift shop?

Pushing those thoughts from her mind, Ruby stared at herself in her "mirror." She was already much thinner, anxiety and the denial of food shedding the pounds quickly. She could see her ribs now—all of them—and her arms looked bony too. Ruby wondered how long she could survive down here, and once more visions of escape filled her thoughts. Her scrawny body and the sunken features in her face demanded action. She was beginning to look like one of those poor kids you see on charity appeals.

Her plan was in play and tonight she would see if he had gone for it. The anticipation was horrible. Had he got what she needed? And, more important, if he had, would she have the courage to see it through?

73

She slipped her key in the lock and teased the door open. She should really have gone back to the station after the discoveries on the beach—to brief Stephen and talk to Media Liaison—but she couldn't face it. Her mouth was dry, her head was pounding and she just wanted to shut the world out for a while.

Yet again, Helen Grace had made her look a fool. She had argued vigorously not to waste time and resources digging up the beach and though neither she, Helen nor Stephen would ever mention it again, it would be remembered by both. For Helen it would confirm her impression that her boss was a politician and desk jockey rather than a real copper, but more worryingly it would set back her relations with Stephen. He knew her well and had always liked her, but lately she had come to question where his loyalties lay. Was he attracted to Helen? Many men were, despite the fact that she was totally unobtainable. Or was he just seduced by her status as the heroic face of Southampton policing? Once more, Helen had proved that she had a nose for the big, career-defining cases. And if she managed to bring in another serial killer, it would burnish Stephen's reputation still further. Leaving her as the bad guy who nearly messed the whole thing up.

Opening the fridge, Ceri Harwood took a large swig of Chardonnay straight from the bottle, then held the chilled glass against her raging head. It felt nice and suddenly all she wanted to do was to find her husband, Tim, snuggle up on the sofa and finish the rest of it. This cheering thought roused her to action and she climbed the stairs two at a time. Tim often worked at home and was constantly badgering her to get home early so they could spend more time together. She seldom obliged—how could she in her position?—but having bunked off work, she felt exhilarated by the thought of surprising him with her sudden appearance.

She was halfway up the last flight of stairs to the attic office when she paused. The office was quiet, but there were noises coming from elsewhere. From their bedroom. She could hear Tim, but also female tones too. Laughing, talking and more besides.

Ceri willed herself to move, but her feet stayed firmly planted to the stairs. What does one do in these situations? Slink away or confront? She wanted to do the former—God, she wanted to do that—but some vestige of personal pride now forced her to choose the latter course. Summoning her courage, she marched forward, turned the handle and stepped inside.

The confusion started as soon as she entered. Surprise, then shock, then panicked apologies, as the naked lovers scrambled to make themselves decent. Tim was already halfway across the room, trying to steer her from the bedroom, but she didn't see him. She had eyes only for his lover. The woman she had been tasked with buttering up on numerous occasions, when she dined at their house. Lucy White.

Shrugging off her husband, Ceri Harwood stumbled downstairs to the kitchen. Her first thought was for the girls—she didn't want them walking into this—so she found herself texting another school mum to see if she could pick them up. She invented a lame excuse for the sudden emergency, which brought her up short. Was this how it would be now—lying to cover up her hurt and Tim's transgression? What *were* you supposed to tell your children in these situations?

Ceri sat down on the hard kitchen chair. None of this felt remotely real, but as she heard the front door shut quietly and Lucy's gentle footsteps clip-clopping down the steps to freedom, she knew that it was. This day had started badly, got steadily worse and ended in utter horror.

All that she had to look forward to now was the fallout.

74

They were closeted away in a snug at the back of the restaurant, away from prying eyes. Helen's first instinct had been to ask Daniel Briers to come to the station, but she'd thought better of it. Too little privacy and far too formal—she loathed the cheerless beige walls of the relatives' room, which seemed to sap the strength and optimism of everyone who set foot in it. So though an upmarket eatery was an unusual place to brief Daniel on developments, Helen felt she had made the right choice. Their relationship had already progressed well beyond the customary formality.

Daniel listened carefully as Helen talked him through the discoveries on the beach. She had been light on the detail—alive to the further torment she could see she was inflicting—but the thrust of her message was clear.

"He's a serial offender? A . . . serial killer?" Daniel closed his eyes as he said the words.

"That's our belief."

"Good God, what must she have gone through?"

He looked up at her with an expression that was part anguish, part need. Like with all relatives in these awful situations, once the worst has been confirmed, Daniel had hoped for a swift conviction and a clear, understandable explanation. A domestic incident. A crime of passion. A hit-and-run. But to imagine your daughter as the victim—the plaything—of a serial killer . . . that was too much for anyone to take on board.

"What did he do to them?"

Helen noted how he talked about "them," as if in his mind the new bodies on the beach were somehow divorced from Pippa's case. She didn't blame him for that—she'd do exactly the same in his shoes—but to her it was clear that all three women had fallen prey to a prolific and practiced killer. The circumstances of their burials, the careful way they had been stripped of all identifying features and, most disturbingly, the bluebird tattoo that they'd found on all three corpses—it was the same guy.

"We're still looking into that," Helen replied, avoiding all mention of mortuaries and postmortems. "But there's no sign he inflicted violence upon them and it doesn't appear he was sexually motivated—"

"So, what—he just starved them to death?"

"I don't know, Daniel, but we'll find out."

Daniel took this in, but said nothing, staring at his feet. Instinctively Helen tried to climb inside his head, imagining the awful situations that were playing out for Daniel—his daughter, alone and scared, facing a slow, lingering death. Hoping against hope that the only person who really loved her—her daddy—would rescue her from a living nightmare. When did she realize that no one was coming?

"You will catch him, won't you?" he said finally, his voice breaking even as he did so.

"I gave you my word. Pippa will have justice."

He looked up at her, his eyes full of tears. Taking her hand in his, he simply said:

"Bless you, Helen. Bless you."

75

He laid out his haul on the bed. It was like an Aladdin's cave of cheap cosmetics and looked exotic and glamorous in the dingy basement. He couldn't help a feeling of quiet satisfaction. She had asked him for something and he had delivered more than she could have dreamed of.

She was grinning from ear to ear. Singing his praises, showering him with compliments. How foolish their petty disagreements and squabbling seemed now. Why had he ever been worried? She just needed a bit of breaking in. But the effort was worth the reward and he basked now in the warm glow of her approbation.

"I wasn't quite sure what you wanted, so I bought a job lot. Mascara, lipstick, eyelash curlers, nail stuff."

He loved all the colors—the gold tubes, the deep red lipsticks, the shocking pink nail varnish. The femininity of it all thrilled him and aroused him.

"Thank you."

"If you like these, then we could think about other things too. Some new clothes, perhaps some underwear . . ."

He said this last bit quickly, not wanting to appear embarrassed in front of her, before listing other luxuries and trinkets that she might like. All the while he could feel his erection growing. The thought of her as his little piece of heaven, hidden away from the world, was too much.

He excused himself and hurried out. Once the heavy door was locked and bolted behind him, he leaned against the cold metal, enjoying its soothing feel. He had been through so much, suffered so horribly, but finally everything was going to be okay. She was *his* now.

76

What the fuck was he doing out there?

Ruby sat on the bed, her body rigid with tension. Her captor had shut and locked the door, so why wasn't he going anywhere? Her eyes were fixed on the wicket hatch—any moment she expected it to snap open. The full claustrophobia of her situation suddenly hit home. She had no control here.

Still no sound, no movement. Had she misjudged the situation? Did he not trust her? She looked at the spread of cosmetics on the bed. Ridiculous baubles to tart up a gruesome reality. She had assumed their purchase signaled something—a willingness to trust her—but now she wasn't so sure. She had built this up in her head too much for it to fall at the first hurdle.

Then footsteps walking softly away. Finally disappearing altogether. Still, Ruby sat stock-still. Not quite believing it. Not wanting to rush things, in case he suddenly returned.

But the silence remained undisturbed, so she quickly reached down and snatched up the eyelash curlers. She tested and probed them with her fingers—as she'd hoped they were the cheap high street kind, rather than anything professional. Seizing the curved shaper head, she pushed and pulled, trying to loosen it. But it wouldn't break. Cursing, Ruby lifted the iron leg of the bedstead and pushed it down firmly onto the shaper head, pinning it to the floor, before pulling the rest of the shaper back hard. With a satisfying snap it came free. Lifting the bed once more, she took out the shaper head and pressed down on it with her heel. Gently at first, but then with greater force, stamping down on the small piece of metal. The hard, dusty floor produced only a dull thud, and oddly Ruby felt totally safe from detection. Adrenaline was making her reckless.

She paused now, wiping the sheen of sweat from her brow. Lifting her foot, she saw that the curved piece of metal was now flat.

Scooping it up, she heaved the sheets, blanket and eventually the mattress off the iron bed frame. Time was of the essence now. Crouching down, she examined the exposed bed frame. It was a heavy, metal frame—four legs, a bedstead and a headboard. The bedstead was connected to the headboard by two metal screws. They had been screwed very tight and had proved immovable thus far, but now Ruby set to work on them, jamming the flattened shaper into the slot of the screw and turning it as hard as she could.

Nothing. No give at all. Already Ruby could feel tears creeping up on her. She renewed her efforts. A few seconds later, she relented, cursing. Surely all this hadn't been for nothing?

Summoning up her last shreds of determination, Ruby applied

herself once more. Her fingers protested as she twisted for all she was worth, the thin metal sides of the shaper cutting into them. She strained harder, could feel the skin on her fingers splitting now; then finally it happened. The screw began to move. Begrudgingly at first, then with alacrity and before long she held it in her hand.

One down, three to go.

77

Lloyd knew something was seriously wrong the moment she opened the door to him. Ceri Harwood was always so well presented, so terrifyingly in control of herself and her situation, that he was momentarily lost for words. He had never seen her look rattled and he had *certainly* never seen her drunk before. She blamed her slurred speech on pills she was taking for a head cold, but Lloyd could smell the wine on her breath.

She had obviously forgotten they were supposed to be meeting tonight, which angered him—how could she be so bloody cavalier? She looked at him blankly at first, as if trying to place him, then without saying a word turned and headed back inside. Lloyd felt a fool standing there, clutching his small Jiffy bag, like an unwanted postman. What was he supposed to do? Enter or wait here? Had he been dismissed? Or welcomed?

Lloyd stepped inside quickly. He was here to do a job and leave—no point lingering where people might see him. A black face in this part of town would excite more interest than usual and he wanted to be as anonymous as possible.

"Hello?" His voice seemed to echo in the spacious and well-appointed home.

"Downstairs" was the listless reply from within.

He walked down a precipitous spiral staircase to the large basement kitchen. He chided himself for it, but he felt deeply uncomfortable here. He had no problem with rich people, with folk enjoying the fruits of their labor, but it was so alien to him. He had never known luxury or privilege. He wouldn't know what to do with a house this size even if he had one.

"Drink?"

Harwood smiled grimly at him as she filled a glass to the brim.

"I'm okay—I need to get back."

"Nonsense," Harwood said, pushing the glass into his hand. "So, what's the news from the front?"

Lloyd looked down at the glass in his hand, and anger flared through him. She had no right to play games with him. "The bodies have both been exhumed now and are with Jim Grieves. We haven't officially ID'd them yet, but we're ninety-nine percent sure they are Roisin Murphy and Isobel Lansley."

Harwood drained her glass. "Press?"

"Nothing yet, but we've closed off the beach again, so it won't be long before we're fielding questions. Have we discussed a media strategy with Liaison?"

"Just give the hacks signed copies of Helen's mug shot. That should do the job."

Lloyd realized she was attempting humor, which only made this whole situation more surreal. Suddenly he wanted to be out of this place. He had no idea what had occasioned this burst of uncharacteristic behavior, but he didn't like it. For the first time he realized that perhaps Harwood wasn't quite as in control of the situation as she had claimed to be.

"Here." He held out the Jiffy package to her.

"Put it on the side," she said, gesturing toward the obscenely large marble-topped island, before wandering off to the fridge once more.

"What the fuck do you think you're playing at?" Finally Lloyd's anger had erupted. "Do you have any idea how dangerous this is? For me? For us? If you're so bloody uninterested, why did you start all this?"

Harwood paused and turned. She looked surprised, rather than offended, by his words. She shot a look at the package, and her face softened. Slowly she made her way back over to him.

"Forgive me, Lloyd," she said gently. "It's been the worst of all days."

She seemed uncertain whether to go on. For his part, Lloyd wasn't sure what to say.

"I know how this must look. But I am grateful for everything you've done. I know I can always rely on you." She looked at him warmly. "So let's forget my bad behavior, have a drink and talk about something else, shall we?"

"I don't want to intrude. Especially if Tim's at home and—"

"I kicked him out."

Lloyd was speechless once more. She didn't seem keen to elaborate further. Harwood took a step closer to him, her nose now only a couple of inches from his.

"So why don't you sit down on the sofa, have a drink and relax?"

As she said it she ran her finger down his face, brushing his lips and chin before coming to rest on his chest. Her eyes sparkled fiercely at him, but he felt no desire for her, just a mixture of horror and pity.

Gently taking her hand from him, he placed his still-full glass in hers and said:

"I really must be getting home."

78

Jim Grieves never said very much, but today he was unusually taciturn. The reason for this was obvious—two partially decomposed women lay on neighboring slabs in his mortuary. This meant a sudden spike in workload for Jim—which he never appreciated—but more than that it meant a depressing few hours spent in the company of two young people who should have had their whole lives ahead of them. Fifty-something Jim was truculent and sarcastic, navigating his job with gallows humor, but he had grown-up girls of his own and Helen could tell that he was affected by the latest arrivals to the mortuary.

"Roisin Murphy and Isobel Lansley," Jim began. "Missing Persons had their dental records on file. I've sent off DNA samples to double-check, but it's them."

Helen nodded. "How long?"

"Roisin about two years. Isobel less—a year to eighteen months."

Two more girls kept alive from beyond the grave through tweets and texts. It gave Helen no satisfaction to see that she had been right about the killer's need for fresh victims.

"I'm going to need a bit longer to give you cause of death. But both are likely to have suffered some kind of organ failure. They've been starved and kept in darkness. Like Pippa's, their eyes have deteriorated; they have a complete absence of vitamin D in their systems; their skin is leathery. At some point their bodies just shut down—I'll pin it down further as we go on."

Helen knew this was coming, but it still upset her.

"We do have something here that we didn't have with Pippa. All three bodies were washed clean—either by the killer or by Mother Nature—but I found something odd on Isobel. Two of the hairs in her fringe were stuck together. Nothing unusual in that—wet sand is sticky—but this was stuck together with some kind of solvent."

"Any idea what it is?"

"Not a clue," he replied cheerily. "Not my department. But I've sent it off for tests. I've told them we need it back within hours. You can imagine what they said to that."

For the first time today, Helen smiled. Jim enjoyed nothing more than winding up the lab crew, whom he unfairly dismissed as automatons.

"What about the tattoo?" she said, pressing on.

"Similar pigments as used on Pippa. Hard to say if he used the same needle—if there's bacteria on the needle, that may help us decide either way—but one thing's clear: he's getting better at it. Isobel's tattoo was much more skilled than Pippa's."

Helen took this in.

"Truth be told," Jim continued, "you can buy these inks and needles online or in scores of stores in Hampshire. They are all pretty generic and I'm not sure that's going to take you anywhere. If I were you I'd concentrate on the design. Find out why the bluebird is important to him."

Helen left shortly after, having thanked Jim for his endeavors. He was right, of course, though it didn't take them any further forward. They had done the necessary checks on the tattoo—nobody sporting a bluebird tattoo had been arrested in recent history, nor was there any record of bodies turning up that were decorated in this way. Computerized records only went back ten to fifteen years, so it might be that the evidence was out there somewhere, predating computerization, but she couldn't allot valuable manpower to sifting the archive, when the result of this line of investigation was so doubtful.

There was, however, one card left she could play, though it wasn't a card she was particularly looking forward to using. She was still pondering how to approach this when her phone rang.

On the other end was an excited DC Sanderson.

79

Lloyd was halfway down the stone steps when he heard her calling after him.

"Lloyd?"

He had left so abruptly—rudely—that he wasn't surprised. Instinct had taken over—he just wanted to be away. Still, he paused now. She was his boss after all. She stood in the doorway beckoning to him, as if keen not to be seen by the neighbors. Suppressing his irritation, he slowly climbed the steps, until he was standing in front of her. Why did he feel like he'd been summoned to the headmaster's office? *He'd* done nothing wrong.

"A word before you go."

To Lloyd's eyes, Harwood suddenly seemed much more cold-eyed and in control than she had been even five minutes ago. Something of the steely professional was returning, in spite of her obvious intoxication.

"We'll forget today ever happened. It's business as usual from now on."

She chose her words carefully and delivered them with emphasis and conviction. Lloyd could feel himself getting sucked in once more.

"I appreciate everything you've done for me," she continued evenly. "And it would be a shame for our close working relationship to be compromised in any way, wouldn't you agree?"

Lloyd nodded, though he was feeling the very opposite. Perhaps Harwood sensed this, for now she leaned closer, her lips almost brushing his ear.

"Don't turn on me, Lloyd."

Then she retreated, shutting the front door firmly behind her.

Driving home, Lloyd cursed himself for his stupidity. Why had he ever got involved with Harwood? Was he really so stupid as to have thought that he could come out of this thing unscathed? It had seemed so simple at first, but now he could see he'd been a fool. Had he come to believe his own hype—the Teflon kid who sailed through life climbing ever upward, never a mark against his name? There was a joke that followed him everywhere—a joke that infuriated him by its knowing racism—that he was "whiter than white." The Goody Two-shoes, flawless in his prowess and reputation. Lloyd knew it made him unpopular, but oddly it was a badge he clung to now, reminding himself that it meant he was better and more committed than those other jokers. Had he thrown that all away now?

Parking up, Lloyd walked to his front door. The lights were on in the living room, which meant his father was still up. Lloyd felt a flash of irritation—why did he insist on staying up so late?—then a wave of shame. Why should he criticize his dad when it was *himself* he was furious with?

"How was your day?"

Caleb turned to his son, switching the TV off immediately. It was as if he'd been waiting for Lloyd—waiting for some company—all day and was now seizing on it eagerly. His siblings never visited, work friends no longer called round, which meant that like many old people his father was alone for most of the day. Lloyd had tried to encourage him to enroll in clubs, he'd even tried to get paid help to visit at one stage, but his father had pooh-poohed the idea. He didn't have anything to say to new people, he said. He just wanted to spend time with family. Which in practice meant Lloyd.

"Usual," Lloyd replied casually.

"You sure? You look . . . a bit beaten up, son."

Lloyd shrugged. "A few issues at work. No big deal."

"Problems with a case?"

"No, just . . . staff issues," Lloyd answered.

"Want to talk about it?"

"Thanks, Dad, but to be honest, I just want to go to bed—I'm bushed."

Caleb said nothing and Lloyd stayed where he was, as if awaiting his father's permission to leave.

"You can confide in me, you know, son. I know I haven't always been easy on you, but . . . you can talk to me. I'd *like* to talk."

Did Lloyd imagine it or was there a slight quiver in his dad's voice? Did he really feel that lonely? That shut out by his own son? He stole a look at his father, who dropped his eyes to the floor quickly.

Lloyd stayed for a few minutes more, chatting about this and that, then took himself off to bed. The truth was, he really didn't want to talk, didn't want to dwell on his reckless foolishness in getting into bed with Harwood. Which of course only made him hate himself more.

Today he felt like a failure, both as a police officer and as a son.

80

Sanderson wondered if she was staring into the eyes of a killer. He met her gaze, then looked away quickly, settling instead on Helen, who sat across the desk from him.

Andrew Simpson had been visibly unnerved to find police officers waiting for him in his office when he returned to close up for the day. During Sanderson's first visit, he had been confident, precise and helpful—now he was on his guard. This no longer felt *routine.*

"How well did you know Roisin Murphy?" Helen asked, skipping the niceties.

"I don't know her."

"But you were her landlord?"

"That doesn't mean I know her, though. Most of my business is done online. I meet the clients once, then sign the contracts and that's it."

"No more contact."

"Not unless they've got a serious complaint. If it's minor problems—leaks, boilers, what have you—it's handled by my men."

"Men like Nathan Price."

"That's right. I was very surprised to hear he'd been arrested and charged with underage—"

"We're not here to talk about Nathan Price. We're here to talk about you, Andrew."

Sanderson suppressed a smile. She loved watching Helen when she had her game face on. Because she was tall, athletic and pretty, people thought she would be genial and pleasant—and often she was. But there was a steel within Helen and an unwavering focus that unnerved people under interrogation. They could find no way to distract her, no purchase of any kind with which to drag the interrogation to areas where they felt more secure. She looked at you with such intensity and such purpose—Sanderson had seen many a criminal give up the ghost before they had even begun.

"So, for the record, you only met Roisin once?"

"Once or twice," Andrew conceded, fingering his tie.

Helen nodded, writing this down in her notepad. The subtle shift from "once" had been noted.

"And Isobel Lansley?"

"Same."

Monosyllabic now—that was a good sign. A sign that they had him boxed into a corner already.

"What percentage of your tenants are female?" Sanderson asked, finally entering the fray. She had let Helen put the wind up him, but it was her lead and she wanted to direct the conversation now.

"I couldn't say."

"Hazard a guess," Sanderson responded.

"I don't know—fifty to sixty percent."

"We have a court order here allowing us full access to your tenancy lists."

Andrew Simpson stared at her.

"So when we look through your records, you're confident that roughly fifty to sixty percent of your tenants will be female?" she repeated.

Sanderson caught the swift glance Andrew Simpson shot at the CID officers outside, who were meticulously leafing through his filing cabinets. His anxious secretary stood over them, all at sea at this sudden and unexpected intrusion.

"Maybe not fifty to sixty percent," he eventually replied. "It's hard to remember off the top—"

"How many?" Helen interjected.

"About ninety percent or so."

Sanderson shot a look at Helen, but her boss didn't react. The phrase hung in the air. Then, with a very slight nod, Helen gave Sanderson the license to proceed.

"About ninety percent. Possibly even a touch more, I'm guessing," Sanderson continued. "That's statistically highly unlikely if they are randomly selected. Why are so many of your clients female?"

The "your" was slightly louder than the rest of her sentence.

"Because they're less trouble. They are cleaner, more organized, more reliable—"

"Not always," Sanderson shot back. "Pippa Briers left you in the lurch, didn't she?"

Simpson paused, then:

"Yes."

"What about Roisin Murphy? Did she give you proper notice?"

"Not that I remember," he conceded.

"And Isobel Lansley?"

"I'd have to look at my records . . ."

Sanderson glared at him.

"But I don't think so," he conceded.

Silence. A long pregnant silence.

"You should know that the bodies of Roisin Murphy and Isobel Lansley were discovered earlier today. Like Pippa Briers, they were tenants of yours. Is there anything you'd like to tell us about them?" Helen said.

Simpson shook his head firmly. Sanderson noted the first beads of sweat appearing on his forehead.

"We estimate they were murdered within the last two to three years. I believe you've known them both for a while longer than that. Is that correct?"

"I've already said I didn't 'know' them. Yes, they've been tenants of mine for several years, but—"

"Tell me about Isobel Lansley's flat," Helen interrupted. "What state was it in when you gained access to it after her disappearance?"

"It was okay. She always kept things nice and neat. She was very fastidious."

"I thought you said you didn't know her?" Helen said quickly.

"I don't. What I mean is that it was very clean and tidy when I went in."

"No signs of a struggle. Broken furniture or anything?"

"No."

"The lock on the front door was intact? No windows forced open."

"No, nothing like that."

"So either they let their killer in . . . or he let himself in?"

Andrew Simpson said nothing.

"Presumably you have keys to all your properties?"

"Of course," he replied, though he didn't look happy admitting it. "Sometimes I lend them to workmen if there's a job needs doing—"

"But it wouldn't be hard for you to get extra sets cut if you needed to."

Simpson shrugged.

"My guess is they were all abducted by someone who had access. Would you say that's a fair assumption?" Helen continued.

"You're the police officer," he replied evenly.

Helen nodded.

"How many flats do you own in the Southampton area?" Sanderson continued.

"Forty-two" was the swift response.

"And do you own any other properties?"

"No. Other than my house, of course."

"And you live in Becksford?"

"That's right."

"Nice and quiet round there, isn't it?"

Andrew nodded, watching Helen carefully. Helen returned his gaze, enjoying the tension in the room. Then, without warning, she got up. "That'll do for now. I'm afraid we'll have to leave a couple of officers here to gather the necessary paperwork. But thank you—you've been very helpful."

Sanderson smiled her thanks too. Nothing unnerved suspects more than gratitude and courtesy. She followed Helen's lead, shaking Simpson's hand, then left the office with her. Both were silent as they walked back to the car. But conversation wasn't necessary—Sanderson knew her superior well and could tell without asking that she was feeling the buzz too. At long last they were getting somewhere.

81

It was late and Ceri Harwood was alone in the darkness. After her unpleasant interview with Lloyd Fortune, she had poured the rest of the wine down the sink and collapsed onto the sofa. She lay there now, hangover slowly taking effect, chiding herself for her weakness and lack of control. To be drunk in the middle of the day was bad enough—to be drunk in front of a junior officer was unforgivable. What was he thinking now? Had her warnings hit home? Had she pushed him *away*? The thought made her feel sick.

As she cursed herself, her eyes drifted toward the island and the small Jiffy package sitting on top of it. In all the chaos and emotion, she had forgotten about it. Part of her couldn't be bothered with it now—so much had happened in the last few hours to render previous preoccupations meaningless. Tim's betrayal had changed her horizons forever. And yet . . . there was something within her that suggested this might yet be her salvation. A way to assert herself against a world that delighted in hurting her.

Picking herself up off the sofa, she crossed over to the island and ripped the envelope open. As expected, inside was a tiny cassette. Fishing it out, she sought out her handheld player and slipped the tape inside.

She was too wound up to sit—her body tense with anticipation—so she paced up and down having pressed Play. At first there was nothing—just the sound of fabric scratching against the microphone. She knew there must be more—Lloyd wouldn't have hurried it over if it was blank—but still it made her worry.

Then the voices started. A man's voice—odd, regional, unfamiliar—and a woman's. The conversation was staccato and punctuated by silences as challenges were laid down and decisions made. The pair seemed to be coming to an agreement, despite their differences. As they did so, a smile tugged at the corners of Ceri's mouth.

She listened some more. The pair didn't exactly shake hands, but the deal had been done. She had heard it straight from the horse's mouth. What a bizarre day it had been. So unsettling, so distressing, and yet here amid the wreckage of her life she had found the one thing she craved—the thing she had been searching for for months.

The means to destroy Helen Grace.

82

It was ten p.m. and the incident room was deserted except for two lonely figures. Helen and DC Sanderson sat huddled at the DI's desk, poring over the photocopied documents that the team had garnered from Simpson's files.

He had lied to them—that much was clear. He didn't have forty-two flats—he had over fifty. Some he owned the freehold to—having carved a decaying house into five tiny, dilapidated flats—others he was just the letting agent for. Interestingly he also owned a number of derelict properties—lockups, outbuildings, even a barn or two—dotted around the county. Some were rural, some were urban, but all were isolated.

As Helen skimmed the list that Sanderson had compiled, she was seized with a desire to search them all. In an ideal world she would have been on the phone to a POLSA team already—scrambling the chopper, the cadaver dogs, the heat-seeking equipment—but that would have been a massive commitment of resources over that many properties. She wouldn't be allowed to call up that kind of firepower without rock-solid evidence, and besides, she wasn't sure she'd get the warrant anyway. They had one connection between Simpson and the dead women—a strong connection admittedly—but as yet no hard evidence linking the landlord to any instances of abduction or murder. He had no criminal record; there were no witnesses linking him to anything untoward and no picture yet of his having an unhealthy interest in young women. Helen had already instructed McAndrew to take a forensics unit back to Ruby's flat. If they could place Simpson in her flat, then they'd have something to work with, especially as he had sworn blind he hadn't been in that flat in years.

So, much as Helen was tempted to go kicking down doors, she knew that she would have to go about this in the old-fashioned way.

"Round up as many of the team as you can," she said to Sanderson. "And pull in uniform too. I want every one of the properties on this list checked out. Knock on doors, ask around, find out if anyone's seen or heard anything unusual at these places. Shouts, cries, lights on late at night. Do whatever you have to—just give me something to work with."

Sanderson was already on her feet, ready to bash the phones and corral the troops. "Does that mean you won't be joining us?"

"Love to, but I've got something much more unpleasant in mind."

Sanderson turned, intrigued.

"I've got a date with Emilia Garanita."

83

Emilia Garanita cast her eye over yesterday's front page again. She had been allowed so few headlines recently—she was sure the editor was punishing her for her disloyalty—that she allowed herself to wallow in this one. It was a good cover with a great photo—the fluttering police cordon and then not one, but two crime scenes beyond it in the near and middle distance. It captured the magnitude of the crime perfectly, the bleakness of the beach and the loneliness of the graves serving to underline the fact that once more Hampshire Police was hunting a serial killer. Emilia had felt that old excitement when writing the copy—finally a major story to sink her teeth into.

Emilia lowered the paper to find Helen Grace walking toward her. It was a moment of pure serendipity that momentarily struck her dumb: Southampton Central's hunter-in-chief striding toward her, fresh from the investigation. In the past, Emilia would have greeted her with sarcasm and snide innuendo, but not now. She ushered Helen into the vacant editor's office, shutting the door behind her.

"I need your help."

As usual, her former adversary cut to the chase. Despite their difficult past, Emilia was the first to admit that she and Helen Grace shared some attributes. Women working in male-dominated industries, they both possessed a directness and courage that others of their sex lacked.

"Happy to do whatever I can," Emilia replied breezily.

"We need to better understand the significance of a tattoo that is present on all three victims."

"The bluebird tattoo," Emilia responded.

"Exactly. We haven't been able to link it to any previous victims or offenders. So it could be a dead end. It may even be a ruse, designed to throw us off the scent."

Emilia nodded sagely, swallowing a smile. Helen Grace had never been this open with her before about an ongoing investigation. Was she worried this time? Stumped? Or was this the start of a rapprochement in their relationship?

"Or," Helen continued, "it may be significant. If it is, then odds on there is someone out there who knows what it means. Who saw it on a friend or colleague or family member. I know it's a long shot, but presuming the killer lives locally, we were hoping the *Evening News* might go big on this. Capture the attention of the public—"

"And rattle the killer too?"

"Perhaps."

So much and no more. Emilia was enjoying being back in the game.

"I'll talk to my editor, but I know he'll be happy to help. This is a big public-interest story."

And a juicy one too, Emilia thought, but didn't say.

Helen left shortly afterward, the rough approach having been agreed between them. Emilia knew that usually this would be a job for Media Liaison, but Helen had come to her personally. Had her past vendetta against Helen been erased from her rap sheet? Emilia felt the old excitement returning. This could play well for her at the paper—and, who knew, perhaps beyond—so as Emilia sat at her desk, next leader article already half-written, she made a silent vow to ride this story as hard as she could.

84

Ruby hadn't slept a wink all night. She had been exhausted by her efforts, and under normal consequences would have sparked out, but hope and adrenaline were keeping her awake. Time was elastic down here—she imagined the minutes and hours passing steadily but had no idea what time it really was. So she tried to stop herself counting and think of other things.

She thought of things she would do when she was free. All the dreams she had postponed out of fear, insecurity or lack of resources. To hell with hesitation now. Silly as it was, she pictured herself in Tokyo. She had always wanted to go to Japan. Why, she couldn't say, but she had once gone as far as buying a "Teach Yourself Japanese" CD and had listened to it religiously one summer. She had forgotten almost all of it, of course, but there were some words she retained. She still loved the sound of them. On-ay-guy-shee-mass.

Kon-eech-ee-wa. She smiled to herself as she rolled the words around her mouth, enjoying their familiarity.

Movement upstairs. A sound, then another. Was it morning? It could just be him wandering around. He wasn't a good sleeper and she heard him walking around at all hours. But the fact that he had been silent for so long gave her hope that the night had finally passed.

This was it, then. Ruby clutched her weapon a little tighter. She would only get one shot at this, so she would have to get it right. Stupidly she found herself smiling again, excitement overcoming caution. Was she crazy to hope? Could it all end so simply? She tried to quell her sense of anticipation—to fail now would be too much to bear—but she couldn't help it. She had won his trust. She had the element of surprise. And something inside was telling her that she would be home by nightfall.

85

He lay in bed, staring at the ceiling. A slick, rust-colored patch of damp stared back at him. He took in its contours, its shadings of color, and saw in its form a million different things—an island, a cloud, a sailing boat, a unicorn. He was amused at his eccentricity, lying in bed dreaming up nonsense when there was so much to be done, but he made no attempt to stop. It had been so long since he'd allowed himself the luxury of happiness—why not indulge himself?

How dark and unremitting his life had been since Summer left. How had he endured so many years of misery and loneliness? It seemed crazy to think now that he had survived more than a decade without her. He had been ripped apart by her desertion of him and he blushed still at the thought of his younger self cradling Summer in his arms, slapping her face to wake her. He had been unable to speak for a month after it happened, mute with shock at this sudden betrayal. He was surprised to find that, even now, if he really concentrated he could summon the distinctive, acrid smell of the vomit that had coated her that night.

His first thought on realizing she had left him was to kill himself. It was the obvious thing to do and there had been many points since when he regretted losing his nerve. He had gone to a DIY store and bought everything he needed, but when it came to the crunch, something held him back. At the time he rationalized this as Summer intervening, pulling him back from the brink. But now he wondered if it was just plain cowardice. He didn't know whether it was a sign of strength or disloyalty that he was still breathing. Still trying to be happy.

Many were the times since then that he had lain in this bed and imagined himself back there. When he thought of that space—their small attic room with the ill-fitting floorboards and rotting joists—he always pictured himself as being horizontal. Lying on his tummy, spying through the floorboards at the goings-on below, or lying on his back with Summer, staring at the ceiling, imagining themselves anywhere but there.

There was so much junk in that small room—left by the previous occupants—and he and Summer had made a little sanctuary for themselves out of the discarded objects. A roll of musty carpet, an old tea chest, an old-fashioned doll's house, a saggy beanbag—they made a little circle of them and hid in the middle, safe from the world, cocooned in secrecy and love. They had read of fairy circles and lucky charms. They had liked the idea so much they had stolen a well-thumbed book from the library—laughing like idiots as they outran the fat librarian—and then, plucking nonsense fantasy words from it, they had cast spells over *their* little circle, hoping to render it secure and impregnable.

Once safe, they had turned their attention to the toys within the magic circle. They stole valuable items from Dixons—Game Boys—as well as books, dolls and Top Trumps from other children—but oddly the thing they kept coming back to was the doll's house. They had inherited it in poor condition. The plastic windowpanes were long gone and there were childish scribblings in biro on the roof that wouldn't come off however hard they scrubbed. But for all that they loved it, not least because inside were two small figures. One dressed in pink, one dressed in blue.

They adopted one each, naming them appropriately, and began to play with reality, imagining themselves in faraway places, living unfamiliar, glamorous lives. King and queen of all they surveyed. It was an arresting fantasy and they played it every day, until other interests took over. It was their world—their special world—and he still felt a deep pang of shame whenever he pictured the doll's house's sad end—smashed into a hundred pieces by his hand. He had destroyed those four walls with venom—his only regret at the time was that he didn't have any matches to turn it to ash. What a fool he'd been. There was nothing in this moldering house—aboveground at least—that was precious to him. He would have coveted that doll's house had he still possessed it.

The alarm clock snapped into action, forcing him out of his daydreaming. He hadn't slept much but oddly had enjoyed the strange half sleep that often conjured up strange memories. But there was no time to indulge himself. He was due in at work soon and he was determined not to do anything that would attract attention. The police focus was so intense now that he would have to be scrupulous not to arouse suspicion. He must be on time and on the button—just another day at the coal face as far as the wider world was concerned.

However, if he was quick, he could just sneak in a quick visit downstairs. He hated the idea of her being lonely, so, dressing quickly, he put a comb through his hair and hurried out of the bedroom. He had a spring in his step, a lightness in his heart—today was going to be a good day.

86

It's hard to watch someone implode. But the worst thing you can do is look away. There's no point pretending it isn't happening—you have to front up to it, take them by the hand and lead them to a better place. Aided by DC McAndrew, Helen Grace was doing just that.

Sinead Murphy was crumbling in front of them, broken by the final confirmation of her daughter's death. Helen was glad she hadn't shared the news last night. This had been her first instinct on leaving the mortuary, but she always shied away from doing these things late in the day. Best to give people the awful news early so that your FLO has a shot at creating some kind of order, to give friends and family time to assemble, before the unforgiving night sets in. Then at least you have a chance of leaving the bereaved relatives on an even keel.

Looking at Sinead, who was drawing hard on her third cigarette of their visit, Helen wondered if that was stupidly optimistic. Roisin had been conceived in difficult circumstances and her father was long gone before her first birthday. History had repeated itself with Roisin. Her ex-boyfriend, Bryan, had split with Roisin before their baby boy—Kenton—was walking. Bryan now sat awkwardly on the sofa, flanking the combustible mother-in-law he had never got on with. They made a strange couple—overweight Sinead crying into her cup of tea as the scrawny Bryan stared at his feet. He clearly didn't know what to feel about the mother of his child, who had booted him out, but was now dead. Despite his looks, appearance and emotional deadness, Helen felt some sympathy for him. It was a horrible situation for everyone.

None more so than for Kenton—the toddler now playing with Kinect bricks on the mud-brown carpet. His whole life had been topsy-turvy and things would only get worse now. His mother was no longer missing; she was a murder victim. Helen knew well how that fact would haunt him as he grew up. Helen had hated her parents most of the time, but their death at the hands of her sister had ensured that they frequently appeared in her daydreams and nightmares, silently accusing *both* their daughters of betraying them. More than that, the brutal murder of someone close to you—by blood if not affection—colors your view of life. The fact that people who *should* be with you have been brutally snatched away leaves you ill at ease, forever looking over your shoulder.

"How did Roisin handle motherhood?"

Sinead would be closed to them soon—a total collapse looked imminent—so Helen pressed on, wanting to get as much information out of her as she could.

After a long silence, Sinead finally replied:

"It wasn't easy. She was still so young. None of her mates had kids. She just wanted to party, y'know? Don't get me wrong. She loved Kenton to bits, but she wasn't ready for him."

"So when she went missing, you didn't report it at first?"

Sinead shook her head and took another long drag on her cigarette. "She'd been finding it tough. Kenton was never a good sleeper and Roisin always hated mornings," she continued, smiling briefly at the memory of her grumpy daughter. "She tweeted saying she had to get away for a while, so it wasn't that surprising . . ."

"But?"

"But it still didn't feel right. Kenton was here alone in the flat. *All night*. If she really wanted to get away, I felt sure she would have brought him to me. I would have kicked up a fuss—I've got problems of my own—but she knows I would never have turned him away. I would have done what I could."

Helen didn't doubt it—Sinead's love for her grandson shone through—the one bright spot in this whole story. "So you were worried?"

Sinead nodded, then went on:

"But I didn't want to contact the authorities, didn't want to get Roisin into any trouble. She didn't have much and relied on benefits to feed the boy."

Bryan shifted uneasily in his seat—Sinead's judgment of him was coming through loud and clear.

"What did *you* think, Bryan?" Helen said, shifting the focus to him. "When you heard Roisin was missing?"

Bryan shrugged—he clearly wanted this to be over as quickly as possible.

"Were you surprised?"

"Guess so."

"Why?"

"Because . . . because this was all she had. The flat, the kid."

"Your son?"

"Sure."

Helen looked at him. She felt there was more here. That his surliness was more than just awkwardness. "You weren't living with her when she went missing?"

"Nah, we'd split."

"How long was this before . . . ?"

"About six months."

"And where were you living at the time?"

"With friends."

Helen was starting to get irritated by his determined nonengagement, but she swallowed her frustration and persevered. "Did she ever mention anything to you that subsequently you've thought was suspicious? Was she scared of anyone? Was she in trouble?"

"No," he replied, shrugging.

Helen took this in, then:

"So, when Roisin went missing, who had keys to the flat?" Helen said it lightly, but it was this that interested her most of all.

"I did, of course," Sinead confirmed.

"Bryan?"

"She made me give my set back."

"Do you still have your key, Sinead?"

"Of course. I've got all her things boxed up," she said, a touch indignantly.

"I'm going to have to look at whatever you have—I hope you understand," Helen said.

Sinead looked at Helen for a moment—it was clear that handing over the treasured keepsakes of her daughter would be hard—

then she rose and headed upstairs with McAndrew, sense finally prevailing.

"Were there any burglaries? Break-ins?" Helen continued, turning back to Bryan.

Bryan shook his head.

"Did she mention anyone hanging around? Did she ever have to change the locks? Or express any fears for her security?"

"No, nothing like that," Bryan replied. "She was okay."

"I'm going to need you to write down the names of everyone she was in touch with," Helen continued as Sinead rejoined them. "We'll need to check them all out, see if anyone had reason to want to harm Roisin."

The pair promised to help, for once singing from the same hymn sheet. Helen rose, thanking them for their time, and headed for the door. She paused in the hallway to look at the boxes of possessions—three of them—that now encapsulated Roisin's short life. Helen was suddenly overwhelmed with sadness—for her, for her son—and was pleased to make her excuses and leave. As she walked away, she turned to look once more at the bereaved family through the living room window. Bryan was getting ready to leave, Sinead had her head in her hands and beyond them playing happily on the sofa was Kenton, utterly oblivious to it all.

87

There she was—slumbering as usual. Snapping the wicket hatch shut, he drew the bolts and unlocked the door. He was still scrupulous about security, despite the thawing in their relations, and never hung around. He had paid the price for carelessness before.

"Summer?"

Shaking his head, he shut the door, locking it quietly behind him. Summer had never been a morning person. Sometimes it irritated him; other times he found it entertaining. Today he was in an indulgent mood.

"Time to get up. We haven't got much time, but I can get you something nice for breakfast if you like. I can do pancakes . . ."

Pancakes had always been her favorite. Why shouldn't he spoil her now and again?

"Summer?"

He hurried over to her. He had reached her bedside and now leaned over her.

"Talk to me, Summer. Are you unwell?"

He pulled back the sheet—but discovered only a rolled-up blanket underneath. Before he could process this, he heard footsteps coming up fast behind. He started to turn—but too late. The hard metal bit into the back of his head and he collapsed heavily to the floor.

He tried to raise himself but was reeling with shock. Ruby didn't hesitate, bringing the long metal strut crashing down on his head again. It was heavy and normally she would have struggled to lift it, but fired by adrenaline she wheeled it freely now, bringing it down on the back of his head for a third time. This time he hit the floor and didn't get up.

Dropping her weapon, Ruby fell to her knees, thrusting her hand into his trouser pocket. A creature of habit, he always kept the keys in his right trouser pocket. But he had fallen forward and they were trapped underneath his body. Ruby was suddenly panicking. Why hadn't she thought of this? Could she be frustrated by something so stupidly obvious?

He groaned, lifting his hand to the back of his head. Summoning her strength, Ruby put her shoulder under his thigh, levering his body off the floor. He was heavy—heavier than she'd been expecting, given his slight frame—and for a moment the pair hung in suspension, wobbling ridiculously to and fro. Then with a savage grunt, she rolled him over. Thrusting her hand into his pocket, she found the keys—tearing them from him.

Now she was heading for the door. Her hand shook as she tried to slip the key into the lock. Her captor groaned once more. Closing her eyes, Ruby willed her hand to be still. This time the key found its groove and slid inside. She turned it hard to the left. But it wouldn't move. In desperation, Ruby tried the other way, twisting it as hard as she could. But still it refused to budge. Looking down at the key ring, Ruby suddenly realized that she had chosen the wrong key.

She tugged at the offending key—but it was jammed in the lock now. Her captor was starting to move—Ruby could hear him behind her, slowly pulling himself up off the floor. Ruby felt paralyzed—sheer terror robbing her of the ability to move. He was cursing and spitting, fury replacing his disorientation and shock. If she hesitated any longer . . .

Ruby pulled at the key with all her might and suddenly it came loose, sending her stumbling backward toward her captor. She felt his hand grasp her leg, his fingers scrabbling for a proper hold on her. Kicking him roughly away, she hared back to the door.

Selecting the second key, she slipped it into the lock. She twisted it hard, but the lock was old and stiff, resisting her endeavors stubbornly. Using both hands now, screaming in desperation, she forced the key counterclockwise and . . . finally the lock turned. Ruby hauled the door open.

Her first instinct was to bolt, but she caught herself, turning back to remove the key from the lock. If she could lock him in, then she would be safe. She tugged the keys out quickly, but as she did so, they spilled from her grasp, landing only a few inches from her captor. She took a couple of steps toward them, then stopped dead. He was already on his hands and knees, scrambling toward her. Snatching up the keys greedily, she turned and ran for her life.

Sprinting down the short dingy corridor, she soon came to another locked door. She had been expecting this. He always shut this door quietly, presumably to conceal its existence from her, but she had heard it *and* noted the second key on his key ring. She slipped this key into the lock—her hand was steadier now—and, swinging the door open, ran through it to freedom.

She was surprised to find a long tunnel stretching out in front of her. She upped her pace, desperate to be away from this place. The exertion exhausted her. She hadn't moved a muscle in days, wasn't used to this sudden burst of activity. But she could sense that liberation was close at hand and pushed herself on.

Then she came to an abrupt halt, staring uncomprehendingly at what lay in front of her. She was at a *junction*. Three separate corridors led off from this point—all of them disappearing into gloom. One of them must lead out of this hell. But which one?

Summoning the last vestiges of her courage and energy, Ruby plunged down the right-hand corridor, disappearing fast into the inky darkness.

88

It was the smell that hit you first. An overwhelming smell of damp, spiced up with bad drains and the thick smell of fried food. DC Sanderson stepped out of the moldering living room and poked her head into the kitchen—she immediately noted that the ceiling was coated with years of grease and cigarette smoke.

The Kurdish family who lived in this sorry excuse for a flat eyed her suspiciously, saying little. Sanderson presumed they were illegal immigrants but wasn't going to push it. They didn't look like scammers and certainly hadn't washed up in the land of milk and honey. She wondered if they had lived in better conditions at home, but decided against asking them.

Sanderson wasn't here to cause them trouble—she had bigger fish to fry. For the last two hours, she and a taciturn DC Lucas had supervised a Hampshire-wide sweep of Simpson's properties, knocking on doors, inveigling their way inside, asking questions of the suspicious occupants. The task was so vast that Sanderson and Lucas had put themselves on the front line as well. Sanderson had offered to do their rounds together—for company and security—but Lucas had declined.

"We can get through them quicker if we split up."

Sanderson agreed, pretending to take her reasoning at face value. But she knew something else was going on. DC Lucas had overplayed her hand in bossing Sanderson around, claiming a superiority that never really existed. And things had changed a lot in the last day or so. DS Fortune had been largely absent, appearing distracted even when he *was* in the office, whereas Helen Grace seemed to be ever present, driving the investigation forward. This put Sanderson at a distinct advantage, being a long-term ally of DI Grace, and Lucas very much in the shade. If Lucas was bright she would be making strides to befriend Sanderson—perhaps even going as far as to apologize—but Sanderson suspected this was not in her lexicon. Too young and too insecure to show weakness.

So they did their rounds alone. The Kurdish family's command of English was limited, so after a few fruitless questions, Sanderson completed her tour of the flat. There were far more people living here than was safe or probably legal—a whole extended family crammed into four cramped rooms in conditions that could not even be described as basic. Simpson had complied with some of the legal obligations required of him as a landlord. The doors were fire doors, there were fire detectors in every room—including the bathroom, which was often skipped by cost-cutters—and the tenants did have a proper tenancy agreement. But that was the limit of the love and attention Simpson lavished on his tenants. Without exception, the flats Andrew Simpson owned or ran were hovels—there was no other word for them. Wallpaper had long since peeled off; the floorboards were increasingly exposed as the dirty carpets wore away; the lightbulbs hung naked and unadorned in cheerless rooms.

Not for the first time that day, Sanderson was assailed by feelings of guilt—guilt at her good fortune. She wasn't rich, but she had a decent flat, a little car, nice clothes—all the trappings of a modern, urban lifestyle. These poor people had only poverty and degradation. She felt ashamed that they had traveled so far and found only this. But mingling with her guilt were feelings of anger too. Anger toward Andrew Simpson. Many landlords were guilty of neglect, but this was on a different level. She knew he was unpleasant, grasping and grubby—but even so Sanderson was shocked to realize that this man was prepared to treat fellow human beings as little more than animals.

89

Ruby's heart stopped as soon as she saw it. A dead end. She had sprinted the length of the right-hand corridor, only to find she had chosen badly. The gloomy tunnel looked like it belonged in a mine—rough earth floor and walls with industrial lights secured to the wooden joists supporting the ceiling—and ended in some kind of storage area. It was piled high with plastic bottles, empty sacks and other detritus. Turning on her heel, Ruby ran back to the junction as fast as she could. Her lungs were burning, her breath short and erratic, but she had to keep going. She only had one shot at this.

Her captor's groaning was louder than it had been before. Had he made it out of her cell now? Was he coming toward her? For a moment, Ruby was frozen with indecision, the fear that he would catch her suddenly robbing her of her energy and conviction.

Footsteps. Now she could definitely hear footsteps. Turning, she plunged down the central passage. Her legs threatened to buckle, but her desire to live drove her forward. Down the passage, round the corner, she sprinted on and on. Surely this had to be right? This tunnel was longer than the last one and she could feel cool air ahead of her. Cool, fresh air. Yes, this *must* be the one.

Ruby turned a bend and now tears—tears of naked fear—sprang to her eyes. Another dead end—a kind of air vent—but no means of escape. For a moment, desolation swept over, and then suddenly Ruby was seized with a thought. Perhaps this air vent *was* a way out after all. She rammed her fingers into the grille and pulled as hard as she could, pushing her leg up against the rough wall to provide extra leverage. Nothing. The grille was secured with numerous heavy-duty screws, and without a screwdriver, she was powerless to move it. Ruby rested her pounding head against the grille, the fresh air mocking her, as it ran over her tearstained face. Was this it? If he found her, he would kill her; Ruby was sure of that. She would never see her family, her friends . . . She would never see daylight again.

All was still now. She listened intently. No more groaning. No more footsteps. Suddenly a thought occurred to her. What if he had taken the right-hand passage, leaving the left-hand one unguarded? The soft earth of the floor would have shown up her tracks—surely he would have pursued her down that passageway first?

Keeping close to the wall, Ruby crept back toward the junction, pausing every second step to listen. Her eyes darted this way and that, her ears strained, but there was no sign of him. She went a little farther. Then farther still. She was only ten yards from the junction. She tried to calm her breathing, bracing herself for one last burst of energy. It was now or never.

She bolted from her hiding place, veering sharply to her right around the corner. Without hesitation, she sprinted down the left-hand corridor. He would probably have heard her movement, so there was nothing for it but to put her head down and run.

A noise made her look up and suddenly she came to a juddering halt. He hadn't gone down the right-hand passageway—he had raced straight for the exit. And there he was now standing in front of her, blocking her path.

Ruby turned to run, but he was on her in a flash. She felt his rough hand yank her head back, then reeled as his fist crunched into her face. As the blows rained down, Ruby slumped to the floor. She made no attempt to defend herself. She simply closed her eyes, took the blows and patiently waited for death.

90

"Okay, let's pull together what we've got."

It was lunchtime and Helen had gathered the team in the incident room. Sanderson and Lucas had returned from their hunt; McAndrew had sifted Roisin's possessions—it was the first time in a while that the whole unit had been in there. Helen watched them as they assembled—taking in who stood next to who, who avoided who and more besides. It was clear to her that there was still unease within the team. Division? Cliques? It was too early to say, but it alarmed her. She had no time—Ruby had no time—for internal squabbling.

"So we have three confirmed victims and one missing woman. Pippa Briers was murdered three to four years ago, Roisin Murphy roughly two years ago. Isobel Lansley is our most recent victim—Jim Grieves estimates she was murdered within the last eighteen months. They all share a look—black hair, blue eyes—and each murder victim has a distinctive bluebird tattoo on her left shoulder. DC McAndrew's diligent work with Roisin's family and ex has helped confirm that Roisin did *not* have that tattoo when she went missing. Same goes for Pippa."

"And Lansley?" questioned DC Lucas.

"We're yet to interview her parents. They're based in Namibia—have been for some years—but we've informed them of developments and we're flying them over," DC Grounds replied.

"Sooner rather than later, please," DS Fortune chivvied.

"So we can assume that the killer tattooed the women," Helen continued. "Why? To mark them as *his*? To make them resemble someone else? For entertainment? What is its significance?"

Silence from the team, so Helen carried on. "What is the importance of their look? Why them? I would like Lucas and McAndrew to lead on breaking down these women's lives to see if we can pinpoint where he might have come into contact with them. What were these women's regular commitments—where did they work, socialize, exercise? We need chapter and verse so we can compare for overlap."

McAndrew and Lucas nodded, though neither looked overjoyed. Helen didn't care—she was going to force this team to work together.

"Next up, access. According to Sinead Murphy, Roisin had four keys to her council flat. Sinead had one in her purse. The other three were recovered from her flat, after she vanished—we found them in her boxed possessions."

"So she knew her abductor?" DS Fortune offered.

"It's possible, as there was no sign of a break-in or a struggle at her flat. But Roisin had a small social circle and hadn't mentioned anyone she knew who worried her or who were new on the scene. So we should also think about people you might let into your flat.

People in uniform—police officers, paramedics, gas and electricity inspectors, charity workers. Would these women let these kinds of people in? Let's go back to the families, see what we can glean."

"How does he get them out?" Finally DC Stevens had spoken. He didn't say much, Helen thought to herself, but his question was on the money.

"Isobel Lansley had traces of something sticky in her hair. We sent it off for tests and found that it was an industrial solvent," Helen replied. "It's called trichloroethylene."

"What's it used for?" Sanderson asked.

"All manner of things," Helen answered. "Cleaning work surfaces, degreasing metal parts; you find it in boot polish and dry-cleaning chemicals. Plus, historically people have used it to get high."

"And would it knock you out?"

"It was trialed as an alternative to chloroform in the 1920s, a form of anesthetic, before being taken on by industry—so there's no question it could incapacitate you. As with chloroform, a soaked rag over the mouth and nose would do the trick."

The team was silent once more. This latest development was sinister and unnerving.

"To administer it, he would have to get close to them," said DC Lucas, picking up the thread. "But there were no breakages, no sign of a struggle in Ruby's flat, so . . ."

"She must have trusted them enough to let them get close," DS Fortune offered.

"Or the victims were already asleep," Sanderson interrupted. "We know Ruby had had a big night out. She could have conked out and then . . ."

More silence.

"Let's go back to the flats," Helen continued. "I know this was a while ago, but check if any of the long-term residents remember seeing any authority figures around the flats late at night. Anything that struck them as unusual. There has to be a reason why this guy never leaves a trace. How does he get in?"

The team broke up, directed to their tasks by an energized DS Fortune. Helen watched them go. Progress had been modest, but finally they had a few pieces of the jigsaw, providing the unit with a well-needed morale boost. Perhaps they were finally inching close to understanding their killer's MO.

Helen's reflections were interrupted by her mobile phone ringing. She was surprised to see it was James calling. Her downstairs neighbor, a handsome junior doctor at South Hants Hospital, had been friendly at first, but had backed off when it became clear that Helen had no interest in being another notch on his bedpost. Puzzled, Helen answered it quickly.

"James?"

"You better get back here, Helen."

"Why, what's up? Please don't tell me there's been another leak."

"They're in your flat."

"Who?"

"Police. Half a dozen of them. You need to get back here *now*."

91

Helen took the stairs three at a time. By the time she reached the top floor, she was sweating slightly, but she didn't hesitate—bursting through the doors. She had been expecting the worst, but even so the sight that met her eyes rendered her speechless.

Her flat—her precious flat—was being turned over. Six officers, all sheathed in forensics suits, were taking the place apart. Opening desk drawers, checking under tables, bagging her laptop and iPad.

"Would someone explain to me what the fuck is going on?" Helen roared, holding up her warrant card. "I'm a detective inspector with Hampshire Police, this is my flat and *you* are in the wrong place."

"Actually we're in the right place," a middle-aged woman with a bad haircut shot back, holding up *her* warrant card. "DS Lawton, Anti-Corruption."

Helen stared at the ID but couldn't take it in. "Anti-Corruption?"

"Exactly, and we have a warrant to search your flat."

Helen snatched the piece of paper from Lawton's hand and scanned it, searching for details of the who, what, why. Predictably it was bland and uninformative. "Why are you here? What are you looking for?"

The searching officers didn't even bother to respond to that one.

"I am currently running a major investigation. I don't know what you *think* you're doing, but I can assure you that Hampshire Police are going to kick you all the way back to whatever hole you—"

"Cool your boots, DI Grace. We know who you are and what you're up to. But know this—it was one of your own lot that called us in, so perhaps you could let us get on with our job and save the abuse for someone else?"

With a scowl, Lawton turned back to the task in hand. Helen stood stock-still, reeling from this latest revelation. She was none the wiser as to their intent, but now at least it was clear to her who was ultimately responsible.

92

"You have no right do this. Whatever has happened between us in the past, you have no right to spread lies about me."

An incandescent Helen faced Ceri Harwood across her desk. "I'm going to make an official complaint to Fisher—"

"What makes you think I've been telling lies?" Harwood replied coolly. Helen was unnerved by her tone, but carried on nevertheless.

"Anti-Corruption? Really? I think my record shows which side of the fence I'm on."

She was referring to Harwood's predecessor—Detective Superintendent Whittaker—whom she had rightly handed to Anti-Corruption on a plate.

"Which makes your actions all the more surprising, Helen."

Still that coolness.

"What do you mean?"

"I'd like to play you something," Harwood replied. "The original is with Anti-Corruption, hence this morning's fun and games. I made this copy for our files."

Helen tensed as Harwood pressed Play on her small portable player. What game was this?

Silence, then shuffling, then finally voices. Helen immediately recognized her voice—and that of DI Tom Marsh. For a moment, Helen was struck dumb. Why the hell would he have been recording their conversation? He had no idea Helen was going to doorstep him in Northamptonshire . . .

She had been set up. DI Marsh had been in on it from the start—he had recorded Helen asking him to leak classified information to her, to compromise ongoing undercover work, to risk the lives of serving officers . . . The charge list was endless. And Harwood had it all on tape.

"I told you not to go near this. No, I ordered you not to go near Robert Stonehill," Harwood continued. "But you ignored me. I'm not sure yet how you accessed the file on him, but I'll find out."

Immediately Helen thought of Charlie. What had she dragged her into?

"File?" Helen queried, keeping her expression as neutral as possible.

"Don't be coy, Helen. The only way you could know about the involvement of DI Marsh is from having read the unredacted file."

"I don't recall any file."

"Good God, Helen, if that's the best you can do, you really are for the high jump. Anti-Corruption is going through your flat with a fine-tooth comb—when they find the evidence they need, then you'll be gone. And not a moment too soon."

Helen stared at her superior. There was something different about her today. Even at the point of her triumph, she looked weary and empty. As if her own hatred had eaten her from within. She had laid a complex trap to catch Helen and it had worked. So why did she seem so dispirited?

"Was any of it true?" Helen said. "The fight in Northampton? Robert's association with the police?"

"I'm afraid that's classified."

And no doubt would remain so. Helen's anger was spiking now. The thought of how her personal life—her deepest vulnerabilities—had been used against her made her blood boil. She had underestimated Harwood's thirst for vengeance and was reaping the reward for her complacency.

"Obviously while this is ongoing, you will be suspended from the investigation—"

"I don't think so."

Harwood laughed. "I admire your balls, Helen, but I'm not sure that's your decision really. Once we're done here, I am due to meet Fisher to rubber-stamp your suspension. He's across all this obviously—"

"Then no doubt he'll be aware what a foolish move that would be. From a publicity view, it wouldn't play well, would it? You suspended me before and look what happened—I found Ella Matthews while you were running round in circles. I reminded Emilia Garanita of that the other day—I'm sure the *Evening News* would take a dim view of Southampton Central's most successful police officer being suspended with such a major investigation in play. I'm sure they would also be interested to hear that I am the victim of a campaign of relentless harassment, despite a total lack of evidence against me, because of your personal vendetta against me—"

"Are you serious? You were caught red-handed!" Harwood fired back.

"A hypothetical conversation between two officers, during which nothing of note was revealed—"

"You accessed a classified file. In contravention of a direct order."

"So where is it?"

For the first time, Harwood paused. Did Helen detect a sliver of doubt?

"If I took the file it, produce it. Then you can throw the book at me. But until then, I suggest you get back in your box and let me do my job. There's a young woman's life at stake, and anything—or anyone—who impedes our search for her had better be prepared to face the consequences if things go wrong. I wouldn't want that on my conscience. Or my face attached to *that* story."

A long pause. Harwood said nothing, but Helen could tell that she had planted a seed of doubt. Harwood would never allow anything to tarnish her public image or professional reputation. Safety first was her motto and Helen knew it.

"You will stay on the investigation *for now*," Harwood eventually conceded. "But you are to cooperate fully with Anti-Corruption. Specifically you will provide me now with all your passwords and encryption codes so that the team can fully access your laptops, phones, tablets and more besides. You will also desist from going back to your flat or discussing this with any serving officers. If you disobey any of these orders, in any way, I will have your badge. Is that clear?"

Helen marched down the corridor, still burning with anger. Life constantly surprised her with its inventive sadism, but she had never expected *this*. How much must Harwood despise her to act in this manner? She was intent on destroying her and yet even now, as Helen's future at Southampton Central hung by a thread, Helen was filled with a defiant sense of purpose.

Suddenly she knew exactly what she needed to do, if she was to tilt the battle in her favor, once and for all.

93

DS Lloyd Fortune shifted uneasily in his seat. He never liked public appeals, and this one was more harrowing than most. Roisin's smiling face beamed out from the screens behind them, the backdrop to Sinead Murphy's emotional appeal for information. Sinead had managed three sentences before breaking down, and since then progress had been halting. It made for good TV and might jog someone's memory or stir their conscience, but it was difficult to watch. It was as if Sinead had been gutted like a fish—all her optimism, her strength, ripped from her by the tragic turn of events. The happy memories of Roisin that she now rehearsed seemed to hurt her still further—they were offered to prompt others into coming forward, but Lloyd feared they only served to underline her own guilt and increase her misery.

When she began talking about Kenton, things got worse. Sinead was almost inaudible now because of the heavy sobbing, and the onus was on Lloyd to step in. But it was hard to do so without looking unfeeling or callous. Despite his good looks and articulacy, Lloyd was camera-shy and hated being in the spotlight. It made him anxious: he was inclined to clam up for fear of making a fool of himself, which he knew from experience made him look remote or haughty. Whenever he was approached to front poster campaigns designed to draw in new black and ethnic-minority officers to the force, he tried to wriggle out of it, usually with little success. People seemed obsessed with putting him in the public eye, hence the endless media training, and once again Harwood had insisted he front today's appeal, despite the fact that really it should be Helen Grace filling his chair.

Sinead had come to a complete halt now, so finally Lloyd leaned over, placing a reassuring arm on hers while redirecting her attention to the script they had signed off on before the press conference began. Sinead looked at him through sodden eyelashes, then, summoning some last vestige of composure, continued her appeal.

"Roisin was a beautiful . . . caring mother and daughter."

Another long pause, as Sinead drew breath.

"She has been cruelly taken from us, and someone out there knows why. If you have any information about my Roisin's disappearance . . . please, please contact the police. She had suffered so much in her short life. A father who abandoned her. A boyfriend who did the same. She deserved so much more from life, but never got it."

Finally she looked up from the table and stared right into the nearest TV camera. "Don't let her murder go unpunished."

94

"Don't let her murder go unpunished." The blubbering bitch seemed to look directly at him as she said it. He swore violently at her. What did she and her slut of a daughter know about suffering?

The exertion of shouting at the TV brought the pain crashing back again. He was lying on the sofa in the filthy living room, an ice pack clamped to the back of his head. Empty packets of Naproxen, superstrength ibuprofen that he'd been prescribed some years earlier, littered the floor. He had taken four times the recommended dose, but it didn't seem to be making much difference. It was like the worst migraine he'd ever had—a deep, insistent throbbing at the back of the skull.

Worse than all this, however, was the pain of Summer's betrayal. How had he been tricked so easily? And so cruelly? She seemed to have returned to him, to want to please him, but actually she was carefully planning her attack, waiting until his heart was open and his guard was down.

Despite the fact that he was concussed, he had dragged her back to her cell by her hair and once there delivered a beating that was savage and unremitting. It shocked him to realize that he had no idea how long it went on for or even if she had survived the attack. Eventually he had run out of steam and then the full extent of her subterfuge became clear. How she had removed the metal strut from the side of the bed, then propped up the bed with one of the chairs to make it look intact so she could enjoy the element of surprise. What a mug he had been—all those cosmetic purchases from Boots had been designed to lay her hands on something metal. Why had he not seen this?

Rising from the sofa, stuffing two more Naproxen in his mouth, he vowed not to be so naive again. She had tricked him once—he wouldn't let her do so again. From now on things were going to be very different.

95

Ruby lay in the darkness. She was sweating and shivering, her body reacting with confusion to the severe blood loss and fractured bones. She had lost consciousness early on in the attack, repeated rabbit punches to her face and neck ending the fight quickly. When she had eventually come to, the pain was kept momentarily at bay by the shock—and horror—of finding that she was still alive. For the first time in her life she truly wished she were dead.

Had he broken her jaw? Her ribs? She couldn't tell. Everything hurt and everywhere was sticky—cloyed blood clinging doggedly to her mouth, face and hair. Why had he spared her? She had attacked him. Would have killed him if she had had more presence of mind. Would he come back to finish the job?

Suddenly Ruby was pushing herself up. She hadn't thought to—she was acting on instinct now, the thought of more suffering driving her on. Pain coursed through her—shooting from her rib cage to the very center of her brain—but she managed to get to her hands and knees. Immediately she vomited, but she was on the move now and paid no heed to that, turning away and crawling toward the bed. It was still propped up by the chair and seemed to offer her sanctuary now. Swiftly she scuttled underneath, pulling the blanket down around her, hiding her from view.

She wasn't safe here, but it felt better to be concealed. Clasping her hands together, Ruby found herself muttering mangled prayers once more. Her words were garbled, their meaning confused, but the sentiment was clear. This time Ruby wasn't praying for deliverance. She was praying for death.

96

DC Sanderson scanned this way and that, searching for danger. The lockup she was scoping was at the end of a needle-strewn alleyway in Portswood. There was no street lighting, no CCTV. You could vanish off the face of the earth here and no one would be any the wiser. She cursed herself for continuing her survey of Simpson's properties alone—she should never have allowed station politics to jeopardize her safety. That was the first rule in the book.

She turned to leave, anxious to be out of this fetid alleyway. She had had high hopes for this property. It was remote and isolated, and had not appeared in their first sweep of Simpson's holdings. For reasons that weren't clear, the freehold for this property seemed to be in Simpson's late wife's name. This might have been a historic oversight or for tax purposes, but Sanderson doubted it. Everything Simpson did was premeditated and controlled. Nothing was left to chance. But on arrival it quickly became clear that there were no potential witnesses in this part of town and there was little hope of gaining access. There was only one entrance and this was covered in padlocks and chains—there was no way of circumventing the lack of a search warrant.

Halfway down the alley, Sanderson paused, her gaze drifting up toward a small window in the side of the building. The dirty window, cracked and broken, hung slightly open. It wasn't large but was wide enough for the slender Sanderson to slip through.

A wheelie bin lay abandoned nearby. What had once been in it? Food waste? A dead dog? She couldn't tell, but the maggots didn't seem to care. Swallowing her nausea and slamming the lid shut, she dragged it under the window and climbed on top. From here it was a short jump to the windowsill. Her fingers slipped off first time and she nearly toppled off the wheelie bin as a result, but the second time round she gripped the sill forcefully. Using the toe of her boots to grip in the worn mortar holes of the brickwork, she scrabbled up fast and ten seconds later she was inside.

As she landed, a cloud of dust rose to greet her, creeping into her nose and eyes and causing her to sneeze violently. The noise seemed to echo round the deserted lockup, underlining her isolation and vulnerability. Plucking her iPhone from her zip pocket, she used its torch to look around her.

My God, what is this place?

Every square inch of it was taken up with boxes that rose from floor to ceiling. All of them marked and labeled. Sanderson examined the one nearest her. Despite the dust, the label looked new, the writing fresh. Sanderson hesitated. She knew examining the box's contents was opening a legal can of worms—especially if whatever she discovered found its way into a court case. But Sanderson figured that that horse had bolted with her breaking and entering. Besides, Ruby had to be their first priority now.

Putting on a pair of plastic gloves, she teased open the box. What had she expected to find? Bloodstained clothes? A kidnap kit? A confession written in blood? Whatever she had been hoping for, she was still surprised by what she found. The whole box was stacked full of tapes. Videotapes.

Sanderson hadn't seen CCTV at any of Simpson's properties thus far, so she was immediately intrigued. As she looked at the spine, her curiosity rose still further—*September 2013* was written on it in blue biro. Flicking through a dozen other tapes, she saw a pattern emerging: *June 2013*, *August 2013*. Opening one up, she examined the tape—no labels—then looked at the inner sleeve.

And stopped in her tracks. Written in biro on the sleeve—a single word that changed everything.

Ruby.

97

Charlie knew something was up the minute she entered the house. She'd just returned from the newsagent—today's *Evening News* had a big spread about the bluebird tattoo lead in the "Bodies on the Beach" case and Charlie was looking forward to reading the details—but something about the feel of the house was . . . wrong. Was this a legacy of her years of police work? Or the result of her abduction by Marianne? Her senses were particularly acute now and she could tell she was not alone in the house.

She remained stock-still, trying to quieten her breathing, which was loud and fast. Her police baton was upstairs at the bottom of a drawer, so she turned now and edged back toward the front door she'd just entered, taking care not to tread on the creaky floorboard on the left. In days gone by, she would have confronted an intruder without hesitation or fear, but there was no question of that now with her swollen belly. But as she laid her hand on the latch—

"Charlie."

A female voice. Helen's voice. Charlie turned, ready to tear a strip off her boss for scaring the life out of her, but when she saw the anxiety on her face, she swallowed the rebuke.

"I'm so sorry. I didn't mean to scare you. I had to see you, but I couldn't risk contacting you directly."

Intrigued, Charlie ushered her into the living room. "What's going on?"

Helen gestured for them to sit down. Once on the sofa, she moved in close. "Harwood's called in Anti-Corruption. They are ripping my flat apart as we speak."

"But why . . . ?"

"The whole Robert thing . . ." Helen paused briefly as the cruelty of Harwood's scheme hit home once more. "The whole thing was faked."

Charlie stared at her, disbelieving.

"I don't think there was a fight in Northampton. I don't think Robert ever lived there," Helen continued. "The whole thing was designed to lure me into accessing classified material—"

"Giving grounds for dismissal."

Helen nodded. Charlie shook her head—could Harwood really stoop this low?

"What have they got on you?"

"A tape recording of my meet with DI Marsh. On its own, it's not enough. She needs to prove I've got the file, hence the search at my flat."

Now Charlie knew why Helen had come.

"I'll do it now," she said, rising.

"Thank you," Helen said, heading back toward the kitchen. She paused in the doorway:

"Oh, and, Charlie, I'd get the lock on your back door sorted. Child's play."

Charlie took the rebuke in good humor and hurried upstairs. Anti-Corruption might make the connection between Helen and her or they might not, but there was no point in taking chances. She thanked God now that Helen had seen fit to trust the photocopied file to her for safekeeping. If she hadn't, she would have been suspended or worse by now. And Charlie and Sally Mason would have been in the firing line too. Steve wouldn't necessarily have minded, but it wasn't how Charlie intended her career to end. She owed it to all of them to put this thing to bed once and for all.

She was all fingers and thumbs as she lit the fire lighters, stacked underneath the logs in their fireplace. It was an odd time of year for a log fire, but needs must. Eventually the match struck, the paraffin ignited and in minutes the fire was crackling nicely. Charlie didn't hesitate, feeding the pages of the faked report, then even the file itself, into the flames. She was oddly tense as she watched the papers catch and curl, as if Anti-Corruption might burst in at any moment. But the house—the street—was quiet and before long the papers were reduced to ash. Charlie wondered if it was enough. They had foiled Harwood's initial attempt to bring Helen down, but how complex was this scheme? And was there anything they had overlooked? The thought of Southampton Central without Helen was absurd and yet this now seemed to be Harwood's mission. And Charlie knew from experience that when Harwood wanted something badly enough, she generally got it.

98

It was an ambush. As soon as he opened the door, she was on him, warrant card shoved roughly in his face.

"Good morning, Mr. Simpson. Not at work today?"

For a moment, Andrew Simpson said nothing, too shocked by the sudden appearance of a police officer on his doorstep to respond. He swayed slightly as if unsteady on his feet.

"I went to your work," Sanderson continued, "but they said you were running late. I hope I haven't caught you at a bad time."

"Not at all," he replied quickly.

"Good. Because I have a few more questions for you about Ruby Sprackling. May I come in?"

A heavy silence followed Sanderson's request. Was that fear in Simpson's eyes? Suspicion? Sanderson gazed over his shoulder to take in the interior. It was a mess. But was it embarrassment or something more sinister that prompted Simpson to pull the door closer behind him, cutting off her view?

"Do you have a warrant?"

"No. But it won't take me long to get one—"

"Then I suggest we do this elsewhere."

Sanderson stared at him—trying to provoke a reaction with her evident irritation and suspicion, but he didn't blink, looking straight back at her with hard, unflinching eyes.

"It'll create a lot of paperwork if we go to the station," Sanderson said. "Which will take up far more of your time. It really would be simpler if I just popped in—"

"We'll do it at the station. Do you have a car?"

"Yes," Sanderson said resignedly.

"Then let's go," said Simpson, slamming the door decisively behind him.

99

Ruby came to with a start—a noise from upstairs startling her. How long had she been out of it? And what did that noise mean?

He had not returned to her since the beating, which surprised her. What was he up to? she wondered. Since she first encountered him—that awful day—she'd had the sense that he was holding himself back, keeping something in. She had glimpsed the emotion at times—sparks of desire, flashes of anger—but he had always managed to rein it in. To appear in control and in command. Not now. As he had laid in to her, Ruby had seen real fury, a desire to destroy her—which was why she'd been surprised to find she was still alive when she came to. Now that she had crushed his fantasy, now that she had duped him, what was there to hold him back?

The thought made Ruby shudder. She had no fear of death anymore, but she was sickened by the thought of more pain. Most of her bones felt broken already, but who was to say what further pain he might inflict, if he put his mind to it? She closed her eyes, trying to block out the thought of him falling on her in vengeance. Memories of his desire for her made her whimper. *Please, God, not that . . .*

The soft tickle of cool air made Ruby turn. The broken brick stared back at her. Shifting over to the wall, she pulled the loose fragments free. Taking the letters and cards from the hidey-hole, she laid them out on the floor next to her. She was in no doubt that she would die down here now—all that was left for her was to leave some kind of message, some kind of marker that she had lived—and died—in this strange, fabricated world. Locating the felt-tip pen, she removed the lid and shook it violently. Then, finding a spare square of blank paper, she began to write.

Nothing.

She shook the pen again, this time licking the end with her tongue. The bitter taste of ink cheered her and she began to write. But after three letters—*My n*—the ink ran out and no amount of coaxing could yield any more. It had run dry.

Ruby lay amid the letters, despondent, furious and utterly bereft. She made no attempt to conceal the letters—what was the point? They were all she had now. Her only connection to a world beyond her captor. She would leave them where they were, fanned out around her on the floor. She would spend the rest of her days in the company of three dead girls.

100

The woman entered the dirty bathroom. She locked the door, then began to undress. Soon she was naked. Standing in front of the cracked cabinet mirror, she regarded herself. Leaning in, she turned this way and that as if searching for imperfections. Then, tiring of this self-examination, she climbed into the bath. Pulling the clear plastic shower curtain round, she turned on the shower. A begrudgingly small jet of water squeezed out of the showerhead, running over her face, neck and body.

Helen stopped the tape. The young woman on the tape was Ruby. And the whole scene had been watched from on high, from a God-like vantage point.

"Are there cameras in all the smoke detectors? Or just in the bathrooms and bedrooms?" Helen asked him, her voice neutral despite her contempt.

Andrew Simpson, flanked by his lawyer, said nothing.

"We have a full list here of your properties. If you want us to go round and check, we will. I'm sure your tenants would be very interested to learn that you're spying on th—"

"Just the bedrooms and bathrooms."

"How many properties?"

Another pause, then:

"Twenty."

Helen shook her head. She wanted Simpson to know what she thought of him, hoped she might rile him. But he just stared at her with those dead eyes. Sanderson had always questioned why ninety percent of Simpson's tenants were female. Now it all made sense.

"How long has this been going on? And before you think of lying to me," Helen continued quickly, "I have a team of officers at your lockup on Valmont Road. So be under no illusions—we know the extent of your 'activities.'"

Simpson stared at his hands—Helen was intrigued to see they were covered in small cuts—then looked up.

"Over ten years now."

"How many tapes do you have?"

"Hundreds."

"Why do you do it, Andrew?"

Simpson paused and looked at his brief, who gave him a gentle nod.

"Because I like to look at them," he said quietly.

"How do you feel when you watch these tapes?"

"How do you think?"

"Do you masturbate when you watch them?"

"Sometimes."

"Why does it arouse you? Is it their bodies? The fact that they don't know you're watching? Or is it the power you have over them?"

Simpson held her gaze for a second. "No comment."

"Oh, you're going to have to do a bit better than that, Andrew," Sanderson said, taking up the baton. "I've seen the inside of your lockup. I know what obsession looks like. Why do you do it?"

"My client has declined to comment, so I suggest we move on," his lawyer interjected. He was a man of nearly sixty, overweight and overbearing—a telling testimony to Simpson's casual misogyny. He liked to look at women but clearly would never have one as his lawyer. Sanderson looked at her notes and changed tack.

"When we first questioned you about Ruby Sprackling, why did you direct us toward Nathan Price?"

"I answered your questions. You asked me about him. I told you the truth. He had the keys to Ruby's flat—"

"You didn't have an extra set cut? Just in case you needed to pop in and check that the fire sensors were working?"

"No," Simpson replied, refusing to rise to her sarcasm.

"We won't find any extra sets at your house, in your possessions?"

"No, I've told you."

Sanderson sat back and looked at him, disbelief writ large on her face. "Where were you on Friday night?"

"I was at home."

"Do you live alone?"

"Yes."

"And you were alone all night?"

"Correct."

"Did you take your car out at any point?"

"No."

"Do you own any other vehicles?"

"No."

But he looked twitchy when he said it. Helen looked at Sanderson, who wrote a brief note in her notebook.

"We've also found footage of Roisin Murphy, Pippa Briers and Isobel Lansley in your collection. The three dead women from Carsholt Beach. Ever been there?"

"Don't like beaches," Simpson shot back.

"We'll see. The sand there has a very specific mineral content. If we find any samples in your house or car, we'll be able to tell where it's from. How many hours of tape do you have of Ruby?"

Simpson looked surprised by Helen's sudden change of tack.

"You can be honest with me, Andrew."

Simpson's face twitched slightly at the sound of his name. Perhaps he didn't like women calling him by his first name? Or perhaps he didn't like his name? Was there something deeper going on here? Helen made a mental note to get to the bottom of this.

"I don't know."

"Is it a lot? A little? Somewhere in between?"

"A lot."

"Did you like her more than the others?"

Andrew looked away.

"You know she has a mother and father, a sister and a brother, who are missing her, right? People who love her."

Helen let the words hang in the air.

"I know you coveted her, Andrew. I know you took her. But I'm asking you now to let her go. Show that you're a bigger man than people say. Show that you can be merciful."

Simpson looked at Helen, as if trying to read her. Helen hated to be supplicatory to a man like Simpson, but if he liked his women subservient, then so be it.

"I have no idea where she is. I don't know anything about these girls."

"Oh, I'd say you do," Helen said. "I'd say you know an awful lot about them. What they look like naked, what they look like when they use the toilet. What they look like when they make love, when they masturbate. You know all these things, Andrew. And more."

Simpson stared at his hands once more, to avoid Helen's fierce gaze. Was that a flicker of shame she saw?

"And guess what? Pretty soon the whole world is going to know too. When they put you in the witness box, they won't let up, Andrew. They'll ask you about the home movies, about the underwear and jewelry you stole, about what you did when you thought about these girls. Imagine for a second what that will be like. The judge, the jurors, the press, the public gallery all looking at you as they force you to talk about what you liked to do —"

"Inspector, please don't bully my client," said the lawyer, attempting to intervene.

"But I can help you, Andrew," Helen continued, unabashed. "I can save you all that scrutiny. All that humiliation."

Still Andrew Simpson didn't look up.

"But I need you to help me. I need you to tell me where I can find Ruby. If she's still alive, then there is a deal to be done here. Set her free, accept a guilty plea and those details will never leave this room. They will be our secret."

Finally Simpson looked up at Helen. She was unnerved to see defiance in his eyes.

"I don't know where she is."

"Is that the best you can do?"

"You've got nothing on me," he spat back sharply.

"These women were all your tenants. You stalked them, spied on them—you knew everything about them. Their routines, their habits, their vulnerabilities. They went missing from your properties—no struggle, no break-ins—because you had the keys. You took them, kept them and when you tired of them, you killed them."

"You know nothing."

"I know that you're a dirty little pervert. Your mum's still alive, isn't she, Andrew? How do you think she'll feel when all this comes out?"

"Fuck you."

"I don't have time for this. Neither does Ruby. So I'm going to ask you again—where is she?"

"I've said all I'm going to say to you. And if you threaten me again, you stupid bitch—"

"Where is she?"

Helen was halfway across the table, her hand grabbing Simpson by the collar. But Sanderson was on her feet quickly, hauling Helen off Simpson, who had instinctively raised his fist to retaliate.

"I think we'll leave it there for now," Sanderson said quickly, heading Simpson's irate lawyer off at the pass. "In the meantime, I'd advise your client to think very carefully about cooperating."

Sanderson flicked off the tape, but paused as she followed Helen out the door. "It's the only play he's got left."

101

Tim was waiting for her when Ceri Harwood got home. He had been trying to contact her all day—in the end she'd had to turn her mobile off. She knew at the time that she was just postponing the moment when she had to face him again.

It had been a long day. The confrontation with Helen Grace had left Ceri feeling dispirited and, more than that, concerned. She had fantasized about that moment for months—ever since she started this whole thing—and it had proved a big letdown. There was too much defiance, too much certainty in Helen's voice that she would survive this latest attack. The fact that Anti-Corruption had found no trace of the missing file since then only made matters worse.

"I've been calling you."

"I know," Ceri said without enthusiasm, dropping her bag on the floor and sinking into the sofa. She knew they had to have this conversation, but she couldn't face it. She was dog-tired—all she could think about was crawling into bed and shutting out the world.

"We need to talk."

Was there a more unpleasant phrase in the English language?

"So talk," Ceri said, staring at the ceiling.

"I'm so sorry, Ceri. That you had to see that. That you should find out that way. I . . . I should have said something to you before. I meant to, but we never seem to be in the same place at the same time."

"So this is my fault?"

"Of course not. Of course not, darling."

"Don't you dare."

The look Ceri shot him was so severe that Tim held up his hands in surrender, acknowledging his mistake. "What I'm trying to say is I should have told you. But it's a function of our lives that we don't spend as much time together as we used to."

There was more than an element of truth in this, but Ceri was damned if she was going to admit it.

"I'm not blaming anyone," he continued. "My business needs me and your job is incredibly demanding."

"Why did you bring her here?" Ceri demanded, tired of his self-justification.

"Because I'm stupid. Because I didn't think."

"Why her?"

A long pause. Ceri watched her husband closely as he searched for the right words. This was the only question she really wanted an answer to.

"Because I like her. And because she wants to spend time with me."

"And the fact that she's young and pretty has nothing to do with it."

"No, it's not that. I know you won't believe me. But I didn't chase her. She approached me."

"How nice."

"Please, Ceri. I'm trying to explain. I didn't want to hurt you. I haven't been unfaithful before. To be honest, I never thought I would be. Didn't want to be one of those men."

"How disappointed you must be."

"But she wanted to spend time with me. And that was very appealing."

"And I don't?"

"Do you?"

Ceri was so shocked by the response that initially she wasn't sure what to say. "Of course I do. You're my husband."

"I haven't been that for a long time."

"Clearly."

"I wasn't talking about me, Ceri."

Ceri stared at him. Now he looked unrepentant, which unnerved her more.

"We've hardly seen each other the last couple of years. We've been living together but . . . we're ships that pass in the night. We do stuff with the kids at weekends, but when do *we* actually see each other?"

"In case you hadn't noticed I had one of the biggest cases of my career last year."

"I know that. Ella Matthews was a big deal. But that was ten months ago. And I don't see you any more now than I did then."

"Come on, Tim, you know what happened after the shooting. The public inquiry, the IPCC hearing—"

"That all finished a long time ago. Ella Matthews isn't the problem. It's this place."

"This house?"

"Southampton. Ever since we moved here, things haven't been right."

"I thought you liked it down here. We're close to your parents, the kids love it, you like the sailing—"

"Okay, *you've* not been right."

Ceri stared at him. She wanted to refute his assertion, to shout and scream at his stupid, knowing face. But there was a grain of truth in what he was saying. Her eyes flicked to her bag in the hall, then back to Tim once more.

"I brought someone else into this marriage. And I take full responsibility for that and the pain it's caused you. But you've done it too."

"I've done no such th—"

"You think the rest of the world is obsessed with Helen Grace. You're always complaining about *that*. But it's you who's obsessed, Ceri. It's you who has driven us apart. And unless you face up to that, then we haven't got a chance."

102

"I've let you down."

Helen stood in Daniel Briers's hotel room.

"I'm sure you did what you thought was best," Daniel said.

Helen looked up, trying to see if he was angry with her, but his tone was hard to read. She wanted him to say that he forgave her, to brush away her feelings of inadequacy and shame. But he remained silent.

"We'll question Simpson again in the morning—see if a night in prison has any effect on him. He's staring down the barrel of a long trial, so if he's got any sense he'll play ball . . ."

But did Helen believe it? Simpson had seemed so defiant, so determined not to acknowledge any culpability. Would he hold out and try to beat the rap? Or was there something else going on here? Was this the defiance of *innocence*? It seemed unlikely—he fitted the profile in so many ways—and yet this nagging thought lingered, unnerving Helen.

Daniel remained silent, so Helen continued:

"Anyway, I'm sorry for making the situation worse for you. If I'd stayed calm, perhaps I could have got him to cooperate. There's no excuse for it. Sometimes I . . . I just see red. I can't help it. It's in my DNA."

Helen wasn't sure how much she should share, how much Daniel already knew about her, but she felt compelled to explain her debacle in the interview suite.

"Sometimes when I'm in there, sitting across the table from a guy like Simpson, it's like I'm twelve years old again. I feel the helplessness, the despair, that someone like Ruby is experiencing and . . . I see myself and Marianne. In that flat. I remember the things my father did, the things he wanted to do, the things Marianne had to do to protect me. I see these men, I think of her and . . . I break inside."

Helen didn't look up, didn't want to see Daniel's reaction. She just wanted to tell him who she was, once and for all.

"Part of me wants to destroy them. I know that sounds terrible, but it's true. Their arrogance, their violence, makes me feel sick. I should be able to contain myself, but those feelings are always there. There's a hatred inside me. I don't want it, but I can't get rid of it. Does that make sense to you?"

Finally she looked up. What was she hoping for? Understanding? Censure? Anger? She would have settled for any or all of these, but to Helen's surprise Daniel was looking out the window. Helen was shocked by his blank expression—he looked *bored.*

A long silence, then Daniel turned to her, finally taking in the fact that she had finished talking.

"Sorry, you don't need to hear all this," Helen said, anger jostling with her deep feelings of embarrassment. She had never confessed her innermost feelings like this before.

"No, I'd like to hear more about you," Daniel replied quickly, but Helen could see the lie.

"I shouldn't have come here . . ."

"Helen, wait—"

But Helen was already at the door. Turning the handle, she muttered:

"I'm sorry, Daniel."

And with that, she was gone.

103

Helen walked away from the hotel as fast as she could. What a fool. What a stupid, naive, desperate fool. What kind of copper was she? To latch on to the vulnerability and grief of a bereaved father and somehow hope to find something for herself there? She had wanted to feed off it. No, that wasn't right. She had hoped to find comfort in it, a sense of peace, a place to belong.

What must he think of her now? She had badly misjudged the situation, imposing her own neediness on a man who had neither feeling nor thought for her. He was bored by her weakness, and who could blame him for that? He had enough to deal with as it was.

Helen approached her bike—she didn't know where she was going, but she just wanted to be away from here, away from the scene of her latest mistake. But as she unlocked her helmet, she saw it. In her side mirror, a figure approaching her fast. He had come from the shadows, had the element of surprise and was nearly upon her. Without hesitation, she spun round, swinging her helmet in a fast, decisive arc. The man raised his hands, but too late—the helmet connecting forcefully with his head. He reeled backward and, dropping the helmet, Helen was on him in a flash, forcing him down to the pavement. She raised her clenched fist and brought it down in a rabbit punch to the neck.

But her blow lost its impact, her arm slowing on its downward trajectory as she recognized her assailant.

Jake.

Her blow glanced off his neck and he now raised his hands to his face to fend off further attack. A deep cut over his left eye was already bleeding heavily.

"Jesus Christ, Jake. What the hell are you doing? I could have killed you."

"You're telling me," he countered angrily, pushing her off and clambering unsteadily to his feet.

"What on earth are you doing here? Creeping up on me like that?"

"Were you with *him*?"

And suddenly it all made sense.

"Dear God—have you been following me?"

Jake stared at her, defiant, but he didn't deny it.

"How long have you—"

"Nearly a week."

Helen hung her head. Had she had a sense that someone was following her? Yes, that car on the return from Northampton. She had dismissed this and other vague inklings of alarm. She never gave them much credence—she knew how to take care of herself—and she never expected it to be Jake. Hadn't they come to an arrangement?

"Do you love him?" Jake asked, shattering her illusions.

"For God's sake, Jake, it's nothing like th—"

"Do you?"

"Go to hell," Helen spat back, turning and climbing onto her bike.

"Please don't go. We need to talk."

Helen paused for a second, then slipped on her helmet. "There's nothing more to say."

She climbed on her bike and sped off, Jake growing smaller and smaller in her mirrors. Right now if he vanished altogether she wouldn't have cared. This evening had proved one thing and one thing alone. Her life was one massive, bad joke. And the gods would never tire of laughing at her.

104

She slid the laptop out of the case and placed it carefully on the kitchen table. She was alone now—the house felt crushingly silent—but even so she hesitated. Was it weakness to give in? Or was it just acknowledging a basic truth?

Tim had left an hour ago. He had said his piece and gone. Events were moving so quickly now and despite the endless chats that would have to take place—the window dressing of a marriage breakup—she could tell already that Tim had made up his mind. There would be no way back from this. He didn't love her anymore. It seemed strange to think such a bald, nasty thought, but that didn't stop it being true. He had found someone who made him joyful and happy. That was no longer the case with his wife.

Strangely Ceri didn't want to fight for him. Not because she didn't love him—she did and the thought of being a discarded wife stung bitterly—but because she had always shied away from a losing battle. Why prolong the agony? She chided herself for such resignation—wasn't it the done thing for a betrayed wife to fight for her man?—but suddenly she didn't seem to have the energy or will. What was happening to her?

She crossed to the fridge and poured herself a glass of water. Her emotions were all over the place today—deep misery mixed with a strange sense of anticipation—and she wanted a moment to gather herself. She seemed to be constantly on the point of either laughing or crying today. Pulling herself together, she walked back to the kitchen table and sat down.

She pressed the On button and the laptop buzzed into life. Immediately a dialogue box popped up, asking for the master password. Ceri's fingers hovered over the keyboard. It was bad enough having Helen's laptop here—"borrowed" from her contact in Anti-Corruption—but it was much worse still to actually access her private files.

Helen had provided her with all her password protection information, so with a little shiver of transgression Ceri typed in the master password. Immediately Helen's desktop opened up in front of her. She clicked on the first file and was confronted by another box, demanding an encryption code. Harwood dutifully entered it and the file came up on the screen. But it was of little interest—just a contacts sheet. Shaking her head, Harwood persevered, opening and closing files, entering more and more passwords, slowly delving deeper and deeper into Helen's system.

She was now accessing the most hidden material, the inner workings of Helen's mind and soul. She drank in her detailed journal of her time stalking, then befriending, Robert Stonehill. She read the many e-mails she had sent to him, desperately trying to locate him.

And deeper still, she found the real pay dirt. A diary Helen had kept on and off since she first started in the force, chronicling her pride in her uniform, the feeling of security and power the job gave her, as well as her deep doubts about herself, as her career progressed.

It was late now, but Ceri read on, drinking in Helen's confessions of anger, self-loathing and recrimination that nestled amid the moments of happincss and optimism. Helen really was cursed, Ceri thought, despite all her success, driven by a desire to expel demons that forever eluded her. All those years in that flat, in the care homes, had left her raw and bruised. It gave Ceri no little satisfaction to realize that some of these wounds would never fully heal.

She sat in darkness, her glass of water untouched, and clicked on the next page. She was careless of all around her, hooked in now to her examination of Helen Grace. Her exchange with Tim was already long forgotten, and for a moment it was as if he didn't even exist.

105

It's hard to be inconspicuous, when you are the size of a small whale. This was one very good reason why heavily pregnant officers tended to find themselves assigned to desk jobs.

It was early morning and the inhabitants of Georges Avenue were slowly surfacing. Curtains were being drawn, cups of tea drained and the early birds were now climbing into their cars and vans, occasionally shooting a quizzical look at the pregnant stranger leaning against the lamppost.

Charlie suddenly felt tired and foolish. They had only one car and even though her boyfriend, Steve, wasn't using it, Charlie had avoided it. Steve loved that car and kept meticulous care of it. He wasn't a controlling person, but he would nevertheless have noticed the spike in miles on the clock that a journey to and from Northampton would have caused. So she had taken a cab, then a train, then another cab—eventually being deposited in a Northamptonshire village with nothing to do but wait. It had cost her money, her feet ached and a headache was brewing and yet . . . she had felt compelled to come here. Unwittingly she had played a part in a conspiracy that might yet claim Helen's scalp. If there was a chance that she could now influence proceedings, Charlie had to seize it.

She heard the front door shut and looked up. DI Tom Marsh paused as he walked to his car, turning back to wave to his wife, who now appeared in the front window. Charlie found herself marching toward him.

"Can I help you?" DI Marsh looked at her quizzically. "Have you come to see Rose?"

"No, Tom, I've come to see you."

Suddenly Marsh looked less certain. Out of the corner of her eye, Charlie could see his wife watching on from the front window. She wondered what romantic crimes Marsh had been guilty of previously and whether this could be used to her advantage. Being confronted by an angry pregnant woman wouldn't look good to his wife—or his neighbors.

"I'm sorry, I don't know who you are and I've got to get to work," he said, attempting to brush past her. But Charlie caught hold of his arm firmly, stopping him in his tracks.

"You don't know me, but I am a police officer and a friend of DI Grace."

Charlie was pleased to see the color fading from Marsh's face.

"You have played your part in a nasty little conspiracy and I'm happy to fill your wife in on your role—she looks pretty intrigued already—but I guess that would involve you confessing how much you were paid by them. Does she know you take bribes?"

Marsh shot an anxious look to his wife. Her face asked a thousand questions and Charlie was amused to see sweat breaking out on Marsh's forehead.

"But I'll spare you that indignity if you tell me when and where Harwood first contacted you. If you can give me that and corroborate it in writing—"

"Harwood? I don't know any Harwood."

"Come off it, Tom. I know she contacted you, warned you Helen would find you, asked you to record—"

"I never met with a woman," Marsh interrupted. The front door was now opening and Marsh shot another anxious glance toward it.

"Then who? Who told you to record your conversation?"

"He said he was called DI Latham, but I never believed him. I'd recognize him again if I saw him though. Tall black guy with a South Coast accent."

"A tall black guy?"

"You heard me," Marsh spat back, turning to face his concerned wife.

"What's going on, Tom?" Rose Marsh said, her eyes fixed on Charlie and her bump.

"Sorry to have bothered you. I can't raise anyone at number eighty, wondered if you knew when they might be back?"

Charlie smiled an awkward thanks and walked off, not caring much if her lie had been believed. A little domestic trouble was the least Marsh deserved. As she pulled out her mobile to ring for a cab, Charlie's mind was already spooling forward to what she had to do next.

It was time for a one-to-one with Lloyd Fortune.

106

The two men sat in silence, breakfast laid out in front of them. Lloyd always made breakfast for his father—tea, soft-boiled eggs, brown toast, day after day—and often he was comforted by the regularity of this routine. Today, however, he was on edge.

He had hardly slept last night. And the night before had been little better. Ever since his exchange with Ceri Harwood at her house, he'd been gripped by a deep feeling of unease. The fact that she had propositioned him sexually was bad enough, but this was just the foreplay to something infinitely more serious and alarming. Rock-solid Ceri Harwood, who had insisted that only good would come of him participating in her scheme to remove the "cancer" of Helen Grace from Southampton Central, was now rocking, personal traumas and professional disappointments colliding in a perfect storm. What a fool he'd been to take her at her word. But she had seemed so sure and as she spoke the road had seemed to open up in front of Lloyd. Taking Helen's place, he would have been the youngest DI Hampshire Police had ever had—finally he would be able to look his dad in the eye.

He looked up from his untouched breakfast to find Caleb staring at him.

"Are you afraid of me, son?"

"Of course not," Lloyd replied eagerly, but his response sounded unconvincing.

"Then why won't you talk to me?"

Lloyd looked down at his plate. There were a million answers to this. Fear that he might not be loved. But how could he say any of this to his dad?

"You've been chewing on this work problem for days now. Tell me about it. Perhaps I can help."

"Dad . . ."

"Please, son. I don't like to see my favorite child unhappy."

Lloyd could feel himself blushing—with embarrassment and shame. It wasn't right for a parent to talk about favorite children, and it made his feelings of guilt ten times worse. "I'm worried I've let you down."

"You've never done that. I may not always show it and I know I push you, but—"

"I've betrayed you and betrayed myself."

The bitterness in his voice was loud and clear. Caleb said nothing, eyeing his son warily, his face full of misgivings.

"I've acted unprofessionally . . . illegally. In pursuit of a higher rank, more prestige. But . . . I've done the wrong thing, Dad. Sacrificed someone else to serve my own ends."

There it was—out in the open.

"What I did runs contrary to everything you ever taught me . . . everything I ever wanted to be. And now I can't look at you."

Lloyd continued to stare at his plate, expecting admonishment. But to his surprise he felt his father's rough hand, lifting his chin. He found himself looking into his dad's weathered face and saw kindness there, not judgment.

"Who did you do it for, son? For me? Or for yourself?"

"It's the same thing," Lloyd replied truthfully. Instantly he saw a wave of—what was it? Shame? Regret?—pass across his father's face.

"Then if you want to blame anyone, blame me," Caleb said softly.

"This isn't your doing. It's down to me."

"No, it isn't. It's me. I've always pushed you so hard. I wanted you to be a better man than I was."

To his shame, Lloyd felt his eyes fill with tears. "What do you mean? You're the best man I know."

"Don't say that." Caleb's voice shook as he said this. But was it anger or something else making it shake?

"I know you have always looked up to me, Lloyd," he continued slowly, "and I love you for that. But I have only been hard on you, expected so much of you, because of what I was."

"You worked every day to provide for us. Broke your health, your body—"

"It wasn't work that broke me," he said, silencing Lloyd. "It wasn't work."

"Then what?" Lloyd asked, suddenly uncertain and unnerved.

There was a long silence, then:

"I've never told a soul this. Not even your late mother," he eventually went on. "But I was a thief."

Lloyd stared at him in disbelief. He knew what the words meant, but still they didn't make any sense.

"In those days, when you worked at the docks, you had to belong. To a team. To a gang."

Lloyd stared at him, wondering what was coming next.

"I chose the latter, lifting a little stock here, a little stock there, as they passed through my area. I handed the goods on and got extra money in return. I needed the money for you all, but that doesn't mean I don't regret it. That time my back was broken. I didn't fall. It was a punishment beating by a rival gang. I did what I had to to survive and if I was hard on you, it's because I wanted you to be so much more than me. Do you understand?"

Lloyd nodded, but his emotions lagged behind his brain. He didn't know what to think or feel.

"And I've hated myself for lying to you and your mother. Even your layabout brother and sister. But try to understand . . . sometimes you find you've gone too far down one road and there's no way back. So don't judge yourself by my standards. You're ten times the man I'll ever be."

Now there were tears in Caleb's eyes. Lloyd wept too, without embarrassment, holding on to his father's arm. He cried for the lies he'd been told, for the feelings of inadequacy he'd felt for so many years. But mostly he cried because of his stupidity, knowing now that he had sacrificed his career in the worship of a false god.

107

Helen could feel Sanderson's eyes crawling all over her, searching for any hint of instability or violence. They were sitting opposite Andrew Simpson once more and, although nothing had been said out loud, Helen knew her junior officer was alive to the danger of another explosion from Helen. She didn't blame Sanderson for this. After a sleepless night, Helen looked even more exhausted and on edge than she had the night before. No wonder her colleague looked nervous.

Simpson was impassive as usual, though he appeared much more strained than before. He kept rubbing his face with his hand and massaging his temples: he appeared stressed, unhappy—he looked like he was in pain.

"So, do you want the good news or the bad news, Andrew?"

Simpson looked at Helen warily, unsure what game she had elected to play this morning.

"The good news for you is that our POLSA teams have searched every inch of your properties and found no sign of Ruby Sprackling. The bad news is they have found enough evidence of illegal surveillance and pornographic file-sharing to make the CPS very excited indeed."

Did Helen see the lawyer's grim smile wobble a little? She hoped so.

"So the bottom line is that they will begin drawing up charges this afternoon, unless I can give them a compelling reason not to do so."

"Meaning?" Finally the lawyer spoke.

"Meaning cooperation. I want to go over every file, every video, every detail of these girls' lives with you. I want chapter and verse on their activities, as well as yours. Obviously you don't have to decide right this minute. You'll need to confer with your legal tea—"

"Okay." It was said quietly but firmly.

"Louder, please, Mr. Simpson. For the tape."

"Okay, I'll cooperate," he said wearily. Helen was pleased to see his defiance ebbing away. Perhaps a night in the cells had had the desired effect after all. She turned to Sanderson and gave her the nod to begin. Her junior had also had a sleepless night but had spent it more profitably, poring over the details of Simpson's decade of snooping and stalking.

"Do you like novelty, Mr. Simpson? Or are you a creature of habit?"

Simpson looked at Sanderson quizzically, before finally replying:

"Both, I suppose."

"But when it comes to the girls?"

"Novelty, I suppose."

"Why?"

"I get bored."

"Of seeing the same girls?"

He shrugged but didn't deny it.

"So you have varied viewing habits. And always plenty of tenants moving out and new ones moving in."

"Sure."

"Do you have a type, Andrew?"

It was offered casually, but Helen could tell that Sanderson was a hundred percent focused on his answer—as was she.

"There are all sorts of girls on your tapes. Large, small, white, black, dark hair, blondes. Do you favor any particular type of girl?"

"I'm not fussy . . . but probably blondes. Especially if it's dyed, so the rest of their hair is, well . . ."

He petered out, suddenly aware of the two women looking at him. For the first time in all their dealings, he blushed.

Helen rose.

"For the purposes of the tape, DI Grace is leaving the room," Helen said. "DC Sanderson will continue and remember the pact we've made, Mr. Simpson. Chapter and verse."

She stared at him intently and he met her gaze, nodding gently. Sanderson resumed the questioning before Helen had even quitted the room, but Helen's mind was already elsewhere. Sanderson's burning of the midnight oil had thrown up one unpleasant but undeniable truth—Simpson *didn't* have a type. The killer they were hunting was compelled to abduct women with black hair and blue eyes, but

Simpson by contrast seemed to crave novelty, rather than specific body shapes, eye color or hair type. It was almost as if the look of his subjects wasn't important to him—just the fact that he could watch them undetected. Which meant that her nagging fears were probably true—Andrew Simpson was innocent of the beach murders. And of Ruby Sprackling's abduction.

108

"I have made the decision to release Andrew Simpson on bail, once he's finished assisting us."

The assembled team reacted with surprise and unease. They had heard rumors to this effect, but Helen's statement still took them aback.

"He will be tailed of course and other charges are still pending. If he cooperates fully and helps us conclude the investigation, we may review those charges. But," Helen carried on, ignoring the dirty looks crossing the faces of some of the female officers, "unless you hear otherwise from me, Andrew Simpson is no longer our prime suspect."

There was a brief buzz of chatter and reaction as her words sank in. Helen found her eyes drifting to Lloyd Fortune. As her DS, he should have been by her side, spearheading the investigation with her, but he had been strangely absent of late—both physically and mentally. Like her, he also looked exhausted.

"Andrew Simpson wasn't fussy in the girls he targeted and both DC Sanderson and I believe that he no longer fits our offender profile."

"So we're back to square one," DC Lucas chipped in unhelpfully.

"Not quite," Helen countered quickly, alive to the effect that dead ends can have on team morale. "We know the killer's type. And we know he abducts these girls with practiced ease, which suggests he had access to their properties or had the girls' confidence."

"Which is unlikely, as they were all so different," DC McAndrew contributed.

"Let's test that theory," Helen continued. "Pippa Briers was a young professional. Roisin a single mum on benefits. Ruby Sprackling was a wild child. Isobel Lansley seems to be an introverted student who seldom left the flat. How are we getting on with her parents?"

"They're flying in this morning. Should be here by the afternoon," DC Edwards replied.

"Good. So we've got four very different women, who lived miles apart, but shared a look and lived alone. How does he get to them? Let's start with Pippa."

"Lived in Merry Oak, worked in Sun First Travel in the WestQuay. Liked to socialize in Bedford Heights," Lucas shot back.

"Find out who her doctor was. Her dentist. Friends, colleagues, book groups—start from the ground and work up. What about Roisin?"

"Lived alone in a council flat in Brokenford. A number of boyfriends, some of whom seemed to overlap. Roisin liked the attention. Never had a job, attended a few free baby groups, went to the post office once a week to get her benefits. Spent the rest of her time window-shopping, drinking and dreaming of being elsewhere."

"Okay, run down the boyfriends—every single one of them. Find out who worked at the post office, who was at those mother and baby groups. Ruby we know about, but let's go over everything again—old school friends, Shanelle Harvey's boyfriends, anyone who knew where she lived, how she lived . . . What do we know about Isobel?"

There was an awkward silence before DC McAndrew eventually replied, "Very little really. Lived alone, kept herself to herself. Had fifteen followers on Twitter."

Helen noticed a couple of the younger officers smirk. Fifteen followers was the equivalent of social death to them.

"Student at the Oceanography Center. Was halfway through her course when she went missing. Her parents funded her, so she didn't have to work to support herself. From anecdotal evidence we've gathered so far, she went to lectures and then went straight home again."

"Okay, let's focus our fire on her. She didn't drink, club, socialize. So what professionals did she come into contact with that might link her to the other women? How is he doing it? How is he getting access to them? Isobel had traces of trichloroethylene in her hair—is that important? Does whoever's behind this have access to this anesthetic or derivative of it for their work? Check and double-check."

There was a brief lull as Helen came to a close. "What are you waiting for?"

The team sprang into action, hurrying off to check and recheck their leads. Helen was furious at herself for wasting so much time on Price and Simpson. She hadn't really had a choice, but this would be of no comfort to Ruby. If that girl died, Helen knew she would never forgive herself. Would this last throw of the dice finally yield results or were they already too late?

109

The door swung open and Ruby jerked awake. How long had she been asleep? What day was it? Why had *he* returned?

Suddenly the whole bed moved. He had a hold of it now and flung it on its side to reveal Ruby cowering underneath. She blinked into the harsh light, ripped from her sanctuary and thrust out into the open. Slowly her eyes became accustomed to the light and she was surprised to see that he seemed to be shaking with anger. It was as if no time had passed at all.

"Listen carefully, Summer, because this is your last chance."

His voice was harsh and unpleasant.

"You have let me down badly. Very badly indeed. If I had any sense I'd forget all about you. But I'm prepared to forgive you. I know you regret your mistake."

Ruby said nothing. She didn't know where his crazy talk was leading and she was suddenly very tired of this game.

"But I won't be hurt by you again. If you let me down again, you *will* be punished. Do you understand?"

"How will you punish me?" Ruby found herself saying, her words dripping with defiance. It was her talking, yet she had no idea where it was coming from.

"Don't push it. You've done enough har—"

"Will you punish me like you punished Roisin?"

She picked Roisin's crudely drawn Christmas card from the floor, thrusting it at him. "Or like you punished Pippa."

She threw Pippa's makeshift diary at him, a fierce rage overcoming her. He immediately backed off, as if the cards were toxic.

"She was a mistake—"

"Then what does that make me?"

"Don't try to trick me, Summer."

"I'm Ruby Sprackling—"

"Your name is Summer—"

"I'm Ruby Sprackling and I hate your fucking guts."

His hand shot out, forcing Ruby back, back, back, until she collided heavily with the wall. The breath was knocked from her; his hand was squeezing tighter and tighter.

"Say another word and I'll kill you. I swear it," he rasped, flecks of his spit landing on Ruby's face.

"There's nothing you can threaten me with anymore," Ruby spat back. "As far as you're concerned I'm already dead."

From somewhere, Ruby managed to find a grim, victorious smile. It had the desired effect. He dropped her like a stone, watching her collapse to the floor.

He walked away from her quickly, then stopped, turned and

hurried back—kicking her harshly three times in the ribs. As she rolled away from the blows, he bent down, grabbing her by the collar. "You'll regret this."

Dumping her back to the floor, he walked over to the bedside table, snatching up her inhaler.

"No."

Ruby was crawling across the floor toward him now, hand outstretched, beseeching. But he was too quick for her, crossing the room quickly, unlocking the door.

"Good-bye, Ruby."

The door slammed shut behind him.

110

He marched away from the cell, muttering obscenities. He passed through the second door, then turned down the left-hand corridor toward the third and final door. Unlocking and then relocking it, he climbed the ladder back to the ground floor.

The house was even more of a mess than usual and it fitted his mood perfectly. His brain felt scattered. His head throbbed violently. He kicked the kitchen chair savagely; then before he knew what he was doing, he'd picked it up and hurled it against the wall. It broke into several pieces, but he felt nothing. Just a crushing emptiness.

Already he could feel the darkness creeping up on him again. Those familiar feelings of desolation. And deep, deep loneliness. He had been cursed since birth—he knew that. Born to a whore of a mother in bloody degradation, he would never have survived infancy had it not been for Summer. He had always worshipped her—for her love, her patience, her kindness. Now he bitterly regretted her charity—why hadn't she left him to die? Why had she consigned him to *this*?

Was their love a curse? She had been ever present in his life, teaching him to navigate life's many dangers, teaching him to give and receive love. Latterly she had been absent of course, but she always came back to him. In the end, she always came back.

As he snatched up the shattered pieces of the chair, ramming them into the already overflowing kitchen bin, which belched some of its contents onto the floor, he felt the full extent of his foolishness. Why was he so easily duped? She was out there, always so close to him that when one of these girls drifted into his life, purporting to be her, he fell for it. He *believed*. But he couldn't have got it wrong again, could he? He had watched this one for months, seen the emptiness in her life, witnessed the arguments with her so-called family. They didn't know her, didn't understand her, but he did and he'd seen her searching for him. Searching for her missing half. But what if he *was* wrong? He had been so sure . . .

This thought took all the strength from him and suddenly he sank to the floor. Curled up in a ball amid the broken wood, rotting food and dirt, he started to cry. He *never* cried, but today he couldn't help himself. He cried for all the disappointments and anguish over the years. For all the false starts and false idols. And for the girl he had loved and lost.

111

Emilia Garanita stabbed the Off button on her computer and picked up her bag. She was already late—the household would have descended into merry chaos by now, no doubt—and she had spent an unsatisfactory day trying to rehash the "Bodies on the Beach" story to make it look like there were fresh developments.

She was halfway to the door when her desk phone rang. She was very tempted to ignore it—today had been a dead loss—but old instincts die hard. For a journalist a phone call is just a story waiting to happen. So she crossed the room and snatched up the phone.

"Garanita."

"Got a phone call for you. From a woman. About the bluebird tattoo."

Emilia's mood descended still further. Since putting this story in the *Southampton Evening News*, they had had no end of loonies, chancers and wannabe detectives jamming their line with dead-end "leads." Each was as deluded as the last—Emilia had ended up regretting agreeing to help Helen Grace with this one.

"Put her through," Emilia barked, keen to get this charade over with.

"Hello?"

The voice on the other end of the phone was cracked and tremulous.

"Emilia Garanita. How can I help you?"

"Are you the journalist?"

"That's right."

"Asking about the bluebird tattoo?"

"Yes."

A pause, then:

"Is there a reward?"

Emilia sighed inwardly. This conversation was developing in a depressingly familiar way. "Only if the information provided leads to a conviction."

"Yes or no?"

The voice had a sharpness to it now that made Emilia pay attention. "Yes."

"How much?"

"Twenty thousand pounds."

"When would I get it?"

"We can discuss that when you come to my office. But I'd need to know the nature of your information before we meet."

"My daughter had that tattoo. She's dead now. But she definitely had one of those."

Emilia sat back down at her desk, silently pulling her phone from her pocket and opening the Notes app. "What did she look like?"

"Thin, bit tarty, I guess, but she had something. Like her mother." The cracked voice chuckled now, but it sounded bitter, not joyful.

"Hair color? Eyes?"

"She was a striking girl. Black hair and big blue eyes."

Emilia paused, her finger hovering over the screen of her phone. "What did you say her name was?"

"Her name was Summer, God rest her."

"And she's dead, you say?"

"OD'd. Her brother found her."

"She had a brother?" Emilia said, failing to keep the excitement out of her voice. "What was his name? And where is he now?"

There was a long pause; then the woman replied:

"I'll tell you when we meet. You don't get anything for free in this life, my dear."

And with that, she rang off.

112

Ruby lay dead still on the floor. She was shivering uncontrollably, but she made no attempt to move toward the bed. Her lungs burned, her throat was tight and she felt far too faint to stand.

The fight was over now; Ruby knew that. Why had she pushed him so far? Had she thought she could break him? No, she knew that her verbal assault on her captor was the last act of a desperate girl. The death throes of her resistance. She would never see her mum or dad again. Cassie or Conor. If they ever did lay eyes on her again, they would find her here, rotting in this horrible place.

Breathlessness used to panic her—a legacy of those trips to the hospital when she was young—but now she welcomed the feeling. She had never asked for much in life—had never expected much—but she hoped now that she would be granted one small mercy. Slow asphyxiation would be a blessing, a way to cheat him out of further punishments and humiliations. It would be a small victory, but a victory nevertheless.

If she could drift away, here on this floor, then maybe she would see her family again. Perhaps there was an afterlife or somewhere where she could be at peace. Surely that wasn't impossible? She had never believed in anything like that before, but now . . .

But she *didn't* believe it. Never had believed it. And life had taught her not to expect happy endings. Ruby knew in her heart that she would go on suffering until the bitter end. There would be no escape for her, and this place—this strange doll's house—would be her tomb.

113

Lloyd walked to his car, a hundred thoughts tumbling round his head. Anti-Corruption's investigation into Helen was ongoing and yet there she was—still in charge of the investigation and leading it with confidence and vigor. Ceri Harwood meanwhile was nowhere to be seen, having called in sick. Lloyd had thought about calling her, but then sense prevailed. While things were up in the air, the best thing he could do was keep his distance. Still, the lack of clarity made him deeply uneasy. Had he backed the wrong horse? Shaking his doubts away, Lloyd pulled the car door open—there was important work to be done on the Ruby Sprackling case.

He slammed the door shut and turned the key in the ignition. Before he could move off, the passenger door flew open and a woman climbed inside. Lloyd turned and was more than a little surprised to see Charlie making herself comfortable, pulling the door quietly shut behind her.

"Shall we go for a drive, Lloyd?"

She waited until they were well clear of the station before she began. In the heavy silence that preceded this, Lloyd tried to work out if she could know—and if she did, how—but had drawn a blank. Despite this he knew with absolute certainty that she was here to begin the counterattack. She was a loyal ally of Helen Grace's—always had been—and her sudden appearance could only mean the beginning of a new and potentially decisive phase in this secret war.

"I don't think you're a bad person, Lloyd. At least I hope you're not. But what you've done demeans you and the job."

Lloyd said nothing but shot a glance sideways at her. Could she be wearing a wire—was that what this was all about?

"Nobody knows I'm here," Charlie continued, reading his mind. "And I'm not recording this. I think this is better handled off the record, don't you?"

Lloyd paused, then nodded. She sounded genuine, but could he trust her?

"I don't know whether she offered you money or promotion or anything else, and to be honest I don't really care. But sometime soon this thing is going to break—and break big—so everybody needs to get their story straight. It's customary in these situations for those lower down the ladder to carry the can for the incompetence or corruption of those above them. But I don't want that to happen here. I know who set this in motion. I'm only interested in her."

"Okay," Lloyd replied cautiously.

"I won't lie to you, Lloyd. You're on pretty shaky ground here. But there is a way you can save yourself and perhaps keep your badge.

You may view it as an act of disloyalty, but it's the only play there is. You have to turn her over to Anti-Corruption and tell them everything you know. Say you were pressured into it, say she threatened to sack you if you didn't play ball. If you have to embellish a little to save your own skin, so be it, but you have to tell them the truth about *her*. When she first came to you, what she asked you to do, when you first contacted DI Marsh."

There it was. The first piece of solid evidence. It was tossed in casually by Charlie but had a devastating effect on Lloyd.

"I've spoken to Tom Marsh. Went up to his home in Bugbrooke. Met his wife too—Rose, nice lady. He's going to cooperate to save his neck and I would strongly advise you to do the same. You've got until the end of the day to decide. You can drop me off here."

Lloyd slowed the car quickly, bringing it to a halt in the bus lane. As Charlie exited, she said:

"Oh, and this conversation never happened."

She slammed the door and hurried round the car to join the queue for the bus. Lloyd drove away quickly, his eyes scanning the street for CCTV cameras that might have picked up their exchange. Normally so cool under pressure, Lloyd was surprised to find now that his shirt was damp with sweat.

As he drove, he played out different situations in his head, each as bad as the last. Harwood had threatened to break him if he didn't play ball. Now Charlie would throw him to the lions if he didn't expose her. It was a lose-lose situation, but Charlie had forced the issue now and he would have to choose sides.

It was decision time.

114

This was usually a space he dominated. A place where he was in complete control. Which was why it felt so strange to be on the back foot now, to be standing, embarrassed and cowed, in front of her.

On hearing the familiar three rings of the buzzer, Jake had raced to open the door. He had expected Helen to avoid him for a while, to punish him with her absence, but here she was the very next morning. As she entered, her mood had been hard to read—she stared at the floor—but her first concern seemed to be for his well-being, which cheered him. She asked him about his injuries and he filled her in on his late-night trip to A&E. He'd had to have a few stitches above his eye, but the wound would heal quickly and there would be no permanent damage.

Helen was clearly anxious to be away, so Jake wasn't surprised when she cut to the chase, demanding to know the full extent of his surveillance. Jake decided to hide nothing from her—a full and frank confession was the very least she deserved—but as the details tumbled out, the depth of his feeling for her became painfully clear to them both. He hadn't meant to get so involved with her—but he had—and now Helen wouldn't look him in the eye as a result.

"Jake, I'm really grateful for everything you've done for me—"

"Please don't do this, Helen."

Jake could see where this was going and wanted to stop Helen before she could articulate her decision.

"You have helped me more than you know," Helen continued, unabashed. "More than I deserved. But we both know this has to end now."

"Of course. We can go back to how we were, strictly professio—"

"I mean 'we' have to end," Helen interrupted. "We've crossed a line that should never have been crossed."

"Why shouldn't we cross it?" Jake retorted, his swelling anger finally overcoming his sense of shame.

"Because I don't want to. And it's not fair on you to pretend otherwise."

"That's bullshit. I know you, Helen. You're no different from anyone else, but you persist in pushing everyone away."

Helen looked at him as if he were mad, but he had seen her vulnerability, her need for comfort and love—so surely *she* was the mad one?

"I'm sorry, Jake, but I've made up my mind. I don't want to hurt you—that was never my intention—but I won't be coming here anymore."

"Then you'll be on your own forever," he spat back. He hadn't meant to sound bitter, but he did nevertheless. "Because of your pride, because of your fear, you'll be lonely for the rest of your days."

As he spoke, he wrenched the front door open. Her very presence seemed to mock him now and he just wanted her out of sight. And as she departed, walking out of his life forever, he couldn't resist one final shot.

"Good luck, Helen. You're going to need it."

115

Charlie pushed the front door shut behind her and leaned against it. She had been feeling peculiar all day—at sixes and sevens—and now she just felt exhausted. Had she been stupid tackling Lloyd directly? She didn't know him at all well and who was to say he wouldn't have reacted angrily, even violently, to her accusations? She was glad she hadn't thought too deeply about it or she probably wouldn't have gone through with it. And that would have been wrong—she had played an unwitting part in the ambush on Helen and she had been determined to put that right. She didn't want cowardice or caution to stop her. Not that Steve would have seen it like that, if anything had happened.

All she wanted to do was collapse on the sofa, but oddly her legs wouldn't move. Her batteries were dead, as her father would say, and she remained where she was, propping up the front door. Something definitely wasn't right. She felt more than peculiar now; she felt uncomfortable. The baby had been less active today, which had at first worried her, then intrigued her as she had felt the occasional cramp. Was this Braxton Hicks or something more meaningful? She wasn't one to jump the gun, but today did feel different.

She looked down and was surprised to see her leggings stained dark. Placing her hand on her thighs, she found that her legs were wet. She investigated further and there was no doubt about it. Her waters had broken. The time had come.

The baby that she'd craved for so long was finally on her way.

116

She had never anticipated failure. Never seen it in her mind's eye. So when it finally happened, she wasn't quite sure how to behave.

The ring on the doorbell was insistent, but Ceri Harwood had nevertheless ignored it at first. Tim was there, driven home by guilt or uncertainty for another of their "chats," and though she didn't hold out much hope that this was anything more than window dressing, she didn't want a postie or duster salesman interrupting them during such a raw conversation.

But the ringing then became repeated knocking on the door. It was obvious they were in, because the upper windows were open and the sitting room light on, so it seemed fruitless to hide. Ceri armed herself with a dismissive turn of phrase, but as she opened the door, words failed her. She could tell exactly who they were by their bad suits and their somber expressions, but it still came as a bit of a shock when they said:

"Anti-Corruption. Can we come in?"

Ceri Harwood. Head girl. Top of her class at Hendon. The youngest female DCI in the Met. Now staring at failure and, worse than that, possible ruin.

"Tim, we'd better take a rain check on this. There are a few procedural things that need to be sorted out."

But he could tell she was lying. Had she gone pale? She felt like she had. Or perhaps she was just a bad actress—failing to cloak the anxiety that gripped her now?

"Can we do this here?" she asked as her husband watched on, making no attempt to leave.

"Better if we do this down the station," came the sober reply.

"Is that really necessary?" Ceri said, her superior rank surfacing as she fixed them with a beady eye.

"Yes" was the blunt apologetic reply. "We'd prefer it if you came willingly, but if we have to arrest you—"

"Okay, okay."

Now that it had come to this, there was no point in dragging it out. Picking up her bag, she nodded to Tim—and was surprised to find tears pricking her eyes. When she had started this thing, she was so sure that it would achieve the desired result, that she would drive Helen Grace from Southampton Central and be the top dog once more. Successful, untouchable, victorious. She paused on the threshold to smile a sheepish good-bye to Tim, and in that moment she knew—her defeat was total. She had reached the end of the road.

117

He worked the machine furiously, his anger with himself—with the world—unconcealed from all around. People came in and out as usual, but where he would normally exchange pleasantries with them, today he served them in silence, his glowering expression enough to repel any casual conversation.

A sudden sharp pain made him look down. Distracted, he had taken his eye off the machine and the blade had sliced his thumb right open.

"Fuck."

He spat the word out, but it didn't make him feel any better. Blood oozed from the deep cut. Flicking the machine off, he hurried out back, swathing his injured finger in rounds of paper towels. The blood seeped through the pale green toweling, but it looked more black than brown.

Why was he such a failure? Such a waste of space? Was he forever to be on this journey, searching, searching, searching—but finding only misery and crushing desolation? How could he have got it so wrong? He could see now that she wasn't Summer. He had just been trying to convince himself, hoping against hope that her coldness and rough manner were some reserved anger at their long separation. But it had actually been because she was a nasty, worthless slut. Why had he lavished so much care, attention and—yes—love on her, when all she wanted to do was throw it back in his face and return to her peevish little stepfamily, who thought she was nothing but trouble? He knew enough about her to know that she spurned and ridiculed those who tried to help—why hadn't he seen the signs? Why had he exposed himself in this way?

The blood was still oozing from his cut. There was no way he could do any more work today, so he might as well shut up shop. It was far too early to close and there would no doubt be a few shoppers confused by his unusual absence. His first instinct was to say "Stuff them," but caution—his watchword—reasserted itself once more. So, having turned off the till, he started writing out a note blaming "staff sickness" for the temporary closure of the shop. It was hard going—he wasn't used to writing with his left hand—and he was still writing when the ringing bell alerted him to the arrival of a customer.

"We're closed," he barked without looking up.

"The sign said you were open and this won't take a minute."

Her voice was soft and gentle. But he didn't look up, concentrating even harder on his note.

"Please, could you squeeze me in?"

Sighing, he put down his pen. No point creating questions, when it was so easy to serve her and send her on her way. Looking up, he held out his hand.

"Oh, you're bleeding. Are you okay?"

Her voice matched her features, which were delicate and pretty. Her accent was local but subtle and she had a kindness in her expression that instantly put you at your ease. "Can I help at all?"

Still he couldn't speak. It seemed impossible and yet it was true. As if the cosmos *was* listening. This lovely, kind girl who was offering the hand of friendship had walked right into his shop, right into his life. Like he always imagined she would. He let her examine his wound, but as she did so, he never took his gaze off her, transfixed by her delicate nose, her long black hair and those piercing blue eyes.

118

Alastair and Gemma Lansley stood stock-still, barely able to breathe. Helen watched them closely. She could tell that, like Daniel Briers, they had found news of their daughter's death hard to credit. But they had done the right thing and flown over from Windhoek to be confronted by the grim reality of Isobel's murder. She lay on the mortuary slab in front of them, her body discreetly covered, but her pale, thin face unveiled. Her opaque eyes stared up at her parents, giving them none of the love they craved. She had been dead for over a year.

Helen was surprised to see that while Alastair's eyes were already brimful of tears, Gemma's eyes were dry, as if they hadn't yet taken in what they were seeing. Usually it was the other way around, the husband desperately trying to be strong for his wife. But that was not the case here. Helen had already established in their preliminary chats that Alastair was very close to his daughter—his only daughter. When he and his wife had retired abroad, Alastair had hoped that Isobel would eventually join them—a life in the sun—but she had cleaved close to Southampton and her studies. Alastair had picked up a note of cynicism, even weariness in her recent tweets and texts that perhaps tokened a change in attitude to her surroundings, and this had raised his hopes of a reunion. But these had turned out to be somebody else's fabrication—a revelation that was too big, too horrific for this elderly couple to process.

Having concluded the identification, Helen moved them into the relatives' room.

"I know this is hard, but I need you to tell me as much as you can about Isobel. Her friends, her study schedule, her habits. We're working on the assumption that Isobel's attacker was not known to her, but rather someone who she came into contact with in daily life."

"We could have told you that," Gemma Lansley said curtly. "Isobel didn't have any friends."

"Gemma . . . ," her husband murmured, a gentle note of warning in his voice.

"They need the facts, Alastair," she shot back quickly, her voice wobbling for the first time. "There's no point dressing things up."

There was a pause and then Alastair looked straight at Helen.

"When Isobel . . . when she was a teenager, she was the victim of a sexual assault."

"Go on."

"She was walking home from school. Took a shortcut across the heath. The man . . . the man responsible was caught and imprisoned."

"Eight years with time off for good behavior," Gemma added bitterly.

"But it left a lasting impression on Isobel. She hated open spaces, hated to be outside. She hardly ever left her flat and didn't really want to share. She had trust issues, I think the psychiatrist said. Hence she lived alone."

"She had a limited social circle?" Helen asked.

"Limited was the word," Gemma said. "She deliberately cut herself off from her family, her friends—"

"Please, Gemma, you're not helping—"

"Cut herself off from anyone who might have cared for her."

Gemma Lansley lapsed into silence now, overwhelmed by misery and grief.

"So she wouldn't have let someone she didn't know into the flat?"

"Have you been listening, Inspector?" Gemma replied acidly. "She wouldn't let people she *did* know into the flat. She felt safe only when she was alone behind a closed door."

Helen nodded, suddenly feeling huge sympathy for the spiky Gemma. Her bitterness was the result of her daughter closing the door on her. Had she too hoped for a reconciliation, a greater closeness later in life?

"She was security-conscious?" Helen offered gently.

"Of course. She didn't go to great extremes—didn't have the cash—but she had a very strong lock, a spyhole in case anyone rang the doorbell. And she'd always tell deliverymen to leave things on the doorstep. She hated the idea of coming into contact with strangers."

"And yet she must have come into contact with them every day on her way to and from college?"

"She did, but it was on her terms. She always took the same route at the same times of day. She knew the faces along her route extremely well—not that she'd ever talk to them, of course."

Helen tensed, sensing a breakthrough. "Do you remember her route?"

"Of course. We walked it several times with her when we were over. We stayed in a hotel—obviously."

"That's very helpful and if you can I'm going to ask you to sit down with one of my officers and go over that route. It could be of crucial importance to know where she went and what time of day she went there."

Gemma nodded without enthusiasm.

"You think that whoever did this . . . saw her on her route to and from . . ." Alastair petered out, unable to finish this unpleasant thought.

"If she had few friends and was security-conscious, then yes, it might be that he followed her home."

Alastair closed his eyes—not wanting to go there—but Gemma looked straight at Helen. She wanted—she needed—the details. "Did he hurt her? Was there . . . a fight?"

"We don't think so. When we interviewed the tenants, nobody remembered hearing anything like that. There was no sign of a break-in, no sign of a struggle—"

"But that doesn't make sense," Alastair butted in. "She wouldn't let anyone in. They must have forced their way in."

"Unless they had a key."

Gemma's thought hung in the air. Helen had come to the same conclusion already, but hadn't wanted to say it out loud.

"Would she have given a key to anyone? A trusted friend? A figure of authority?" Helen asked.

"Absolutely not. Not even if she'd been threatened with eviction or expulsion from college—she would never compromise her security in that way," Alastair shot back. "I really think you're barking up the wrong—"

"She had her lock changed," Gemma said suddenly.

"When?" Helen asked, without hesitation.

"About . . . about six months before you say she . . ."

"Went missing. Why did she change the locks?"

"Somebody wrecked the old one. Squirted superglue into it. We thought it was kids at the time, but now . . ."

It was all starting to make sense.

"So she got her locks changed?"

"Yes. I remember it was quite a to-do. She asked her college tutor to come round, as she didn't want to be alone with the locksmith. He obviously thought she was mad but obliged anyway."

"Do you remember who changed the lock?"

"No, but the receipt might be in her effects. She was quite particular like that."

"Do you know how many keys were provided?"

"Two, I think. She kept one on her key ring and wore one round her neck as a backup."

"Would she have slept with the key round her neck?"

"No, she wasn't that mad. Why?"

"It might be important, but let's focus on the keys. So you believe there were two and neither was out of her possession."

"No, that's not quite true," Alastair offered. Helen swung her gaze toward him.

"She had some more cut. I know that because she sent one to us. She gave the other one to her landlord, I believe. Much against her better judgment, but those were the rules."

"And do you know where she got the extra keys cut?"

There was a long pause as both parents racked their brains for a half-forgotten memory, the tiny events of yesteryear, before eventually Alastair looked up and wearily said:

"I'm afraid we've no idea."

119

Andrew Simpson looked up sharply as Helen burst into the room. He and Sanderson had been locked in one of the remoter interview suites for hours already—Helen could tell by the musky scent of his BO that filled the room—and his files were spread out like a blossoming fungus across the table.

Helen leaned on the table and, dispensing with formalities, got straight to the point. "Isobel Lansley had her locks changed."

Simpson stared at her, still startled by her sudden arrival; then slowly he nodded. "Her lock was glued up, I think. So she had it changed. What of it?"

His defenses were already up, sensing another attack.

"How do you remember that?"

"What do you mean?"

"You didn't give a shit about your tenants' lives or the hovels they lived in. Why would you remember such a small detail?"

"Because it's in the records, the financial records, I mean. Every time something like that happens, I charge a . . . small fee. For the administrative hassle."

I bet you do, Helen thought to herself, but swallowed the insinuation. "This is really important, Andrew. Did any of the other girls—Ruby, Roisin or Pippa—have their locks changed at any point?"

Andrew thought for a long time. "Roisin definitely did. Was told to by her boyfriend of the time, I believe. And we could check the records of the other two . . ."

Helen was pleased to see that Sanderson was already leafing through Pippa Briers's tenancy file. Her finger ran down the columns at breakneck speed. "There. A twenty-five-pound administration fee. Would that be it?" she said, turning to Simpson.

He looked at it. "Yes, that's it."

"Dated one month before she went missing."

"Because of Nathan Price," Helen said, as the pieces slowly started to fit together. "She was scared of her ex, so she changed the locks to keep him out."

"And look here."

Sanderson was now holding Ruby's tenancy file.

"An administrative charge of twenty-five pounds. Six weeks ago. Just over a month before she went missing."

"No great surprise," Simpson piped up. "That girl was incredibly scatty. She probably lost them or had them pinched. Never knew if she was coming or going."

"He kept an extra key." Helen shivered as she said it out loud. "Say they all got them cut at the same place, somewhere central, somewhere they all knew. What's to stop him cutting an extra one for himself, while doing theirs?"

"Nothing at all."

"And when they came back to collect the keys, all he'd have to do is shut up shop and follow them home."

"He's a textbook stalker," Sanderson said, picking up Helen's thread. "He would then know where they live and could watch them at his leisure. He could find out what their family situation is, if they have partners, flatmates, what their daily routine is—"

"But what separates this guy from ordinary stalkers is that he has a key," Helen interjected. "He could enter their flats whenever he wanted. He could even do dummy runs while they were out, to make sure the abduction was perfect."

"No sign of a struggle, no forced entry."

"No need," Helen said, the awful simplicity of it hitting home. "*Because he was already in their flats when they came home.* He was waiting for them, hiding in a wardrobe, loft, spare room. He was waiting for them to come back and go to sleep."

Helen could scarcely believe it, but it made perfect sense.

"They thought they were back safe at home. But in fact they had just walked right into his trap."

120

He kept a good distance behind, so as not to alert her to his presence. He had eventually found his tongue and responded to her concern for his cut finger, before taking the job from her—a simple boot reheel—promising to have it ready first thing tomorrow as recompense for her kindness and sympathy.

After she left, he'd remained at his workstation for a silent count of twenty, then switched off the shop lights, flipped the *Closed* sign and hurried out, locking the door behind him. Experience had taught him not to dawdle during this process—you risked losing your quarry among the crowds of shoppers, if you were too cautious. You just needed enough time for her to clear the immediate vicinity of the shop.

He scanned left and right, before spotting her a hundred yards away, idly window-shopping. Her crisp navy suit and smartly tied-back hair made her quite distinctive among the loafers and driftwood that usually populated this place. Tired of daydreaming, she moved off again. And he went with her, as always at a discreet distance.

She meandered slowly homeward. She had finished work for the day—she really did look smart and professional—but clearly had no one to rush home to. She stopped to look in various shop windows, to buy a copy of the *Big Issue*, but she looked like she was killing time. As if she was waiting for something to happen. Or someone to come along.

They passed through Bedford Place, then through Portswood to the cheap flats that lay near the university. Though she was well turned out, she clearly wasn't well-off, living among the detritus of the city. This was in character too, he thought to himself, suppressing a smile. You grow older, but you don't really change.

He stopped abruptly. He had momentarily lost himself to memory and inadvertently had walked too close to her. She had stopped at a door—not ten yards from him. If she turned round now, she'd see him. So he upped his pace, thankfully clearing her without exciting her interest. Crossing the street, he chanced a backward look—just in time to see her enter a sorry-looking flat.

Hugging the corner of the street, he found a decent vantage point behind a hedge. He watched with interest as the lights came on up on the first floor. He didn't know whether to stay or go. The working day was coming to an end and workers would be filling the streets soon—he couldn't risk being spotted or, worse, reported. But, as always, she made the decision for him, appearing now in the first-floor window.

There was no way he was leaving now. He had the perfect vantage point—to watch her, to admire her, to drink in every detail of her life. She made no attempt to draw the curtains; she just looked down onto the street below. Looking for hope. Looking for love.

Looking for him.

121

"Why did you lie to me?"

"What do you mean?"

"I asked you to your face if Roisin had ever had her locks changed and you denied that she had. But that wasn't true, was it, Bryan?"

Roisin's awkward ex boyfriend attempted to usher Helen toward a quieter part of the garage, but she stood her ground.

"Why did you lie?"

Bryan shot a look at his fellow mechanics, who stared with undisguised curiosity at the strikingly attractive woman who was now hauling their apprentice over the coals. Was that something resembling respect in their eyes?

"Because of Jamie," he eventually murmured.

"Who's Jamie?"

"Roisin's ex. Before me, I mean. He used to live with her. Still had his key. I . . . I found out he'd been coming round, letting himself in, you know . . ."

He didn't need to elaborate. Roisin needed affection and clearly wasn't picky where she got it from.

"So you made her change the locks."

"I couldn't stop her seeing him, if that's what she wanted. But I wasn't having him thinking he could come and go as he pleased, letting himself in at any time of day or night."

"You do know lying to the police is a serious matter."

"I know all right . . . I didn't want to, but I wasn't going to say nothing with *her* sitting right next to me."

He meant Roisin's mum—his former mother-in-law. Did he clam up to avoid making himself look foolish or to avoid telling Sinead Murphy that her daughter was faithless and generous with her favors? Helen hoped it was the latter.

"Who changed the locks?"

"A mate of mine—Stuart Briggs at LockRite."

"I'll need his contact details."

"Sure, but he's got nothing to do with this."

"We'll see. Did you get any more cut?"

"Sure. We only got two with the lock and her mum needed one, so—"

"Where? Where did you have them cut?" Helen failed to conceal the urgency of her request.

"Roisin did it. But still stung me for the cash."

"Where, Bryan?"

"She showed me the receipt, but it only had the cost on it—five quid or so. It was just a bit of till roll."

Helen stared at Bryan, knowing she would get no more from him. Whoever their killer was, he was meticulous, precise and ultra-cautious. A pro. But this only made Helen more determined to catch him. And as each small piece of the jigsaw fitted together, she felt she was getting closer to the moment when they would finally be face-to-face. At times like this, Helen had no thoughts for her own safety—she would die doing this job; she knew that—and she longed for that encounter. Things were building to a climax now—Helen felt sure of that—and she was determined to be in at the death.

122

"I don't expect your forgiveness and I don't deserve it. I could try to explain myself, my reasons, but I won't embarrass myself. What I did was wrong, pure and simple, so I'll get my things, write my resignation letter and be out of your hair."

Lloyd Fortune hadn't once looked up as he said this, the words tumbling out in a sudden rush. He clearly wanted this to be over as quickly as possible.

Even though he and Helen were closeted away in her office, Lloyd could tell the team outside had half an eye on proceedings and he wanted to be away from their curiosity and censure.

"I would like to know why, Lloyd," Helen said slowly. "Because I think you're a good copper and basically a decent guy, so I would like to know why."

Lloyd hung his head—he had been afraid she might take this line.

"But we don't have time for that now. I've had officers resign on me before because of personal indiscretions, officers who I miss now, so I'm going to ask you not to write that letter."

Lloyd looked up at her, suddenly wrong-footed.

"We have a major investigation going on, which you should be helping me lead. But your focus has been elsewhere—that is what is truly unforgivable."

Lloyd took the hit—he knew it was justified.

"However, we need every available officer on this now. And I believe in second chances. So first we find Ruby. Then we deal with you. Okay?"

"Keys. Let's focus on the keys."

The entire team had been called to the incident room. Helen, flanked by Lloyd Fortune and DC Sanderson, led the discussion.

"We think this is how he gains access, so we need to check out every key cutter in Southampton. It's a big job, but we don't have any other choice. We'll start centrally and work out. To narrow the search a little, let's start with shops that Isobel Lansley passed on her route to and from university. McAndrew?"

"So this is a full breakdown of her route," the reliable DC responded, handing out stapled A4 sheets to the assembled officers. "You'll find a breakdown of the route by street name, plus a map showing her route in red. She left her flat in Dagnall Street, turning right onto Chesterton Avenue past a small parade of shops. She would then walk to the city center along Paxton Road, before cutting through the WestQuay and on to Lower Granton Street. From there . . ."

McAndrew ran through the rest of her route, highlighting possible points of interest. Helen had hauled in a couple of bodies from the data analysis unit and they proved to be a godsend now. They speed-typed, bringing up several possible key-cutting shops en route. Sanderson wrote them up on the board and detailed officers to check them out. Though they were only inching forward, Helen was pleased to see the team finally pulling together. Even Sanderson and Lucas seemed to be getting on.

As the selected officers snatched up their jackets and hurried off, Helen addressed those who remained. "The rest of you will focus on the other girls now. We need to find overlaps with Isobel's route that will narrow the search still further. Pippa might have walked down Chesterton Avenue to get to the city center, and we know she worked in the WestQuay shopping center, so there's two possibles for starters. Let's forensically examine their routines and see what that throws up. Roisin didn't work and neither did Ruby, so where did they go, what did they do?"

Helen paused a moment before she finished, pleased by the sense of determination that shone from the faces of her team now:

"Find the link and we find our man."

123

"First things first—I don't want my name anywhere near this. I've got enough problems as it is."

"Of course. We won't publish anything you don't want us to."

Emilia had told this little white lie many times in her career. Oddly this time she actually meant it—if this lead proved important in cracking the "Bodies on the Beach" case, then her source would get the royal treatment. Emilia surveyed the woman opposite her. She guessed she was in her early fifties, but she looked older. She had a drinker's face—bloodshot and jowelly—and the yellow fingers and teeth of a smoker. Her voice was deep and she was slightly overweight, but there was something in the eyes—a low cunning, a spark of wicked humor—that nevertheless drew you in. If Emilia met this woman on the street, she would hold her purse tight and move on quickly, but she had her professional face on today and looked only too pleased to be seated with her in this grim backstreet pub.

"Another drink, Jane?"

Jane Fraser nodded and soon Emilia was back, clutching a pint of Best and a double Jameson's. The woman threw the whiskey back in one go, then got stuck into the pint.

"So, tell me about the tattoo?"

"How about a little down payment first, eh?" Jane said swiftly.

Emilia had been expecting this and immediately slid a brown envelope across the table. "Five hundred pounds. Best I can do for now."

Jane paused, giving Emilia a filthy look. For a horrible moment, Emilia thought she was going to get up and walk out. But then she picked up the packet and started leafing through the notes and Emilia knew she was fine.

"The tattoo, Jane."

Jane pocketed the money, sniffed unpleasantly, then replied:

"She got it done when she was eleven. She and her brother went to the parlor together—probably half-inched the money from me—and they both got it done. A poxy little bluebird on their shoulders. Just right for those little lovebirds."

Emilia eyed up the prodigious display of tattoos that covered Jane's arms and shoulders. They were not cute—they were aggressive and highly sexual in their content. "Why a bluebird?"

"God knows. Never asked. Perhaps they wanted to fly away together?"

She laughed unpleasantly, before the coughing started up again. Once the fit had relented, she lit up. It was banned in here, of course, but no one in this hole was going to stop her.

"What happened to her?"

"My Summer died, didn't she? Heroin overdose. Ben went looking for her when she didn't come home. Found her in the park. Covered in vomit she was, her eyes clamped shut. Silly sod thought she was asleep. Had to be prised off her by the police in the end—he was convinced she'd wake up and be back to normal any second. Wouldn't let go of her, they said."

"Ben? He's your son?"

Jane grunted a yes.

"Was he an addict too?"

"God, no. Her brother didn't have the balls for that and he was only small when she died. Twelve or so."

Emilia scribbled this down and considered her next question. "What happened to him?"

"Stuck around for a bit, but he and I had never got on, so after a few weeks, he took off."

Emilia had a bad feeling they were winding up to a massive dead end. "And you've not seen him since?"

"Didn't say that, did I? Saw him a few months back—in town, you know."

"So, where does he live?"

"I don't know."

"Come on, Jane. You just said—"

"He wouldn't tell me. Didn't want me hanging about, I guess."

Emilia didn't push it—she could tell more was coming by the sly look on Jane Fraser's face. She pulled Emilia in close, so close she could smell the stink of stale tobacco on her breath as she whispered:

"But I do know where he works."

124

He lay on the dirty bed, his mind full of strange and exciting thoughts. He had been so blind for so long, trying to see gold in the heart of a worthless slut. Now that he could see again, he couldn't stop smiling. He felt light as a feather. He had stood and watched Summer until she closed the curtains and retreated inside. He had then done a couple of circuits of the street, checking for CCTV, street lighting, as well as the names on the bells at her house. Like all the places round there, it had been divided into numerous flats. He had been pleased to see that the names on the top and bottom bells sounded foreign. Far less likely to kick up if they did hear or see anything. But he would make sure they didn't. He was pretty practiced at this now, after all.

As he'd walked home, his head had been full of her. Those bewitching eyes, the tenderness of her touch, her gentle South Coast accent—identical to his of course. He had kissed his fingers and pressed them to his tattoo—then chuckled at the extravagant nature of his tribute. People must think him mad.

As thoughts of her overwhelmed him, he undid his fly and slipped his hand inside his trousers. He had been denying himself for so long, but now it felt so natural, so right. As he closed his eyes and let his mind drift, he saw them back there, two little conspirators hiding in the attic room. Whenever their mother came home, they always scurried up there to avoid her sharp tongue and rough hand. It was their little refuge—she was a heavy smoker and could never be arsed to climb up after them—and for them it was like a magical kingdom. It was only full of junk, but to them it was their world. They would open up the old doll's house and play with the two cracked figures inside, dreaming up all kinds of scenarios in which they lived happily, in splendor and comfort. At these times the dirt and damp of the attic didn't register—they were safe in the cocoon of their fantasy.

Sometimes the fantasy worked; at other times reality intruded—usually because of noises downstairs. They lived at the top of a rickety old terraced house, and the loose, creaking steps in the communal parts always gave them warning of their mother's approach. If she was marching up, it meant she was in a mood or having an episode. If the steps were slow and irregular, it meant she was stoned. And if there was more than one pair of feet, it meant she had "company."

Ben hated drugs, never touched them, but his mother couldn't get enough of them. She funded her habit by fraud, stealing and occasionally bringing foreign sailors home from the dockside bars. They didn't pay much, but they came and went pretty quickly. When she was "entertaining," Ben and Summer would lie dead still, peering through the floorboards into the flat's only bedroom. They didn't understand what they saw at first—believing the men were hurting their mother—but at the end of it everyone seemed happy. And after a while, they began to realize that these grunting, half-naked men were taking pleasure in these acts and that on occasion their mother seemed to be too.

It was only when they were older—Summer was fourteen and Ben eleven—that they truly understood. He had been surprised when Summer slipped her hand into his trousers, but he didn't mind.

Later, they went further, exploring each other's bodies, when their mother was entertaining those men below. Their little private joke. Did their mother suspect anything? If she did, she never said anything. As long as Summer was on hand to run down to the park for her next baggie, that was all that mattered.

The thought of this made him angry. He tried to concentrate on his fantasy, but he could feel his desire ebbing away now. His fury at his mother for dragging Summer away from him into the vile world of drugs still burned strong. He had seen that awful woman not three months ago. He was shocked to see her and his first reaction had been to beat the living hell out of her. He was older, bigger now—she wouldn't have stood a chance. But she wasn't worth it and he had bigger fish to fry, so he'd said a few curt words to her and sent her on her way.

There was no point continuing; he was too angry to focus on pleasure now. Zipping up his trousers, he rose from the bed and headed down to the ground floor. His mind was turning and he walked straight into the old utility area. It looked like a bloody school chemistry lab now and stank as bad too. But he always liked it here. He always felt a sense of achievement in its narrow confines. It had taken him a long time to learn how to distill trichloroethylene, but when he had done so he was childishly pleased with himself. He remembered the first sniff of it—the pleasant light-headed feeling it gave him. He laughed too as he remembered his experiments with dosage. There were numerous rats in the house and he didn't discourage their presence, as they were useful for his experiments. He'd killed a few before he got the saturation levels in the wool right, of course, but practice makes perfect.

This brought him up short. Excited as he was about the future, there was still the present to deal with. Now that the real Summer had returned, *she* was surplus to requirements and he just wanted her out. So, summoning his resolve, he unlocked the basement door and descended into the darkness.

125

"Do you think she's on the level?" Helen's heart was pounding, her tone urgent.

"To be honest I think it's so odd it has to be true."

Emilia and Helen were huddled in the outside courtyard beloved of Southampton Central's smokers. Mercifully they were alone today.

"I don't think Jane Fraser has the imagination to make something like that up. It sounds like the two children were very close. They always shared the same bed, never went to school, they lived in each other's pockets. And I don't blame them, to be honest—their mother had no love for them. Clearly didn't even know who their fathers were, so . . ."

"So they were the world to each other."

Emilia nodded, then continued:

"Apparently the son—Ben—was ungovernable after Summer's death. Police, doctors, social services—nobody could handle him."

"Because he was mad with grief."

"Still is mad with grief," Emilia added, echoing Helen's thoughts.

"And you're sure about this address?"

"Well, I haven't been down there, but I know it."

"Good. Thank you, Emilia."

Helen was halfway to the door when Emilia called out:

"Usual rules?"

"You'll get your exclusive," Helen said over her shoulder as she hurried back into the station.

"So the address is a boot-heeling and key-cutting concession in the WestQuay shopping center. It's called WestKeys."

Nobody groaned at the bad pun. The team was hanging on Helen's words, processing this major development.

"I'll need volunteers for a surveillance unit to go down there." Helen was pleased to see a dozen hands shoot up. "But before we go, let's double-check our facts. Pippa Briers worked in the WestQuay shopping center, so it would have been convenient for her to get her keys cut there. Ditto Isobel Lansley, who walked through the center every day on her way to lectures."

"Roisin Murphy went to a free mums and babies group that was held in the crèche at the shopping center," DC McAndrew chipped in.

"And Ruby?"

"Ruby used to hang out in the center with her mates. Window-shopping, getting up to no good."

"Then it fits. They took their keys there and walked into Ben

Fraser's life. They looked just like his sister, so he kept a key, stalked them, then abducted them."

"But to make them perfect—a replica of his sister—he would have to 'customize' them," DC Sanderson interjected.

"The tattoo," Helen responded, "and possibly more besides."

"Where does he get the stuff, though, the trichloroethylene?" DC Grounds queried.

"Let's think about what Jim Grieves said," Helen countered. "Trichloroethylene is used in cleaning agents, solvents but also boot polish. You could perhaps extract it from boot polish—"

"Without ever drawing attention to yourself. No trail of any kind."

"But why does he starve them? If he loves these girls?"

DC Lucas's question hung in the air for a moment, before Helen replied:

"Why don't we go and ask him?"

126

"Hello, Ruby."

Ruby had crawled into the corner and stared up at her captor with ill-concealed fear.

"Don't be afraid. I'm not going to hurt you."

Ruby kept her eyes riveted to him. The more he insisted he wasn't going to hurt her, the more convinced she was that he would.

He sat down on the bed a few feet away and looked around the room as if seeing it for the first time. "I have a confession to make."

He smiled now, looking for all the world as if he were blissfully happy. "I made a mistake."

Ruby stared at him. What was he up to? Where was this going?

"I got the wrong girl. I shouldn't have taken you. I'm sorry."

He seemed genuinely penitent. And oddly relaxed.

"What are you going to do to me?" Ruby asked, her voice shaking as fear bit.

"What do you think I'm going to do to you?"

He half laughed as he said it, as if she were the one who was mad, not he. "I'm going to let you go."

127

"Is there another way in?" Helen barked, pulling Sanderson aside, her frustration finally getting the better of her.

"Not according to the architect's plans," Sanderson countered.

They had arrived at the WestQuay shopping center discreetly—fifteen officers, all casually dressed as if for shopping—and fanned out, taking up their various vantage points. A few passes confirmed what was obvious straightaway. Despite the fact that it was only five p.m., WestKeys was shut.

They couldn't force the shutters open without causing a scene and possibly alerting the suspect—or friends of his—to their presence. So Helen was keen to find another way in. But the shop was small—a glorified kiosk, really, sandwiched between bigger, brighter outlets—and had no rear entrance.

"Keep our eye on it," said Helen, handing over the surveillance to Sanderson and marching over to DC McAndrew, who stood with her mobile clamped to her ear.

"What have you got?"

McAndrew held her hand over the mouthpiece as she replied: "WestKeys is owned by an Edward Loughton."

"So Ben Fraser is just an employee. Can we raise Loughton? If he can give us a home address for Ben Fraser, then we might still be able to save Ruby."

"Loughton died three years ago. He's got a sister who lives somewhere locally. We're trying to track her down."

McAndrew resumed the call, spelling out the name of the woman they now sought. As she did so, Helen paced up and down. Every delay, every setback would cost them dear now. They were so close to unmasking him, but would it all be for nothing? Thoughts of Alison and Jonathan Sprackling arrowed into her mind now—she could sense their desperation, their longing to be reunited with the girl they had rescued all those years ago. Helen refused to believe that their kindness had been for nothing, that Ruby could be snuffed out as cruelly as the other girls. But she was powerless to influence matters, and the fact that the shop had been shut early filled her with alarm. Any deviation from his normal routine was bad news for them.

And bad news for Ruby.

128

Helen stopped in her tracks as soon as she entered the lobby of the Great Southern. She had been in a world of her own, walking automatically toward the lift bank, but the sight of Daniel Briers at reception brought her to a halt. He had a suitcase with him and by his side stood a tall lady with long dark hair and an elegantly swollen belly.

"Daniel?"

He turned and on seeing Helen smiled—but the look was forced and unconvincing.

"Are you leaving?"

"I am," he replied, failing to look her in the eye. "I wanted to stay for the duration as you know. But obviously I've got other responsibilities, so . . . This is Kristy, my wife."

"DI Helen Grace. I'm running the investigation—"

"I know who you are," Kristy Briers said, shaking hands cursorily with Helen.

"You've got all our contact details, haven't you, in case there's any news . . . ?" Daniel continued. His concern and interest were genuine, but Helen could sense he just wanted to be out of this conversation.

"Of course. In fact, I was just coming here to update you. There have been some significant dev—"

"Do you always update people in hotel rooms? At night?"

Kristy's question was delivered calmly but had an edge to it that was hard to miss.

"No, but I made your husband a promise to keep him up to speed with the very latest developments. And I was honoring that promise."

Helen's tone was even but firm. She had undoubtedly put herself in an awkward position by handling Daniel Briers personally, but they had done nothing wrong, so why should she be castigated for showing compassion?

Pulling the couple aside, Helen told them about the police search for Ben Fraser and her hope that they would soon make an arrest. Daniel asked a few questions, but the conversation swiftly came to a natural conclusion. There was nothing more to say.

"Thank you, Helen. For everything. It would mean the world to me to see justice done."

He spoke from the heart, but the words still sounded strange to Helen. Everything was slightly *off* tonight. Daniel shook her hand formally and with a brief look back walked toward the awaiting car. Kristy made to follow, then paused, turning back to Helen.

"Don't feel too bad. It happens to them all in the end."

"I'm sorry."

"I've been with Daniel for over ten years now. I know what he's like—"

"Kristy, I really don't know what you're allud—"

"The thing about Daniel is that he likes attention. Loves to have a pretty face staring up at him, an arm round his shoulder. Or someone to keep him warm at night. It's like an addiction. There's no other way to explain it. But you should never take it personally. It's not you he's interested in. It's himself."

Kristy stared at Helen. She was victorious, but it was a Pyrrhic victory for a woman who seemed accustomed to betrayal.

"I should probably leave him, but I guess it's a bit too late for that, isn't it?" She patted her belly and looked Helen in the eye. "Don't contact him directly again. If there is any news, get another officer to call. Preferably a male one."

She turned on her heel and walked toward the car. Daniel held the door open for her, shutting it gently behind her once she'd climbed in. A brief apologetic look at Helen and he was gone. Leaving Helen alone and feeling more foolish than ever.

129

Whatever the weather, there is always something nice about Friday morning. The dark clouds that hung over Southampton spat contemptuously on the early-morning workers hurrying through the streets to their shops and offices, yet in spite of this Ben Fraser thought he detected optimism and happiness in their expressions. Only a few more hours and the weekend would begin. Who wouldn't smile at that?

He too had hope in his heart this morning. There was still much to be done, of course—some of it pleasant, some of it not—but when the path is clear in front of you, life is easy. He had risen early, washed and dressed by six a.m. and been on the streets not long afterward. On these early reconnaissance trips, he always wore the regulation uniform of city workers in the summertime—jeans, T-shirt, sunglasses and a record bag casually slung over his right shoulder. He looked for all the world like a young man going places. But there was only one place he was going today.

Blenheim Road in Portswood looked even more drab in the daylight. Last night, it had had a kind of faded glamor, but now it appeared in its true colors—a haven for students and wasters. Impoverished young workers—like Summer—liked it because the rents were cheap, but the whole place had the tired, lazy feel of a student hive. You could almost smell the ganja fumes as you walked up the street, Ben thought to himself.

He had barely been at his vantage point five minutes when Summer appeared. The gods really were smiling on him now. She looked even lovelier than he remembered. Crisp white blouse, smart charcoal suit and long suede boots that *click, click, click*ed down the street away from him.

Ben slipped out from his hiding place and padded down the street after her, seemingly intent on a phone call—on an iPhone that had given up the ghost years ago. He muttered nonsense into it, amusing himself by the random collision of words. He didn't care what he was saying. His real focus was fifty yards ahead of him.

She stopped at a nearby Costa to pick up a latte and a croissant, slipping the latter into her bag to eat at her desk later. Ben wondered if this was her habitual breakfast stop-off—time would tell. She walked to the bus stop and Ben kept pace with her, slipping on to the number 28 bus behind her.

Watching her at close quarters, he felt himself blessed as never before. It had been so long, but here she was. Back where she should be. He took in every detail of her hair, her face, her clothes, her mannerisms, her habits. He noted that she left her bag open, having removed her phone to text. A little trusting, he thought, but not unhelpful—he could glimpse her set of keys within. What else did she have in there? he wondered.

She got off the bus in Nicholstown and Ben was soon padding behind her, making a mental note of her route to the employment agency where she worked. She was so oblivious to his presence, he even managed to clock the key code she tapped in to enter the lobby—all useful information for the future.

Soon she disappeared from view, but Ben wasn't downhearted. It had been a successful trip. Far more successful than he had any right to expect. But luck was with him now and slowly, but surely, he was climbing inside her life.

130

Ruby lay on the bed and smiled. She hadn't slept a wink—she'd been too wired following Ben's visit to even consider that. She was going home. This was the one outcome she had never really expected throughout her incarceration and yet it was true. Soon she would see her mum, dad, Cassie and Conor. She would be back where she belonged.

Her eyes drooped—her body, her brain demanded sleep now—but still Ruby resisted. Previously she had wanted to take refuge in dreams, to escape the grim misery of everyday life down here. But now she feared sleep. If she went to sleep, who was to say that she wouldn't dream that she was still there, with him, trapped in that dark hell?

She pinched herself hard, twice. "Not long now, Ruby," she told herself, pulling her legs off the bed and forcing herself to pace back and forth. Stay awake, stay alert and before long she would see natural light again. The thought made her laugh, although in truth she was a little scared of the idea—surely it would blind her, so accustomed had she become to this dead gloom. But it would be a small price to pay for her freedom.

What had occasioned his sudden change of heart? Had he grown tired of her? Or had there been some development aboveground? Had contact been made? A ransom been paid? It seemed unlikely, but was there another credible explanation? Perhaps even now he was negotiating with them, trading his liberty for Ruby's?

The thought thrilled Ruby. Perhaps he would never come back here again. Safer by far to give up her location and move on, before he could be caught or traced. Surely that was what he'd do? It was what Ruby would do.

For once his absence didn't bother her. Usually she wondered what he was up to—what he was thinking and doing—and how that might impact upon her. But today she didn't. Today she sat quiet and content, dreaming of the future. Dreaming of *her* future.

131

Helen sped through the city center, her Kawasaki cutting a swath through the static traffic. They had finally got an address for Edward Loughton's sister, and Helen was on her way there now. If she could help them locate Fraser, then there was still hope for Ruby.

Helen should have used a pool car—complete with lights and sirens—but it was quicker by bike, and instinct told her to handle this alone. Ben Fraser might live with Alice Loughton for all she knew—they couldn't afford to announce their arrival. Sanderson, McAndrew, Lucas and Edwards would follow close behind in unmarked cars, but Helen would take the lead.

She pulled up sharply by the curb. Melrose Crescent was an impressive street, lined with handsome Victorian villas. Somehow this street had survived the Second World War bombs—a proud reminder of Southampton's architectural past. Edward Loughton had owned a number of shops and had clearly done well for himself. Having no wife or children, he'd bequeathed his estate to his younger sister—though, now aged seventy-four, Alice Loughton could hardly be called young.

Pulling off her helmet and shaking out her long hair, Helen climbed the wide stone steps up to the imposing front door. She rang the bell but resisted rapping the knocker. No point alarming anyone—yet. She waited patiently, jogging from foot to foot as the tension coursed through her.

There was no movement within, so Helen rang the bell again. *Please, God, let her be in.* Still nothing. She turned back to the street and was surprised to see Sanderson and McAndrew pulling up fifty yards away. They had made it here quickly, but had their journey been for nothing?

A sound made her turn. What was that? Footsteps. Yes, definitely, slow, measured footsteps approaching the front door. Through the mottled glass a figure appeared. Some fussing with the locks and then the door crept open, and an elderly woman's face appeared above the security chain.

"Can I help you?" she intoned suspiciously.

"DI Helen Grace," Helen replied, raising her warrant card for inspection.

"What can I do for you?" Alice replied, never once taking her eyes off the warrant card.

"I'd like to talk to you about your brother. And about Ben Fraser."

Her eyes narrowed. Was that suspicion Helen saw there? Anger? The elderly woman stared at her for what seemed like an eternity, then slipped off the chain and opened the door.

"You'd better come in, then."

Nodding her thanks, Helen stepped inside, the heavy door slamming firmly shut behind her.

132

Ben walked toward the WestQuay with a spring in his step. After all the recent trouble, things were shaping up nicely. Summer seemed her usual trusting self and as for Ruby, well . . . she wouldn't be a problem for much longer. She believed she was going to be released, which would buy him a day or so before the shouting and moaning started. When would she realize that she had been abandoned? And how would she react? The first one had resisted for nearly two weeks, banging at the door, screaming and shouting. And the third one was just as bad. The second one was less bright and had given up more quickly, which was much less fun. He liked it when they ranted and raved and begged. He couldn't hear them upstairs, of course, so he had to descend into the basement when he wanted to listen to them. As soon as they heard his footsteps approaching, they started up with the pleading. He would never open the door, though sometimes he teased them, slipping the key into the lock before removing it again. The thought still made Ben smile.

Of course, this time the disposal would be more complicated. Carsholt Beach had been perfect for him in its wild isolation—but events had forced the change. He had already made the decision to bury Ruby in the New Forest. If he took her there in the dead of night, he would be unmolested and he had to admit there was a pleasing symmetry about burying her where he had first burned her clothes. The vegetation was so thick round there, the chance of anyone stumbling upon the burial site was remote.

Ben was so wrapped up in his thoughts that only now did he realize that he had walked straight past his shop and all the way to the end of the arcade. Shaking his head, he turned and began to head back toward WestKeys. He was already late opening—he didn't want to arouse anyone's suspicions by . . .

Suddenly he ground to a halt. Instinctively he turned to look in the shoe shop window next to him. Sweat was already breaking out on his forehead and he was surprised to see his hands were shaking. Was he overreacting? Seeing things that weren't there? He walked into the shoe shop to gather himself and, turning, looked through the shop window back into the concourse. The young black man in the shirt and jacket was sitting at the café opposite WestKeys, but his attention was definitely directed toward the shop, rather than toward the newspaper that sat uselessly on the table in front of him.

Directing his gaze upward, Ben spotted another one. A young woman on the upper concourse. She seemed to be texting, yet her gaze kept straying to the WestKeys frontage. Ben was out of the shoe shop now, walking steadily but quickly past his shop. En route, he saw one more—a young man, sitting by the water feature, looking at his watch, as if waiting for someone.

Ben knew exactly who he was waiting for and wasn't going to give him the satisfaction. Hurrying toward the emergency exit, he burst into the stairwell and ran toward the exit.

133

The incident room was empty, which seemed fitting. Ceri Harwood stood alone, her eyes flicking over the board, taking in the pictures of Pippa, Roisin, Isobel and Ruby. The entire team was out hunting Ben Fraser—this major operation was reaching its climax. With luck, Fraser would soon be in custody, but this thought gave Harwood little pleasure. She would be excluded from the triumph, isolated in defeat.

How had she misjudged things so badly? There had been other DIs, women especially, who had threatened her position before. She had crushed them easily, exiling them from her unit, replacing them with ambitious, compliant officers who would dance to her tune. But Helen Grace had refused to buckle, had always found ways to evade the traps laid for her. Perhaps it was time to acknowledge that she lacked the imagination to deal with Helen Grace. Perhaps she was too bound by protocol, by rules and regulations, to deal with an adversary who was constantly surprising. In the final analysis, she just wasn't good enough to beat her.

It was time to go and see Fisher now. She had typed out her resignation letter, had her excuses ready—the easy lie of wanting to spend more time with her family. That bit almost made her laugh. She had the girls, of course, but their family was fractured now—weekend visits to their dad would be a constant reminder of that. Even now this seemed such an odd thought. They had come to Southampton so full of optimism and yet the end result had been catastrophic for everyone. She would have to rebuild her career, her life, elsewhere now—it was time for someone else to take the lead. *Please, God, Fisher doesn't give the job to Grace,* Ceri Harwood thought as she left the incident room. She had suffered enough indignities already.

134

Alice Loughton stared at Helen Grace. Was that suspicion in her eyes? Or worse, incomprehension? She had said nothing since Helen started outlining the urgent reason for her visit and Helen had a nasty feeling that she wasn't taking in the import of her words. Finally, however, the old woman opened her mouth and said in a croaky whisper:

"You're sure?"

"We are."

"And how long . . . ?"

"We're not sure, but we believe he's been targeting women in the Southampton area for nearly five years."

"I don't believe it."

This was what Helen had been afraid of. "I know it's hard to take in—and I'd like to reiterate that neither you nor your brother is in any trouble—but we do need your help . . ."

"I only met him once or twice, but he always seemed such a gentle boy."

"I appreciate that—"

"Edward found him sleeping in the shopping center. In one of the loading bays. He was only small—fourteen or so. Edward offered to take him back to his mother, but the boy begged him not to. So he went to a hostel instead—"

"Where does he live now, Alice?"

"Edward took an interest in him after," she replied, seeming not to hear Helen's question. "Gave him a job in the shop. He's been working there—Lord knows—well over ten years now. Edward *relied* upon him. He was a damn sight more reliable than some of the people in his other shops."

"I do understand that, Alice, but it's vitally important we talk to him now. If he is innocent, then we can exclude him from our investigation and move on—"

"Edward was like a father to him, which was why he was so generous in his will."

"He left him money?"

"No! Edward didn't like money—not in the way you mean. He liked assets—houses, businesses and so on."

"So he gave Ben Fraser property?"

"Don't look so surprised. It's a tumbledown affair in a dubious part of town, but all these places have their day, don't they, as the town expands? Edward thought it would see Ben right in the long term."

"And do you know where it is?"

"Of course I do. I'm not completely doolally," she replied, giving Helen a hard stare.

"Then tell me, please. A young woman's life is at stake."

The old woman sized Helen up, as if trying to work out if she could trust her or not, before eventually she replied:

"He lives at fourteen Alfreton Terrace. It's not five minutes from here."

135

Ben let out a roar and drove his fist into the glass. The mirror shattered and fell to the floor as the blood oozed from his lacerated knuckles. Without hesitation, he stamped on it, his heavy boots pounding it to oblivion.

How? How? How?

How had they found him so quickly? Those bodies were dug up less than a week ago and already they were staking out his shop. It was purely a matter of luck—and their incompetence—that they hadn't caught him there and then. He let out an anguished howl and drove his head against the exposed brick wall. It couldn't be happening, not when Summer had just come back into his life, when he was so close . . .

How long would it take them to find this place? The home that he had so lovingly constructed for their future happiness? It couldn't be long now. Once they found out who owned the shop, they would talk to that old bitch. If he was lucky she might be barmy by now, but he couldn't take that chance. There was nothing for him to do but disappear.

He still had the van. They wouldn't know about that. And the fake plates would make it hard for them to find him. He could visit Summer tonight. He had never made such a direct approach before, but needs must. If they could be together before the evening news broke, then they might make it away completely.

Marching to the utility room, Ben picked up the squat glass bottle. The rubber bung was still firmly in place and he could see that there was enough clear liquid inside for his needs. He snatched up a couple of old rags and shoved them in his pocket. He turned to leave, then paused. This place would be like a treasure trove when the cops turned up. This distillation unit, his mementos of Summer, not to mention that thing in the doll's house downstairs. Bitterness gripped his heart as he thought of those faceless policemen and -women passing judgment on him as they patiently fingered his possessions . . .

Suddenly Ben knew what he had to do. Throwing the cardboard boxes aside, riffling through the detritus of this small room, he found what he was looking for. A large can of turpentine. And nearby it on the shelf, an old lighter, a relic of his smoking days.

Picking them both up, he stalked over to the trapdoor and hauled it roughly open.

136

Ruby looked up hopefully as the door swung open. *Is this it, then?* But as soon as she saw the look on his face, all hope died within her. He looked at her with ill-disguised contempt and, worse, with intent. Ruby scrabbled off the bed as he approached, bounding toward the other side of the table. But she wasn't quick enough, his left fist slamming into her stomach, knocking the wind out of her.

As she doubled over, his knee connected sharply with her nose and for a moment she blacked out. When she came to, she found herself lying on the floor. Her wrists were pinched and hurting—when she turned she saw that he was securing her bound hands to the metal bedstead.

"Please."

He ignored her, instead producing a battered metal can, whose contents he now poured onto the floor around her. The smell of the clear liquid was overpowering. Suddenly Ruby had an inkling of what he was going to do—but it didn't make any sense. This was *his* doll's house. Why would he destroy something that he'd created? What had gone wrong?

"Please don't do this. I'll do anything. Please don't kill me."

The can was now empty and he tossed it aside. Ruby's pleas seemed to have no effect on him—he now produced a cigarette lighter from his pocket.

"I'll be your Summer. I *am* your Summer. Please don't hurt me."

Still he refused to look at her, instead igniting the lighter. He looked at the dancing flame in his hands and as he did so a thin smile crept over his face. Finally he looked up, his eyes boring into her:

"See you on the other side."

And with that, he tossed the lighter toward her.

137

Helen wrenched the throttle toward her and the bike kicked forward. Cutting down Queen's Drive, she cornered sharply onto the ring road, immediately upping her speed to ninety miles per hour. Finally they had the lead they wanted—the breakthrough they had been searching for since Pippa's body was discovered—and yet Helen suddenly felt with total conviction that every second counted. It was as if time had just sped up, pushing them toward some desperate and uncertain conclusion.

Six unmarked cars followed her. They would arrive silently—no sirens, no lights—and once the Firearms Unit arrived to support them, they would go in swift and hard. There was no telling how a psychopath like Ben Fraser would react to the realization that his carefully constructed universe was about to implode. Many serial predators killed their victims and then themselves. Others tried to take some police officers with them. You could never predict how they would react.

Suddenly Helen saw it and her heart skipped a beat. A thin plume of smoke rising into the sky. He *knew.* Helen didn't know how, couldn't even say for sure yet that the smoke was coming from Alfreton Terrace—and yet what other explanation could there be for this sudden and unexpected sight in a lonely part of town?

There were no school mums or passersby round here, so Helen upped her speed still further, hurtling down Constance Avenue and into Alfreton Terrace. There it was—number 14—a horrible, decaying impression of a Victorian home. Lifeless, rotting and nondescript—apart from the smoke that now seeped from the ill-fitting windows.

Helen leaped off her Kawasaki while it was still moving, the discarded bike sliding awkwardly to a stop in the yard. Sanderson was only a minute or two behind in the car, so Helen squeezed her radio as she ran toward the house. "Call the fire service. I'm going in."

There was a shout of protest from Sanderson, but Helen didn't respond, ramming the radio into her leather jacket as she sprinted toward the door. Without stopping, she launched herself at it. Pain seared through her shoulder as it connected with the heavy wooden door. The door buckled but stood firm, denying her entry. A bolt at the bottom was drawn, barring her way. It suggested that their killer was safety-conscious—and, more than that, that he was within.

Helen drew her baton and kicked at the stubborn bolt. Her steel-capped boots connected aggressively, and after a couple of kicks, the bolt flew off its hinges. The door fell crashing to the ground behind, sending up a huge plume of dust. Helen hurried inside, Sanderson and McAndrew pulling up outside just in time to see her disappear into the burning house.

Helen scanned the front room for signs of life, but there were none. Her only thought was to find a way down. His victims had been kept in darkness, so if there was a basement . . .

She darted her head into the living room, alive to the danger of ambush, but it was empty. She hauled the dirty rug off the floor but, finding nothing, headed straight into the kitchen. It was covered with heavily soiled lino, which looked secure enough, so ignoring it, Helen headed to the back of the house.

And there it was. A trapdoor. It had two bolts on its upper surface to secure it from above, but they had been left unsecured. It was like an open invitation. For the first time, Helen paused. Smoke was billowing out of it and who knew what lay within—was Ruby even there? Was it an ambush—one last stand against those who would deny Ben Fraser his fantasy?

Then a cry. Faint, but urgent. And unquestionably female. Now Helen didn't hesitate, opening the trapdoor and plunging down into the abyss. The metal rungs of the ladder were already heating up, but Helen's leather gloves gave her some protection and she made it to the bottom swiftly.

She lifted the tinted visor of her helmet and looked around. It was an amazing sight—a warren of little corridors leading God knew where. At intervals, bare bulbs covered in plastic casings were attached to the wall, illuminating the path. It was so well manufactured it was almost like being in a mine, a shocking testimony to the concerted, precise nature of Ben Fraser's madness. The thought made Helen shiver and she gripped her baton a little harder.

Another cry, closer this time. Helen plunged forward, hopelessly waving her arm in front of her to clear the smoke that surrounded her. It was filling her nostrils, creeping into her eyes; it was completely intolerable. A fire in these damp conditions would create great billows of smoke. Helen slammed her visor down again—it would make her vision darker, but with it up she couldn't keep her eyes open.

She navigated by sound now, using Ruby's plaintive cries to guide her. Instinctively she wanted to call out to her, to reassure her that help was on its way, but he was down here somewhere. And she dared not announce her presence.

Helen cannoned off a rough dirt wall, her forward momentum suddenly and brutally checked. Using her free hand, she felt her way round the corner, moving carefully but purposefully forward. She had the sense that there was someone with her in the smoke, right behind her, and turning, she swung her baton in wild self-defense. But it connected with nothing, and in the deep gloom Helen could just about make out that she was still alone.

Helen moved forward again. She just wanted to find Ruby and get out of this place. It was getting hotter all the time and harder and harder to breathe. Helen suddenly found herself plunging to the floor, her foot having caught on something solid. In the clear air near the floor, Helen could see she had tripped over the lip of a doorway.

Turning, she could make out another open doorway a few yards ahead of her. The heat was less intense lower down, her vision slightly better, so in spite of the obvious dangers, Helen crawled forward, through the threshold and into the room beyond.

The sight that greeted Helen took her breath away. The room was ablaze. A wooden table and chair had already been consumed by the flames and the other fixtures—an old cooker, an iron bedstead—were next in line. Secured to the heavy bed frame and writhing in agony was the thin frame of Ruby Sprackling. A precise ring of fire encircled her, the killer's sadistic and deliberate method of execution, but Helen was damned if this poor girl was going to die in this hole, so hurdling the flames, she sprinted over to her. As she did so, another wave of heat hit her. The fire was freshly made, but fierce, and they had only seconds before they would be overcome.

Ruby's hands were tied tight with nylon cord, secured to the bed frame with a constrictor knot. Ruby's wrists were already red-raw. There was no way she could wriggle out of the cord's grip, and the bed frame was too strong and too thick to cut through.

Searching desperately for some means of liberation, Helen spotted a small patch of crumbling brickwork in the far wall. Without hesitating, she plunged toward it. Within seconds she was back by Ruby's side, clutching the loose brick in her hand, hammering at the metal bed frame. The strut that Ruby was tethered to protested, then bent before finally snapping in two. Pulling Ruby to her feet, Helen tugged the securing knot up, up and eventually off the severed end of the strut. Immediately Ruby collapsed into Helen's arms, but Helen propped her up, slapping her gently but firmly in the face.

"Stay with me, Ruby."

She half dragged, half walked her through the flames and to the doorway. "Keep going."

Ruby's eyes rolled in their sockets, the smoke filling her lungs, clouding her brain. Helen could tell she wanted to blank out, to sleep, but they had to keep moving. She pinched her hard—eliciting a small reaction—and they moved on once more.

"Not far to go n—"

Helen froze, the words stillborn in her mouth. The lights had suddenly flicked off, plunging them into darkness.

He was down here after all.

138

"Get out of my way."

"You're not going in there."

"For the last time, stand aside or I *will* arrest you."

DC Sanderson was bellowing now, eyeball to eyeball with the fire sergeant who blocked her path. Behind them, black smoke belched from the interior of Ben Fraser's house.

"This is my scene now," he replied, shouting to be heard above the sirens and activity. "This is *my* fire. And until it is under control, you have no authority here. So I would encourage you to step back—"

But Sanderson had already rounded him and was sprinting toward the burning house. There was no way she was leaving Helen alone in there. Her boss had been gone over ten minutes already. The smoke fumes were bad enough out here; what must they be like inside, near the seat of the fire? Helen wouldn't have stayed down there all this time unless something had gone badly wrong.

Sanderson crested the threshold of the house, but even as she did so she felt herself flying backward again, away from the house. A pair of rough hands had her by the shoulders. She lashed out, trying to force her way back into the house, but the heavy, gloved hands of a firefighter dragged her back, pinning her arms by her sides, forcing her to the ground. She continued to thrash, but his knee was now pressed into the small of her back, rendering further resistance futile.

As she lay there pinioned and breathless, the enraged face of the fire sergeant lowered itself to her level.

"If you so much as move a muscle, I will order your colleagues to arrest you. Do I make myself clear?"

Sanderson stared at him, refusing to acknowledge his ultimatum. He was only doing his job, but in her eyes he was condemning Helen to a gruesome death. So when she did finally speak, her response was terse and bitter.

"Go to hell."

139

The darkness clung to them. Smoke filled their lungs. The searing heat was becoming unbearable. Any movement risked announcing their location to the man who was now hunting them. But they had no choice—they had to get out of here.

Switching Ruby to her left side, Helen readied her baton once more. She moved forward, stumbling slightly on the lip of the second doorway. But she didn't hesitate. On and on they went, expecting Ben Fraser to come charging at them at any moment. A change in the heat level made Helen pause. She reached out her hand. She felt a solid dirt wall with space on either side. They were obviously at a junction of some kind. She hadn't spotted one on the way down. Had she taken a wrong turn somehow?

Ruby was now a deadweight, lolling in Helen's aching arm. Reaching down to grasp her ankles, Helen hauled her up and over her shoulder into a fireman's lift. She stumbled slightly with the extra weight, pain ripping through her already damaged shoulder; then, making a split-second decision, she plunged to the left, stumbling forward.

The blow sent her reeling sideways. It was so sudden and savage that she slammed into the side wall, spilling Ruby from her grasp. A second blow to her side landed immediately after, robbing her of breath and cracking her ribs. Now Helen saw him coming at her, a hammer raised, fierce intent in his expression. She raised her baton—but too late—the hammer came crashing down onto her head, sending her reeling backward and shattering her visor. Another blow and she was on the floor, her helmet split.

He raised his hammer again, intent on crushing her skull, but this time Helen lashed out, her baton connecting forcefully with his Adam's apple. For a moment, he appeared stunned, so Helen swung her free arm with all her might, battering the hammer from his grasp. It fell to the floor with a dull thud.

She pulled herself up quickly, but moved straight into his fist, descending upon her with crushing speed. Her head hit the floor hard, the shattered helmet falling apart like a cracked walnut, rendering her defenseless.

Now his hot hands sought out her throat, encircling it and squeezing hard. The smoke was so thick now they could no longer see each other, but at such close quarters it made no odds. They had a hold of each other and were locked in a fight to the death.

Helen rammed the baton against his elbow, trying desperately to break his grip, but he squeezed harder still. At any moment he would crush her larynx and that would be it. Helen thrashed at the side of his head with her baton, but it seemed to have no effect. Her killer would not be denied.

In desperation, Helen rolled sideways as hard as she could,

crashing Ben into the wall. His grip loosened slightly, and pressing her foot against the wall, she swung back forcefully in the opposite direction. This had the desired effect and Ben toppled off onto the floor. Helen scrabbled on top of him, before he could rise, holding her baton at both ends, pushing the thin steel bar down onto his throat with as much strength as she could muster.

She pushed hard, but his fist lashed out, catching her above the left eye. She held firm, increasing the pressure. He was choking now, but Helen didn't let up. His fingers sought out her face, scratching at her eyes, trying to dig into her eye sockets. Helen twisted her head to escape his reach, but he caught her hair, yanking her head down sharply toward his face.

She felt his teeth sink into her left ear and she howled in agony, drinking in plumes of smoke. He was biting so hard—any second now he would bite it clean off. Helen could feel the blood pouring down the side of her face and neck.

Then suddenly his grip weakened. Only slightly, but it was enough to tell Helen she was winning. Pushing down harder on his neck, Helen now felt his mouth open and a small gasp escape as he released his grip on her ear. The fight was over.

Jerking her head up, Helen stumbled away from his corpse, but immediately the tunnel spun around her. She felt faint, nauseated, the smoke filling her mouth and her lungs, rendering her victory meaningless.

She crashed to the floor. Ruby was only a foot from her, but suddenly Helen had no energy to move. The darkness spun around her and for a moment she didn't know where she was. Her face hit the cold concrete and didn't move again.

Helen's eyelids began to droop. Ruby's innocent face would be the last thing she saw. The last thing she would ever see.

140

DC Sanderson stood by the safety barrier, staring daggers at the fire sergeant, who avoided her gaze as he marshaled the activities of the fire teams who had now entered the burning house. Sanderson cursed herself for her stupidity and cowardice. Why had she let Helen go in alone? She knew her boss—she knew that she would plunge inside the house without any fear for her own safety. Why hadn't she spoken up earlier—insisting her boss ride with them—instead of swallowing her concerns? Was it out of respect for her superior, as she'd told herself at the time, or just that she was weak?

She shot a look at McAndrew to see if she looked as guilt-ridden as she did, but suddenly she caught sight of movement by the front door. Vaulting the barrier, she sprinted over to see a fire crew emerging with Ruby in their arms, and moments later, Helen too. Ignoring their repeated warnings to stay back, Sanderson kept pace, desperately searching for signs of life. Ruby had sustained some nasty burns and was clearly unconscious. But what about Helen?

Her boss was covered in soot and dirt. A thick coating of blood clung to the left-hand side of her face, oozing from a deep wound to her ear. Her eyes rolled back in her head—she was unconscious and didn't appear to be breathing.

"What's going on? What's happening?"

The paramedics ignored her questions as they took charge. Sanderson watched on helplessly as they administered oxygen, chest-pumped and searched for a pulse. Why the hell weren't they doing more? Why were they being so measured? Then a brief look from one paramedic to the other—sober and serious. What the hell did that mean?

Oxygen masks were now attached to both women and they were levered up onto the ambulance stretchers and hurried into the respective vehicles. Both ambulances took off at speed and as Sanderson watched them disappear into the distance, she felt tears prick her eyes. This was it, then. Helen's life now hung in the balance. Why *hadn't* she done more?

141

The light was utterly blinding. She held her hand up to shield her eyes from the savage glare, but still multicolored shapes seemed to dance about in front of her. Swiftly she turned away from the water, which burned with the reflection of an unseasonably strong sun, turning her gaze instead to the beach beyond.

Autumn had crept up on them and Steephill Cove was nigh on deserted. Ruby cut a lonely figure standing by the swell of the sea. In her old life she would have balked at the strange isolation of the scene—where were the holidaymakers? The fun? The laughter?—but now it suited her perfectly.

They had driven here almost as soon as Ruby was discharged from the hospital, so strong was her desire to escape the press frenzy in Southampton, to retreat somewhere she felt safe. Her burns were healing well, but she still felt self-conscious about her blistered arms and her short patchy hair. Here she could dress as she pleased, go where she pleased, without the risk of encountering well-wishers who would smile and stare. Everywhere else she was still a newspaper headline—here she could just be Ruby.

Staring at the beautiful beach, framed perfectly by the rugged cliffs, Ruby couldn't help remembering those lonely nights of her incarceration when she'd imagined herself here, daydreams from which she'd been brutally ripped time and again. The fact that her abductor had died twice—first at Helen Grace's hand and then in the fierce conflagration that followed—didn't make Ruby feel any better, or any safer. The memories of her isolation and despair were still too strong to stop herself shaking when she thought of him and her terrible ordeal. He still came to her at night—in vivid, appalling nightmares—and Ruby had hardly slept a wink as a result. Weeks after her liberation, she still felt weak, damaged and unsettled.

But her abductor had not won, and in time she hoped to expunge him from her life completely. It would be a long road—removing the tattoo in the hospital had been the easy bit—and the worst was yet to come. But she *had* won—she must keep telling herself that—and the most eloquent testament to that fact was the view that now stretched out in front of her: this place, this cove, no longer an illusory retreat for her fractured mind, but something real and reassuring. Ruby crouched down, running the wet sand through her fingers over and over again, fighting back tears of relief.

A cry made her look up and there they were—Mum, Dad, Cassie, Conor—meandering their way toward her. They let her have her moments of solitude but were mindful to ensure that she felt loved and supported every moment of every day. Wiping the tears from her eyes, Ruby straightened up and started walking toward them. This was her future now, her happiness.

Finally she had come home.

142

Helen had never seen anyone look so happy. As they strolled across the Common together, the pristine red pram cutting a swath through the fallen leaves, Charlie chatted animatedly about little Jessica's arrival. She laughed at the indignity of a hospital birth, her naked terror during the days immediately afterward and the many lies she had been told about what parenthood was going to be like. The whole process had clearly been bewildering, scary, painful, but through it all slightly amazing too. Given Charlie's history, there was much more riding on this pregnancy than there normally would have been, and Helen was more pleased than she could say that things had worked out so well for her.

Helen had been totally unaware of Charlie's labor, as it had played out during Ruby's rescue. In fact, Helen had first become aware of Charlie's good fortune while lying in the same hospital as she was, awaiting surgery on her ear. The wound that transpired was not too deep and—though it still looked gruesome—would heal in time. Charlie had asked Helen about it, but Helen had moved the conversation on fairly swiftly. After the events of the past few weeks, she wanted to focus on happier thoughts.

So much had changed in such a short period of time. Ceri Harwood had resigned, effective immediately, and had not been seen since. The search was under way for her replacement—Helen having already been offered the post and turned it down. Harwood's disappearance served only to underline the continuing mystery of Robert's whereabouts—now when she thought about Harwood's unpleasant machinations she didn't feel any anger, just a deep sadness at Harwood's having exploited a vacuum in Helen's life for her own selfish ends.

Helen pushed the thought away. She knew she had a tendency to obsess about things that were painful and difficult, but she would not give in to the darkness. Today was a day for celebrating the good things in life. Like the fierce joy Alison Sprackling had exhibited on being reunited with her precious daughter. Or the quiet but equally fierce love that Charlie felt for her baby girl.

Helen had no family to speak of now and at times like this she was wont to distance herself from life, to retreat and hide. But for once she didn't want to. It was a beautiful day and she felt at peace with the world. More than that, she felt connected to it, Charlie having sprung two momentous surprises on her during the course of their morning together. First by asking her to be godmother to Jessica, a request that had rendered Helen temporarily speechless. She had happily accepted the role, of course, once she had recovered from the shock—and a good thing too—for in a subsequent nod to their ever-deepening friendship, Charlie topped off the day's surprises by revealing Jessica's middle name.

Helen.

Don't miss Detective Helen Grace's next chilling case.

LIAR LIAR

Available from New American Library
in June 2016

1

Luke scrambled through the open window and onto the narrow ledge outside. Grasping the plastic gutter above his head, he pulled himself upright. The gutter creaked ominously, threatening to give way at any moment, but Luke couldn't risk letting go. He was dizzy, breathless and very, very scared.

A blast of icy wind roared over him, flapping his thin cotton pajamas like a manic kite. He was already losing the feeling in his feet—the chill from the rough stone creeping up his body—and the sixteen-year-old knew he would have to act quickly if he was to save his life.

Slowly he inched his way forward, peering over the lip of the ledge. The cars, the people below, seemed so small—the hard, unforgiving road so far away. He'd always had a thing about heights, and as he looked down from this top-floor vantage point, his first instinct was to recoil. To turn back into the house. But he stood firm. He couldn't believe what he was contemplating, but he didn't have a choice, so, releasing his grip, he hung his toes over the edge and prepared to jump. He counted down in his head. Three, two, one . . .

Suddenly he lost his nerve, dragging himself back from the brink. His spine connected sharply with the iron window frame and for a moment he rested there, clamping his eyes shut to block out the panic now assailing him. If he jumped, he would die. Surely there had to be another way? Something else he could do? Luke turned back toward the window and looked once more at the horror within.

His attic bedroom was ablaze. It had all happened so quickly that he still couldn't process the sequence of events. He'd gone to bed as usual, but had been awakened shortly afterward by a chorus of smoke alarms. He'd stumbled out of bed, groggy and confused, waving his arms back and forth in a vain attempt to disperse the thick smoke that filled the room. He'd managed to scramble to the door, but even before he got there, he saw that he was too late. The narrow staircase that led up to his bedroom was consumed by fire, huge flames dancing in through the open doorway.

The shivering teenager now watched as his whole life went up in smoke. His schoolbooks, his football kit, his artwork, his beloved Southampton FC posters—all eaten by the flames. With each passing second, the temperature rose still further, the hot smoke and gas gathering in an ominous cloud below the ceiling.

Luke slammed the window shut and for a second the temperature dropped again. But he knew his respite would be brief. When the temperature inside grew too great, the windows would blow out, taking him with them. There was no choice. He had to be bold, so, turning again, he took a step forward and, calling out his mother's name, leaped off the ledge.

2

It was almost midnight and the cemetery was deserted, save for a lonely figure picking her way through the gravestones. Simple crosses sat cheek by jowl with ornate family tombs, many of which were decorated with statues and carvings. The weatherworn cherubs and angels of mercy looked lifeless and sinister in the moonlight, and Helen Grace hurried past them, pulling her scarf tight around her. The scarf had been a Christmas present from her colleague Charlie Brooks and was a godsend on a night like this, when darkness clung to the hilltop cemetery and the temperature plunged ever lower.

The frost was slowly spreading and Helen's feet crunched quietly on the grass as she left the main path, darting left toward the far corner of the cemetery. Before long she was standing in front of a plain headstone, which bore neither name nor dates, just a simple message: FOREVER IN MY THOUGHTS. The rest of the headstone was blank—with no clue as to the deceased's identity, age or even sex. This was how Helen liked it—it was how it had to be—as this was the last resting place of her sister, Marianne.

Many criminals go unclaimed on their death. Others are quickly cremated, their ashes scattered to the winds in an attempt to blot out the very fact of their existence. Others still are buried in faceless HMP cemeteries for the undesirable, but Helen was never going to allow that to happen to her sister. She felt responsible for Marianne's death and was determined not to abandon her.

As she looked down at the simple grave, Helen felt a sharp stab of guilt. The anonymous nature of Marianne's epitaph always got to her—she could feel her sister pointing her finger at her accusingly, chiding Helen for being ashamed of her own flesh and blood. This wasn't true—despite everything, Helen still loved Marianne—but such was the notoriety of her sister's crimes that she'd had to be buried without ceremony, to avoid the prurient interest of journalists or the justifiable ire of her victims' relatives. Safety lay in anonymity—there was no telling what some people might do if they found out where this multiple murderer had finally come to rest.

Helen was the only person present at her sister's committal and would be her sole mourner. Marianne's son was still missing, and as nobody else knew of the grave's existence, it fell to Helen to battle the weeds and honor her memory as best she could. She came here once or twice a week—whenever her shift patterns and hectic work schedule allowed—but always in the dead of night, when there was no chance of being followed or surprised. This was a private, painful duty and Helen had no need of an audience.

Replacing the flowers in the urn, she leaned forward and kissed Marianne's headstone. Straightening up, she offered a few words of love, then turned and hurried on her way. She had wanted to come here—she never ducked her duty—but the winds were arctic tonight and if she stayed here much longer she would suffer for it. Helen loathed illness—her life never seemed to allow for it anyway—and the thought of being tucked up at home in her flat suddenly seemed very attractive indeed. Hurrying back down the path, she vaulted the locked iron gates and made her way back to the car park, now cheerless and deserted save for Helen's Kawasaki.

Reaching her bike, Helen paused to take in the view. You could see the whole of Southampton from the top of Abbey Hill, and this vista always cheered her, especially at night when the lights of the city below twinkled and glistened, full of promise and intrigue.

But not tonight. As Helen looked down at the city that had been her home for so long, she caught her breath. From this high up, she could see not one, not two, but three major fires gripping the city, fierce orange tongues of flame reaching up toward the heavens.

Southampton was ablaze.

3

Thomas Simms slammed the car horn and swore violently. Despite the late hour, the traffic near the airport had been murder, thanks to a truck shedding its load. Having eventually escaped that snarl-up, Thomas had seemed set fair for the short drive back to his home in Millbrook—only to run straight into another jam. It was gone midnight now—where the hell was all this traffic coming from?

He flicked through the local radio stations searching for a traffic bulletin, but, finding nothing save for late-night phone-ins, impatiently switched the radio off. What should he do? There was a shortcut coming up, but it would mean diverting through the Empress Road Industrial Estate, not something he was keen to do, given the prostitutes who'd be there at this time of night. The sight of them, half-naked and shivering, always depressed him and he never felt comfortable sitting at the slow-changing traffic lights, eyed up by pimps and working girls alike. Given the choice, he preferred to stick to the main roads, but the sound of approaching sirens made up his mind. A fire engine and an ambulance were trying to bully their way through the traffic. If they were heading in his direction, that could only mean that there was trouble ahead.

Slipping into first gear, Thomas mounted the lip of the pavement and drove for twenty yards before turning sharply left down a dark, one-way street. Suddenly liberated, he drove too fast, speeding past the thirty-miles-per-hour sign as if it didn't exist, before catching himself and lowering his speed to a more sensible level. If he was lucky, he would be home in five minutes—kissing his wife and kids good night before flopping into bed. There was no point in getting pulled over by the cops now that the end was so nearly in sight.

He worked sixteen-hour days at his import business near the airport, and he missed his family—but he was no fool. So though he was tempted to run the red light on the Empress Road, to escape the unwanted attentions of the scrawny drug addict in hot pants, he waited patiently for the lights to change, distracting himself from the unpleasant sideshow by thinking of the warm, king-size bed that awaited him at home.

He drove through the city center, then picked up the West Quay Road, before finally hitting the home straight. Millbrook wasn't a fancy neighborhood, but the housing was solid Victorian, the neighbors were decent and, best of all, it was quiet. Or at least normally it was. Tonight there seemed to be a lot of people about, the majority of them making their way to Hillside Crescent—his road.

Thomas muttered to himself. Please, God, there wasn't some kind of party going on. A couple of the more expensive houses had been occupied by squatters recently and local residents had been kept awake as a result. But things had been quiet of late, and besides, the people hurrying toward Hillside Crescent were not ravers; they were ordinary mums and dads, some of whom he recognized from the morning run.

The expressions on their faces alarmed him, and as he approached the turning into his road he realized why they were looking so concerned. A huge plume of smoke billowed into the night sky, illuminated by the somber sodium glow of the streetlights. Someone's house was on fire.

No wonder everyone was worried—the housing round here was gentrified Victorian—all scrubbed wooden floorboards and feature staircases. If the fire jumped from one house to the next, then who was to say where it would end? Fear gripped him now as he sped down the street, honking his horn aggressively to clear his path of gawpers. What if the fire was close to his house? Immediately he clamped down his fear, telling himself not to be stupid. Karen would have called him if she was concerned about anything.

The road was blocked now with ambling pedestrians, so Thomas pulled over to the curb and climbed out. Locking the door, he started to jog down the street. The fire was near his house—it had to be, given the direction of the smoke and the concentration of people at the far end of the road. His jog now turned into a full-on sprint as he barged startled onlookers out of his path.

Breaking through the throng, he found himself at the bottom of his drive. The sight that met him took his breath away and he suddenly ground to a halt. His entire house was ablaze, huge flames issuing from every window. It wasn't a fire; it was an inferno.

He found himself moving forward and turned to find his neighbor gripping one of his arms, guiding him gently toward the house. The expression on her face was hideous—a toxic mixture of horror and pity—and it chilled him to the bone. Why was she looking at him like that?

Then Thomas saw him. His boy—his beloved son, Luke—lying on the grass in the front garden. Shaded by the mulberry bush, he lay with his head on the lap of another neighbor, who was talking to him earnestly. It would have been a touching sight, were it not for the crazy angles of Luke's legs, bent nastily back on themselves, and the blood that clung to his face and hands.

"The ambulance is on its way. He's going to be okay."

Thomas didn't know whether his neighbor was lying or not, but he wanted to believe her. He didn't care what injuries his son had sustained as long as he lived.

"It's okay, mate. Dad's here now," he said as he knelt down next to his son.

The ground around Luke was covered with leaves and branches from the mulberry bush and in an instant Thomas realized that his son must have jumped. He must have leaped from the house and landed in the bush. It probably broke his fall—may even have saved his life—but why was he jumping at all? Why hadn't he just run out the front door?

"Where's Mum? And Alice? Luke, where are they, mate?"

For a moment, Luke said nothing, the agony racking his body seeming to rob him of the ability to speak.

"Has anyone seen them?" Thomas cried out, panic rendering his voice high and harsh. "Where the hell are they?"

He looked back at his son, who seemed to be trying to raise himself, in spite of his injuries.

"What is it, Luke?"

Thomas knelt in closer, his ear brushing his son's mouth. Luke struggled for breath, then through gritted teeth finally managed to whisper:

"They're still inside."

4

Helen Grace flashed her warrant card and slipped under the police cordon, walking fast toward the heart of the chaos. Three fire engines were parked up outside Travell's Timber Yard, and over a dozen firefighters were tackling a blaze of monumental proportions. Even from this safe distance, Helen could feel the intense heat—it rolled over her, clinging to her hair, her eyes, her throat, reveling in its power and appetite for destruction.

Travell's Timber Yard was one of the largest in Southampton, a prosperous family business, popular with tradesmen and builders the length of Hampshire. But little or nothing of this successful venture would survive the night. From humble beginnings, this city center outlet had grown year on year, culminating in the construction of a huge warehouse where timber of every variety, shape and size could be found. Helen watched now as this cavernous building raged in flame, its metal skeleton shrieking in the heat, as the windows shattered and fire rained down like confetti from the disintegrating roof.

"Who the hell are you? You can't be here."

Helen turned to see a firefighter from the Hampshire Fire and Rescue Service approaching her. His face was caked in dirt and sweat.

"DI Helen Grace, Major Incident Team, and actually I have every right—"

"I don't care if you're Sherlock Holmes. That roof is going to go any second and I don't want anyone standing nearby when it does."

Helen cast an eye over the roof in question. It was buckling now as the fire ripped through it, seeking new fuel and fresh oxygen. Instinctively she took a step back.

"Keep going. There's nothing for you here."

"Who's in charge?"

"Sergeant Carter, but he's a bit busy at the moment . . ."

"Who's the fire investigation officer on duty?"

"No idea."

He walked back toward the fire engines—two of which were now moving away from the scene.

"You're leaving?" Helen asked, incredulous.

"Nothing we can do here except contain it. So we're being sent elsewhere."

"What are we looking at? Any chance it could have been accidental? An electricity short? Discarded cigarette?"

The exhausted firefighter cast a withering look in her direction. "Three major fires on the same night. All starting within an hour of each other. This wasn't an accident." He fixed her with a fierce stare. "Someone's been having a bit of fun."

The lead fire engine paused as it passed, allowing the firefighter time to clamber up into the passenger seat. He didn't look back at Helen—she was already forgotten, he and his team discussing the trials that still lay ahead. Helen watched the flashing blue lights disappear down the road before returning her attention to the huge conflagration behind.

Seconds later the roof collapsed inward, sending a vast cloud of hot smoke and ash billowing toward her.

About the Author

M. J. Arlidge is the international bestselling author of the Detective Helen Grace Thrillers, including *Pop Goes the Weasel* and his debut, *Eeny Meeny*, which has been sold in twenty-eight countries. He lives in England and has worked in television for the past fifteen years.

CONNECT ONLINE
twitter.com/mjarlidge